LETHAL
EDGE

NEW YORK TIMES AND USA TODAY BESTSELLING AUTHOR

KAYLEA
CROSS

LETHAL EDGE

Copyright © 2020
by Kaylea Cross

* * * * *

Cover Art and Print Formatting:
Sweet 'N Spicy Designs
Developmental edits: Deborah Nemeth
Line Edits: Joan Nichols
Digital Formatting: LK Campbell

* * * * *

ISBN: 979-8666611951

For Katie Reus, who always supports me and my dreams. For being a fierce and loyal friend. And for always being there for me.

Love you bunches.

xo

Author's Note

Welcome to the small mountain town of Rifle Creek, Montana! I hope you'll fall in love with this place, and the new cast of characters I've created.

Happy reading,

Kaylea

help being protective of her, and him being a cop made it ten times as bad. "You're the only niece I've got." She had chosen to go to school here at the University of Montana because it was close to him. Her mother, still back in B.C., entrusted him with keeping an eye on Rylee, and he took his niece's safety and wellbeing seriously.

Rylee tipped her head back to look up at him, her hazel eyes so like his own, and full of adoration. "I'm going to be okay here. But thank you for worrying about me."

Shit, now his damn throat was getting tight. He cleared it. "I know you'll do great." He nodded at the door with a dark look at all the noise coming from the hallway. At least this was an all-girls' dorm. No way in hell would he have let her stay in a co-ed one. "It's them I'm worried about." They sounded like all kinds of trouble.

Rylee grinned and patted his back soothingly. "I'll use the pepper spray you gave me if they get too out of hand."

He squeezed her one last time, then released her. "Good. Keep it on you whenever you leave the dorm. And especially if you go to a party or wherever." She was a mature and responsible kid, but he felt the need to reiterate all of this anyway. "Never ever leave your drink unattended, not even for a second. If you do, toss it and get a fresh one."

He didn't want to scare her, but sexual assaults weren't uncommon on college campuses, and there had been a string of them in the area over the past couple years that still hadn't been solved. He'd worked on a few cases that had seemed to be connected at the end of his time with the Missoula police department, but they'd never found a suspect. Thankfully he hadn't had to deal with that kind of thing yet at his new job in Rifle Creek.

"I know. And I promise I'll think about your offer to certify me with a pistol," she said.

3

She thought it was overkill but wanted to humor him anyway. "How old were you when we last went to the range together? Thirteen?"

"Fifteen, but I still remember most of it." She eyed him, the hint of a smile playing around the edges of her mouth. "I could just call you and have you escort me if I decide to venture out to a party. Of course, then I'd never get a date, because you'd scare off any guy who came within fifty feet of me."

"Deal." He'd make the forty-five-minute drive down here in a heartbeat if she wanted him there. "You don't need to date anyway. College-aged guys are assholes only after one thing, and you're here to study."

She grinned, making her look so much like her mom. "This is why I love you."

He flushed a little at the praise, but her words hit dead center in his chest and warmed him inside and out. "I know you probably can't wait to see the back of your paranoid and overprotective uncle, but how about some pizza before I leave you to fend for yourself?"

Her smile was pure sunshine. "I'd like that."

They ventured out onto campus together and walked the few blocks to a pizza place. The late August sun blazed high in the brilliant blue sky, warm and golden. He managed to withhold another lecture about safety while they ate. She was all grown up and could make her own decisions.

After lunch he hugged her, kissed the top of her head and made himself let her go. "Go get 'em, sweetness. And I'm only a phone call away if you need anything."

"I know. Thanks, Uncle Tater. Love you."

"Love you too." Christ, his whole chest ached as he watched her walk away, all on her own for the first time as she faced her future as a young adult.

He climbed into his truck for the drive back to Rifle Creek, more restless and unsettled than ever. Lately he had started to feel unsatisfied with life, bored and hemmed in, like it no longer fit him.

He hadn't felt this way since leaving the military, during his initial transition back into the civilian world. So the potential business opportunity looming on the horizon couldn't have come at a better time. He was excited at the idea of working with his buddies, setting his own hours and being his own boss.

With Rylee on his mind, he used his truck's hands-free device to call his sister as he left campus. "Just wanted to let you know she's all squared away."

"And how are you holding up?" Tala asked, an amused edge to her tone.

One side of his mouth pulled up. She knew him better than anyone. "Not as well as you are, to be honest."

"Aww. Well, hang in there, Tater. This too shall pass."

He grunted. "When are you coming down to visit? Canadian Thanksgiving?" That was only a few weeks away, in mid-October.

"No, probably not until American Thanksgiving, since Rylee will have some time off then. Can you handle me staying with you for an entire week?"

"I can handle you staying as long as you want." His sister was the greatest, and with their schedules they didn't spend nearly enough time together.

She laughed. "You say that now, but I guarantee I'd drive you nuts inside of a month living in your house. Anyway, I hear Mason's coming into town tomorrow?"

"Yeah, he's driving down from Calgary. You know he'll do anything to avoid flying." His buddy was coming down to scope out a piece of land they and another friend were thinking of turning into an adventure ranch/training facility geared toward private security and contracting groups.

"Can't say I blame him, after what happened."

"No." Mason had never fully recovered from that incident, and Tate was starting to think he never would.

"So you're seriously thinking about starting the business with him and Brax?"

"Yeah." It was time for a change.

"How's that gonna work when Brax is still active duty?"

Braxton was still serving with JTF2, Canada's elite, tier-one unit. "It's tricky, but doable, especially if Mason and I get everything up and running by the time Brax's contract is up. I just feel like I need a change of p—" He broke off when a car suddenly veered out beside him over the double solid line and cut off someone to run the red light.

Horns blared, tired squealed.

Tate only had time to glance in the rearview mirror and tense before the car behind him swerved and slammed into his truck with a sickening crunch that pushed him out into oncoming traffic.

CHAPTER TWO

Nina gasped, her heart jumping into her throat as the loud impact shot the dark gray pickup straight into the middle of the intersection. Thankfully the driver wrenched to the right and sped through it just in time to avoid being hit head-on by someone else.

"Oh my gosh..." The car that had hit the truck was stopped. Traffic was snarled in all directions, and she couldn't tell if anyone was hurt.

She pulled her little SUV over to the curb, put on her hazards and threw open her door, cell phone in hand. The idiot driver who had caused the wreck by running the red light was long gone.

The car that had rear-ended the pickup sat partway through the intersection, blocking traffic in most directions. Other drivers were impatiently veering around it, unwilling to stop and help.

Nina ran past the rear-ender car, noting that the elderly lady behind the wheel looked shocked and shaken, and headed for the pickup to see if the driver was okay.

Just as she neared the back of it, the driver's side

opened and a tall, powerfully built man stepped out. She halted as he turned to face her, a little jolt running through her. He was hot as hell, and thankfully didn't appear hurt.

"Are you all right?" she asked, pushing down her worry.

He nodded, annoyance clear in his expression. His sandy brown hair was longer at the front, the bronze stubble on his jaw glinting in the afternoon sun. The light gray T-shirt he wore hugged his sculpted chest and shoulders, and left most of his muscular arms bare. "I'm fine." He turned toward the car that had hit him.

"She's elderly. I think she's okay—"

"Oh, shit," he muttered, and took off past her.

Nina whirled and followed him, alarm streaking through her when she saw what the problem was. The elderly woman was clearly in some kind of medical distress, grabbing at her chest, her mouth opening and closing, eyes wide with panic.

"Call 911," the hot guy ordered Nina, and ran to help the lady.

Nina's fingers fumbled as she dialed the number. She spoke to the operator, her heart racing as she hurried to the woman's car. Through the windshield the elderly driver appeared to be struggling to breathe. The guy tried the driver's door, but it was locked. Other people had stopped now and were getting out of their vehicles.

The guy ignored everyone, watching the elderly woman as he hurried around the other side, reaching a hand down to his hip. Nina gasped as he drew a pistol from its holster. He slammed the butt of it into the passenger door window, cracking it, then pushed the broken glass in so he could reach inside and unlock the door.

"Ma'am? Are you still there?" the operator asked, jerking Nina from her shock. Coming from California with its strict gun laws, it was still a shock to see weapons being carried around openly here.

"Yes, someone broke a window to get to the woman. He's helping her right now. It looks like she's having trouble breathing. Do you have anyone on the way?"

"A fire crew and ambulance are en route right now."

"All right." God, it looked bad. "Please hurry."

"They'll be there soon, ma'am. Stay on the line with me and let me know what's happening."

"Okay." Nina approached the car, watching anxiously while the man leaned inside it to scoop up the woman in his arms and lifted her out easily. He laid her gently on the ground, talking to her.

Juggling her phone, Nina hurriedly stripped off her jacket, wadded it up and tucked it beneath the woman's head. The man was leaning over the woman, talking to her in a deep, calm voice. He radiated a calm confidence Nina could feel through her distress.

He looked up at her. "See if she's got some ID in the car."

"Right." Nina jumped up and rushed around them to look inside, and found a purse sitting on the passenger seat. The driver's license was inside a wallet.

"Her name is Sophie," Nina said, coming around to kneel next to the woman's head. "Hi, Sophie, I'm Nina," she said, taking the woman's cold, damp hand. The poor thing was still gasping, a sheen of sweat on her face, eyes panicked. "Help is on the way. I'm going to stay with you."

The man looked up at Nina with a grateful half-smile, his hazel-green eyes staring right into hers before focusing on the woman once more. "We'll both stay with you, Sophie. Just try to stay calm, and focus on your breathing."

Sophie continued to gasp, her face pale, eyes full of fear as she stared up at the man. Then her eyelids fluttered, her rasping breaths going quiet as she went limp.

Nina stared at her in horror. *Oh, shit...* Her chest

wasn't moving.

"Sophie?" the man asked, his voice urgent as he checked the pulse in the woman's neck. "Her heart's stopped," he muttered to Nina.

Before she could say anything, he stacked his hands on the center of Sophie's chest and began compressions. Nina clung to the woman's frail, limp hand while she spoke to the operator, then held her breath as the man tried to get Sophie's heart going again.

Sirens sounded in the distance and Nina was aware of the crowd forming around them, whispering and muttering. A fire truck arrived and the firemen ran over.

Nina released Sophie's hand and moved backward out of the way to give them room, heart in her throat. *Hurry, hurry*, she urged them, and updated the operator. "The firemen are here." *Finally*.

Ending the call, she wrapped her arms around her ribs and stood back, watching the scene helplessly. *Come on, Sophie. Fight.*

"Baldwin, hey," one of the firemen said to the pickup driver as he knelt beside Sophie to take over. "When did you start the compressions?"

"Four minutes," Nina said, drawing the fireman's attention. Though it seemed like a lot longer than that.

The fire crew immediately took over and the man stepped back, wiping his forearm across his glistening forehead. Damp spots darkened his T-shirt across his chest and under the arms. For the first time Nina noticed the metal badge clipped to his belt.

A cop. That explained why he'd handled everything so perfectly.

Police cars began arriving. The firemen were still working on Sophie. Nina put her hands to her mouth, her attention glued to the woman. A fireman placed the paddles of a portable defibrillator on Sophie's chest and hit the button.

Sophie's chest surged upward, then dropped. A fireman checked the pulse in her throat. Seconds later, Sophie's eyelids fluttered.

Nina gasped. *Yes. Come on, you can do it*, Nina urged her silently. The firemen eased back a bit as Sophie continued breathing on her own. Her eyes were open.

Nina glanced over just as the pickup driver came up to her. "You all right?" he asked.

He was so big and calm and strong. She wanted to lean into him, soak up some of that strength until she felt steadier. "Yes." She studied his face. "Are you?"

His eyes crinkled at the corners as the hint of a smile tugged at his mouth, framed by all that delicious bronze stubble. "Yeah, I'm okay." He looked back at Sophie. "She's doing great. Look."

Nina nodded, her insides starting to loosen now that Sophie had been brought back from the brink.

Expelling a deep breath, she ran an unsteady hand through her hair. That had been intense.

"Here. Sit down," the cop urged, wrapping his long fingers around her upper arm.

The contact sent a little shockwave of sensation up her arm. "No, I'm okay." Before she could say anything more, other officers came over to begin taking their statements and information.

By the time it was over, Sophie had been loaded into the back of an ambulance and was on her way to the hospital.

"So I'm free to go now?" Nina asked one of the officers. The pickup driver cop was talking to a few others, and they all appeared to know him.

"Yes, we've got your contact information," the officer said.

Nina hesitated, caught the handsome cop's attention to give a little smile and a wave. He said something to the others, then turned and walked toward her.

Watching him come toward her set off a flutter in the pit of her stomach. The way he moved, all purposeful and self-assured, was mesmerizing. She couldn't take her eyes off him.

"You doing okay?" he asked when he got close.

"I'm fine." A little shaken, but better now, and his concern for her warmed her insides. Although the intent way he watched her was making her heart thud all over again. "I didn't see the driver who caused all this, except that it was a dark-haired man. I didn't get a plate or anything, it all happened too fast."

"It's all right. There're cameras in the area the cops can look at." He paused, holding her gaze. "Thanks for your help."

She flushed. "Of course. I'm just glad Sophie's okay. That was so scary."

"It was close. But she's going to be fine now." His tone was a little gruff. Though he didn't need to, he escorted her back to her vehicle and opened her door.

She murmured a thank you and slid into the driver's seat, every cell in her body aware of how close he was. How incredibly masculine he was, and the slight tang of his clean cologne.

He rested a muscular forearm on the doorframe as he leaned down to look at her through the window with those gorgeous hazel eyes, his expression dubious. "You gonna be okay to drive? You seem a little shaken."

Holy moly, the man was something. "I can drive."

He didn't look convinced. "You live nearby?"

"No, I just moved to Rifle Creek, actually."

Surprise lit his eyes. "Really?"

"I literally just moved there last night."

His answering smile made her heart lurch. "Is that right? Well, maybe I'll see you around town, then."

It wasn't even a full smile, just a quirk of his sexy lips, but that admiration and male interest in his eyes were a powerful combination. Good lord, this man was potent. "I'm—"

"Baldwin, need you over here," someone called behind him before she could introduce herself.

He straightened, gave her another quick smile. "Drive safely." He shut her door and sauntered over to whoever had called him.

Nina watched him for a moment, disappointment filling her that she hadn't gotten his name. Or his number. After their brief but intense encounter, she was more interested in him than all the guys she'd dated recently. But maybe she'd only imagined that interest in his eyes?

She shook the thoughts away and started her SUV. Her romantic sensibilities had gotten her into trouble once already, and besides, she had a ton of things to take care of by the end of the weekend.

Monday marked the start of a new teaching semester. After a disastrous finish to her first semester at the University of Montana back in late April, this was another beginning for her.

Life had taught her many things. Most importantly, that happiness was a choice. So she'd chosen to look forward instead of back.

She'd made up her mind four months ago to seize this chance, put the past behind her and take advantage of this fresh new start—and that's exactly what she was going to do.

CHAPTER THREE

Vince finally allowed himself a deep breath when he'd reached the eastern limits of town without being followed or pulled over. Didn't look like anyone was coming after him. Maybe he was still okay.

Damn. That traffic incident was a stark reminder that he was playing a dangerous game. One mistake, one slip, and he would lose everything.

The knots in his stomach eased as he headed for home. He'd been at the campus scoping out a possible new target today, and had seen *her* talking with someone he'd been eyeing that afternoon.

Then she'd looked at him. Right at him. And in that instant, he'd been certain she'd recognized him, so he'd had no choice but to get out of there.

What had they been talking about? It was too much of a coincidence that she'd been talking to his next intended target in front of him. *Had* she recognized him? Been suspicious of him? Warned the other girl to be careful? Called security?

He ran a hand over his mouth as he drove. Seeing the two women talking had spooked him so much that he'd

14

immediately left campus. His heart had damn near stopped two minutes later when he'd seen her following him in her SUV out of the parking lot. He'd had no choice but to take immediate evasive action, even though the ensuing accident would bring unwanted attention.

At least it had allowed him to get away. And he was driving his buddy's car, having borrowed it this morning after telling his friend his own vehicle was in the shop. Anyone looking for him would go to his buddy instead, buying him a little time to get away if it came down to it.

He kept checking his mirrors as he drove out into the suburbs, aware of how lucky he was. No one looking at him would ever suspect what he'd done. He hid his tracks well. And for the most part he led a normal, highly functional life.

With one major exception.

A rush of power and excitement shot through him. Power because he'd gotten away with everything so far. Excitement at the thought of what he'd done, and what he would do again.

He should stop. He knew he had to stop, but the thrill of it was just too damn addicting. He'd always been an adrenaline junkie, and this was an extreme way to get his kicks, fulfill the needs his mundane life and tired marriage never could.

He was going to do it again. Sooner than he should. Because he was too hooked now to wait a safe time period.

Every time he went a little further. Pushed the boundaries, seeking the edge like an addict. Some deeply buried part of him wanting to find out exactly how far he could go and what he could get away with before he was caught.

Every time he did it, he left the area and waited, monitoring the situation to see if he'd been reported as a suspect. So far, nothing. None of the women had been able to identify him, or give enough of a description for the cops to make him a suspect.

Despite everything he'd done, he was still in the clear. And that only made him want it more.

He dropped the car off at his buddy's house and waited for his wife to pick him up. She glanced at him from the driver's seat as he climbed into the front next to her. She looked tired. A little sad.

"Any word on your truck?" she asked, her expression almost hopeful as she scanned his face. Searching for something, a connection he no longer felt. Maybe he never had.

"Yeah, everything's fine. I'll pick it up tomorrow." In reality he'd left it parked at a restaurant ten minutes from their house.

She gave him one last lingering look that made him uncomfortable before pulling onto the street. "Have a good day?"

"Great. You?"

She shrugged. "The usual."

He pretended to pay attention while she ran through the mundane details of her HR job at a local accounting firm. "Anyway, I grabbed groceries on the way home and the girls helped me start dinner. It should be ready by the time we get home."

"Perfect."

He walked into the kitchen ten minutes later, grinned as his six and nine-year-old daughters came running, their faces full of delight at seeing him.

"Daddy!" they cried, racing for him.

Vince bent and spread his arms wide, catching them both. He lifted them, hugging them to his chest as he rubbed his short whiskers across their baby-soft cheeks, smiling at their shrieks and giggles. "My two little butter-beans. You miss me?"

"*Yes*," they chorused, hugging him around the neck with their thin arms.

Giving them each a sound kiss on the cheek, he set them down and grabbed plates and cutlery as they hurried to help their mother get dinner set out. His heart sank as he watched them, an inexplicable wave of sadness hitting him.

Their love was so pure. Even his wife's.

Against all odds she still loved him, was still sticking it out with him even though neither of them had been happy in years. She wouldn't leave, though, because she didn't want to fracture their family, no matter how unfulfilled she was.

He loved her too, in his own way, but it wasn't enough. Not anymore.

He swallowed, a hard, cold ball gathering in the pit of his stomach. From the outside looking in, he had it all. A respectable job. A comfortable home, wife and healthy kids.

Why wasn't that enough? Why did these terrible cravings keep pushing him to the brink when he knew he would eventually lose all of this in the end if he kept going?

But that dark thrill was there inside him, coiling restlessly in his gut. Like a storm gathering. A growing pressure that eventually demanded release.

No. He wouldn't stop. Not yet.

He was going to do it again, maybe in the next few weeks. And in the meantime, he was going to keep a close eye on *her*, because if she eventually remembered enough to identify him, the game—and his life—would be over.

****

Tate finally pulled into his driveway as the sun dropped behind the western edge of the mountains. His head was pounding and his neck and shoulders were stiff as hell.

He'd declined medical attention at the accident scene and refused to go to the hospital to get checked out. It was only a mild whiplash. He'd live. God knew he'd been injured far worse than a minor rear-ender in his thirty-three years on this earth.

As he stepped out of his truck, the top of a graying head and a pair of dark eyes appeared over the top of the side fence. "Hey, man. What the hell happened to your ride?"

Tate grunted, unsurprised that his neighbor had noticed the damage immediately. The old man noticed *everything* around here. While Tate didn't love how everybody knew everyone's business in Rifle Creek, it wasn't all bad, because people around here looked out for one another. And a nosy neighbor could be one hell of an added security measure.

"Hey, Curt." Tate rolled his head from side to side to ease the stiffness in his muscles. Curt Larsen was a Vietnam vet well into his seventies. A grease monkey always tinkering away on something in his garage, in addition to running his hobby farm. He and Tate had immediately liked and respected one another because they had both served in the Corps. "Got rear-ended."

Those dark eyes stayed pinned on him. "You all right?"

He wasn't in the mood for socializing. "I'm okay." Just sore and looking forward to a hot shower and a beer. "How's things?"

"Good. Got another coyote today. Bastards have started digging their way under my back fence again."

"Ah. Well, I'm gonna head in and take a hot shower."

"For sure. Hey, you take your niece to campus yet?"

He withheld an impatient sigh. "Yeah, I was just leaving when I got hit."

Curt nodded, the top of his head and face still the only parts of him visible. "So, back to the bachelor lifestyle, huh?" He bounced his bushy eyebrows.

"Looks like." Not that Tate dated much. Or at all these days. He was too busy with his job as a detective on the Rifle Creek Sheriff's Department, although given his recent restlessness he was starting to wonder if he'd made a mistake in taking the job.

For some reason the mention of his bachelorhood made him think of the woman he'd just met at the accident scene. She was pretty, and seemed like a good person because she'd stayed to help even though she'd clearly been rattled by what was going on.

Yeah, he was definitely in a funk. At one time, Tate would have gotten her number and used the excuse of checking on her to ask her out, but not anymore, thanks to his relationship with his ex.

He was done with trying and failing to meet someone else's impossible standards. At least now he was no longer a constant source of disappointment. His life was peaceful now, and that's exactly how he liked it.

"Why don't you let me take a look at the damage to the rear end?" Curt offered. "Bet I can do the body work for cheaper at my buddy's shop than anyone else. Save you some money and time."

"That'd be great, Curt. Thanks."

"No problem. I'll grab it in the morning. Semper fi, baby."

Tate couldn't help but grin. He'd missed the brotherhood the military had given him. Another reason he was looking forward to seeing if the new business idea was feasible. "Semper fi."

The sight of his home made him sigh with relief. The main part of the house was an old log cabin built in the 1880s. Since then various owners had added to it, but the old logs and chinking in the living room were his favorite part. He'd fallen in love with the place the first time he'd seen it and had turned it into his own space, complete with a woodshop out back he liked to putter around in on the weekends.

He'd just walked into his entryway when his cell phone rang. His work partner, Avery. "Hey."

"Why the hell am I finding out you had an accident from a uniform in Missoula instead of you?" she demanded in her no-nonsense way.

"It's no big deal. Was gonna tell you at the office on Monday." He rubbed the back of his neck.

She huffed out an indignant sound. "Are you hurt?"

"No. Just sore." And he didn't feel like talking to her either.

"You didn't get checked out, did you," she added, sounding irritated.

"Didn't need to."

"You are so stubborn." She sighed. "Look, my new roomie just moved in downstairs, and we could use a hand moving the bigger stuff around."

He grunted. "How much do you really know about her, anyway? You say she's your best friend, but I've never even met her."

"Tate, you cynical bastard," she said on a chuckle. "Why don't you come over for dinner so you can meet her and vet her yourself. And then if you're up to it, you can help us set everything up in the suite after."

He did want to meet this so-called best friend of hers and make sure she wasn't crazy or anything. And a hot, home-cooked meal and some company sounded a hell of a lot more appealing than a takeout pizza in an empty house. With Rylee gone things were going to be too quiet all of a sudden, and he was alone until Mason arrived sometime tomorrow.

"Sure, I can come for dinner. What time?"

CHAPTER FOUR

Tate parked in front of Avery's 1890s brick Queen Anne-style Victorian and grabbed the bottle of her favorite wine. A hot shower had helped, but his muscles were stiff and sore as he headed up the front steps. The old house was solid and while it still needed some work here and there, Avery had made major improvements to the interior since she'd moved in last year.

He knocked twice, received Avery's call to enter, and found her at the marble-topped island in the creamy-white country kitchen. The reno might have been pricey, but in Tate's opinion it was worth every penny. Whatever she was making smelled awesome, a lot better than the basic meals he made for himself on the nights he didn't get takeout.

Light flooded in from large windows over the sink and in the dining area, making the honey-toned oak floors gleam and the chrome fixtures sparkle. "Still the best room in the house."

"I agree." Tall and slender, Avery tucked a lock of her jaw-length strawberry-blond hair behind her ear.

"Here, can you put the salad together while I get the casserole done?"

"Sure." She'd already laid everything out. He got busy chopping veggies and assembling the salad while Avery prepped everything else. "So where's your roomie?" he asked.

"Downstairs unpacking." She shot him a warning look, narrowing her golden eyes a little. "Be nice when you meet her."

He blinked. "I am nice."

"Yeah, you are, deep down. Just lose the suspicious and gruff vibe for tonight, and you'll be great." Footsteps sounded on the stairs on the other side of the door connecting the main floor to the basement suite. "And here she is."

The door opened. Tate looked up, his hands freezing on the salad spoons when he saw the woman from the accident standing there.

She stopped in the kitchen entryway when she saw him, surprise on her face, then a big smile curved her mouth. "Wow, hi again."

He forced himself to keep his eyes on her face instead of letting them trail over the peach-colored dress she wore, hugging her curves and leaving her golden-toned arms and lower legs bare. Her long, coffee-brown hair was swept over one shoulder, trailing over a breast.

"Hi." *This* was Avery's best friend?

"Again?" Avery asked, looking between the two of them.

"We met at the accident scene," Tate explained. "She stopped to make sure the other driver and I were okay."

Avery turned toward the woman, eyes wide. "You didn't tell me you guys met!"

"I didn't know," her friend said, smiling at him.

Neither had Tate. "She was amazingly helpful." He stepped forward and offered his hand, suddenly a lot more interested in Avery's roommate. "I'm Tate, by the way."

She clasped his hand, the touch of her soft, slender fingers making his skin hum. "Nina Benitez."

Latina heritage. He nodded, unable to look away from those big brown eyes. He hadn't noticed before but they had warm golden flecks in them.

"How are you feeling?" she asked, withdrawing her hand but leaving the lingering warmth of her touch.

"I'm okay." Better now. He would definitely be spending more time at Avery's from now on.

She gave him a doubtful look. "Really?"

He lifted a shoulder, covered a wince. "A little stiff and sore. No big deal." It came out a little growly, even though he'd tried to soften his tone.

"Ah yes, the classic alpha male response, refusing to show any form of weakness to others," Avery said with a roll of her eyes. "Do me a favor, Tate. Go into my bathroom, grab two extra-strength Advil and I'll give you something to wash them down with."

He opened his mouth to say something, but Avery shook her head. "Nuh-uh." She pointed a finger down the hall. "Master bathroom medicine cabinet. Go." She thrust a glass of juice at him.

Tate took it and lifted an eyebrow at Nina. "You sure you want to live downstairs from her? If she orders her work partner around like that, imagine how she'll treat a tenant."

Nina grinned, exposing the hint of a dimple at the corner of her mouth. "Trust me, she's got nothing on my mom and sisters. I can take it."

"Glad to hear that. Be back in a sec."

In Avery's master bathroom he found the meds and took two. So, Nina. He already liked her. She had a bright energy about her that seemed to fill up the room.

He tried to remember the things Avery had told him about her, but nothing important came to mind. He was looking forward to getting to know her better tonight.

Avery was pulling something from the oven when he came back to the kitchen. "Did you actually take them?" she asked.

He smothered a chuckle. She knew him too well. "Yeah."

She nodded. "Good. Now I want to hear everything about this afternoon. Let's sit down and eat, I'm starving."

Tate sat at the table directly across from Nina and sipped at his juice. "She's always trying to take care of me," he said to Nina.

"Someone has to," Avery muttered. "Pass the salad. And then you can both fill me in on exactly what happened at the accident scene."

He and Nina relayed everything. "It was crazy," Nina finished with a shake of her head that Tate couldn't help notice made her shiny brown hair swish against her breast. "I've never seen anything like that, and never want to again. Thankfully, it all turned out fine. Sophie's getting a new pacemaker tomorrow."

Tate looked up at her. "How do you know?"

"I talked to her husband. He came to the hospital. The staff was really busy when he first arrived and he was so worried, so I told him what happened. I stayed until after he visited her in the Emergency Room. He's going to text me with updates to let me know how she's doing."

Tate stared at her. "You went to the hospital and stayed there to make sure she was okay," he repeated, wanting to make sure he had it right.

Nina shrugged. "It bothered me that she was all alone after something like that. If it had been my mother or grandmother, I wouldn't want them to be alone. And then when her husband showed up, he was so upset, I couldn't just leave."

Tate looked from her to Avery, who was smiling into her wineglass. She raised her eyebrows at him, and he read her thoughts as clearly as if she'd spoken aloud. *See? Not a psycho.*

Tate shifted his attention back to Nina, impressed and now insanely curious about her. Being a cop wasn't easy, and it was probably true it had made him more cynical and harder edged than he already was. But in his experience, people didn't go out of their way for strangers like that very often. Not without getting something in return.

"Well, I'm glad everything worked out, and that you two could finally meet officially," Avery said, then spoke to him. "And we should be grateful Nina's spending one of her precious Friday nights with us instead of painting the town red," she added with a teasing smile at her friend.

"Is it possible to paint this town red?" Rifle Creek wasn't exactly known for its nightlife. In fact, the local wildlife was far more active at night than the human residents.

"Ha. I'm just saying, she was in high demand back home in San Fran this summer. And I'm sure she's been on a few dates in Missoula since she got back."

"Oh, please," Nina said with a laugh, looking down at her plate.

"Please nothing. How many dates have you been on in the last month alone?" Avery said.

"I don't know. A few."

Tate chewed his food, for some reason disliking the thought of Nina dating all those other guys.

"Uh huh. Any more coming up in the near future? Come on, spill." Avery waved a fork between herself and Tate. "Tate and I don't date much. Or ever, really. And you've got so many awesome stories."

Tate shot her a warning look. *Thanks, Ave, for making me look like an antisocial loser.*

"I do, don't I?" Nina said cheerfully.

"Yes." Avery's eyes twinkled. "The recaps of some

of them have provided me with hours of entertainment."

Nina snickered. "It's not that bad. Well, it's not *all* bad."

"But most of it's pretty bad?" Tate asked, watching her. Why bad? Had some asshole come on too strong? Pushed her to go farther than she wanted to? He bristled at the thought, his hand tightening around his fork.

"Whoa, easy, tiger," Avery said, reaching out to pat his hand before speaking to Nina. "He just mentally jumped to the worst possible conclusion."

Nina's eyes swung to his, and widened. "Oh, no, nothing like…" She paused, a flush hitting her cheeks as she averted her gaze. "Nothing like that. Let's just say there've been a few…flops."

He relaxed, but her reaction didn't completely reassure him. She'd looked away like she was embarrassed about something, and that bothered him. "Define flops," he said in a tone that managed not to sound like a growl, wanting to lighten the mood and keep her talking.

She looked up at him again, her lips curving. "Okay, so for instance, one guy a couple weeks ago kept checking his phone every two minutes. Literally sat there across the table from me at a nice restaurant in town, texting and answering emails. Said it was for work. I mean, I respect hard work and commitment to your work, but if he's gonna be like that on a first date?" She shook her head. "People are usually on their best behavior on a first date, so I wasn't interested in finding out how much worse it would get over time."

No shit. Idiot didn't deserve a text response from her, let alone a second date.

"And did he ask you out again?" Avery asked.

"He did," Nina said, sounding amazed. "He thought it went great and said he couldn't wait to see me again. I couldn't believe it. But it never would have worked out even if he'd been attentive, because his conversation was limited to sports and himself. No thank you."

"So he got the axe."

Nina laughed. "I know that sounds harsh," she said to Tate, waving her hands in front of her in self-defense. "But honestly, even though I'm kind of a serial dater, I don't want to waste my time. I know pretty quick whether a guy has second-date potential or not."

He was getting more interested by the minute. "How quick?"

She thought about it a second. "Within the first ten minutes, give or take."

"Wow, that's...fast."

"I know, I'm brutal. But I've been on enough dates to know when it's not gonna work."

"Have you ever been on one when you knew it would work?" he pressed.

"Not yet," she admitted with a grin. "But when it happens I will."

"And there it is. Nina's a hopeless romantic," Avery said with a fond smile, reaching for her wine glass.

Tate tensed inside slightly, his interest dimming at that description. He had a complicated relationship with romance and still hadn't healed up from his most recent experience.

Nina shrugged and grinned. "Can't help it. I come from a long line of them."

"You're not saying you believe in love at first sight, though," he said, to clarify.

She lifted a shoulder. "I think it happens for some people."

Yeah, if they were nuts. "So how will you know when you meet the right person?"

"I just will, deep inside. If it's meant to be, it will be."

"Well, that's...a nice thought," he managed, unable to think of something more polite to say about it.

"Yes." She titled her head, such warmth in her eyes as she watched him. "Do you believe there's the right match out there for everyone? A soulmate?"

"Nope."

She blinked at his instant response, as if taken off guard. "No?"

"Me neither," Avery said. "Sorry, babe."

Nina shook her head and laughed at them. "You guys are a couple of cynics."

"Yeah, well, a shitty ex and life as a cop will do that to you," Avery said with a wry smile, then patted Tate's muscular shoulder. "But now he and I have each other. Two cynical workaholics, making the world a better place one criminal case at a time." She held up her glass to him. "Cheers, partner."

This was why he loved her. Avery was the shit. "I'll drink to that." Tate tapped his glass to hers.

"So, I know why Avery doesn't date much, but why don't you?" Nina asked him after he'd taken a sip and lowered his glass.

"Too busy," he answered, turning back to his meal. "Rifle Creek's small, but so is the sheriff's department, and that keeps us busy."

"Does it ever," Avery said, and started talking about an incident at work.

Tate was glad for the change in subject. The rest of the meal was great, and the sound of Nina's laughter made him smile. The differences between them were obvious and glaring. She was like sunshine to his clouds, optimistic where he was world-weary. Maybe that was why he found her so interesting—they were total opposites.

After dinner she helped him clear the table and do the dishes while Avery cleaned up around the kitchen. "So, Avery said you've got some furniture that needs moving downstairs?" he said when they finished.

She was standing less than three feet away from him.

Close enough that her light, sweet scent teased him, her nearness creating a hum of awareness deep inside him. "Oh. No, it's fine. I can move it later with some rugs underneath or something. I don't want you moving anything if you're sore—"

"I'm fine," he said, cursing the curt edge to his tone. He'd always been a little on the gruff side, but he'd lost a lot of his social graces since the breakup. "What do you need done?"

Those big brown eyes swung up to his, and held, as if weighing his sincerity. "I'll show you," she said finally.

Tate followed her downstairs, eyeing the shape of her and the way the dress hugged her waist before flaring out over her hips. Curvy hips made for a man's hands to wrap around—

"There's a painting I'd like to hang, but it's too heavy for me."

He jerked his gaze off her ass. "I'll do it. Just show me where you want it."

She led him through to the small living room off the kitchen. "This is it."

"What is it?" Something space-related, but he wasn't sure what.

"The Cat's Eye Nebula. My family all pitched in to buy this original oil for me from an artist in San Fran when I earned my PhD."

Whoa. "In what?"

"Astrophysics. Though I teach that and lower level astronomy at the university."

Well, damn, that was impressive. How had he forgotten those details? Unless Avery had never told him. "So you're a doctor, huh?"

Her lips quirked. "I am. But I'll let you call me Nina instead of Doctor Benitez."

She was adorable, if misguided about her views on love and romance. "Not sure anyone as smart as you has ever lived in this town."

"I like it here already. Avery's going to show me around town in the morning."

"That'll take all of two minutes," he said dryly.

She laughed. "I can't wait. How long have you lived here?"

"About seven months now. It's nice, but it takes some getting used to after living in the city for so long. Did you grow up in San Fran?"

"Yes. My whole family's back there."

"This'll be a big change for you, then."

Avery came down the stairs. "You guys making out okay?"

Her choice of words amused Tate. He wouldn't mind making out with Nina, except they were on totally different pages when it came to relationships and romantic expectations. That made her hands off.

"Good," Nina answered. "Can you help Tate with the painting? I want to set up my telescope."

"You're such a geek, and I love it," Avery said, handing Tate the little hammer from the pink toolbox Nina had placed on the floor next to him. "Go ahead," she told Nina. "Get your geek on."

"Where'd you guys meet, anyway?" Tate asked as he tapped the hanger into place in the wall. If Avery had mentioned it, he couldn't remember.

"At a charity function last Christmas, when I'd first moved to Missoula," Nina called back from the master bedroom. She appeared a moment later carrying her telescope. "We bonded instantly."

"Instantly," Avery agreed with a dry smile at Tate.

"We totally did," Nina argued. "And then we became besties. When I mentioned to Avery a few weeks back that I was looking for another place to live, she immediately offered me this suite."

"You won't mind the commute?" Tate asked, lifting

the heavy, framed picture while Avery "helped." At least with her height she could hold her side at the right level.

"Not at all. Living alone isn't for me. I like having Avery right upstairs, and even with the forty-five-minute commute each day, the lower rent still puts me farther ahead financially every month."

He nodded and hooked the wire at the back of the painting over the hook on the wall. Avery was still "helping" by tilting the painting up on one side. "Be more than that in winter."

"Still worth it. I love the idea of small-town life, it's so charming." She set her telescope in front of the French doors leading to the back patio.

"What's next?" Tate asked, letting Avery fiddle with the alignment.

"My bed frame and headboard."

"Lead the way."

Her bedroom was painted a soft, sunny yellow that matched what he'd seen of her personality so far. He followed her inside and got to work putting the frame together, noticing the framed photos on the shelves on the far wall, along with a brightly-colored, striped blanket and some terra cotta figurines of suns and moons similar to ones he'd seen in Mexico.

"That your family?" Two people who had to be her parents, two young women who looked a lot like Nina, and some kids he guessed were her nieces and nephews.

"Yes. We're really close." She glanced at the pictures, a fond smile on her face. "I just spent the entire summer back home."

"You must miss them."

"I do, though it feels good to be out of their well-meaning but prying scrutiny."

He grunted in reply and finished the frame and attached the headboard to it while she unpacked a few boxes. "Which wall do you want this against?"

"Here." She gestured to the one opposite the window.

She helped him move it into position, and he was struck by how strange it was to be in her most intimate space like this. He'd be lying if he said he didn't find her attractive, but there were too many obstacles between them to act on it, especially with her being Avery's roommate and best friend.

"So tell me about this family of hopeless romantics you come from," he said as he headed out into the living room to move the armoire.

She brightened and told him about her parents and siblings, nieces and nephews. "It's a big family. Sometimes they drive me crazy, but we love each other anyway. My grandparents immigrated to California from Mexico. My parents were high school sweethearts in San Fran. Met in sophomore year and got married right after graduation. I've got two sisters, both happily married with kids. I'm the outlier. Nerd academic still holding out for my own prince charming, but I can't help it. They've set the bar high, and I'm not going to settle for anything less than what they've got."

He made a sound to let her know he was listening and kept moving the armoire into place, even though he thought her expectations were totally unrealistic and were bound to lead to disappointment.

"What about your parents? Are they still together?"

And here was yet another instance of them being opposites. "Divorced when I was a kid." Another reason he wasn't a big believer in true love and soulmates or whatever.

Her encouraging smile fell. "Oh."

He didn't like that he'd made her smile disappear. "My mom moved me down here right after. My half-sister lives with our dad in Kelowna, B.C."

"Are you close with your mom?"

"I was." He glanced away. "She died of breast cancer last fall."

"Oh, I'm so sorry." She sounded horrified.

He nodded but didn't say anything else. The loss was still pretty fresh and he didn't like talking about it. "This okay?" he asked, straightening and stepping back from the armoire. The meds Avery had given him weren't really helping. A bitch of a headache was pulsing in his temples and the back of his head.

Her grateful smile hit him right in the chest. "Perfect, thanks. I really appreciate your help. This would have taken me forever."

"It's no problem. Anything else?" He should go.

"No, that's it. What can I get you as a thank you?"

"Nothing. Seriously, it's no big deal. Don't worry about it."

"But I'd like to."

She looked so sincere. And almost hopeful. He didn't have the heart to dismiss it again. "Then I'll think about it."

"Good."

She looked even more beautiful than she had five minutes ago. He really needed to leave. "Well, I'm gonna head home, then. Nice to meet you finally. Guess I'll see you around."

"Yes. Have a good night."

She followed him out, even walked around the side of the house with him, and waved as he drove away. His last sight of her was as she turned away in the rearview mirror.

It wasn't his last thought of her, however. Tate couldn't get her out of his mind, even after he was home alone in bed. Even though he tried to stop thinking about her.

Even though they were opposites in almost every way and it would never work out between them.

CHAPTER FIVE

Tate pried his eyes open when his cell rang on his bedside table the next morning. Avery. "Hey," he mumbled, still half-asleep as he squinted at the logs and chinking in the wall beside his bed. Damn, he was sore. "What's up?"

"We've got a call. Since you don't have wheels at the moment, I'm on the way to get you."

It was seven in the morning on a Saturday. Curt had taken the truck in last night. "Was there a murder?" It was the only reason he could think of to warrant a response in Rifle Creek at this time of the morning.

"Your neighbor's apparently been terrorizing the area again by, quote, 'holding a shooting spree in the middle of the night.' You and I are supposed to deal with it ASAP."

Tate groaned and flopped back onto his pillow. "Curt?"

"Who else?"

He closed his eyes and sighed. "Let me guess, Mrs. Engleman filed the complaint." The elderly widow was a recent addition to Rifle Creek and wasn't shy about letting the Sheriff's Office know when something bothered her. Which was often. And mostly pertained to Curt, whose rear property line abutted hers.

"Yep. Can you call him and get his side of things before I get there? It'll save us time."

"Yeah, all right. How long do I have?"

"Seven minutes. But only because I'm stopping to get you coffee on the way."

"You're a goddess."

"I know. Now call him. I'll be there soon." She ended the call.

Tate dialed Curt, taking stock of all his aches and pains while he waited for his neighbor to answer. Damn, he was sore through his neck and shoulders and down either side of his spine. "Hey, Curt, sorry to call so early."

"No, it's great timing," Curt answered in his usual brisk way. Pneumatic tools buzzed in the background. "Figured I'd get an early start on your truck."

"That's great." He rubbed his eyes. "Listen, I'm calling about something else. The department got a complaint from—"

"That damn woman. I guess she'd rather lose her precious powder puff of a lapdog and her chickens to the coyotes, then?" Curt snapped. "That damn woman became the bane of my fucking existence the day she moved in behind me. I've lived on this land since nineteen-eighty-one, and never had any trouble with a single soul until her. *She's* the problem, *not* me."

Okay, well, be that as it may... "Can you give me your side of the story? It would help to know before I go talk to her."

Curt huffed out a frustrated sigh and relayed his version of events. They were as Tate expected. "Okay, thanks. I'll make a note of all that in the official report."

"Listen, just tell her to remove that stick up her ass

and wake up to reality. This is the wild Rocky Mountains, not suburban Atlanta. Damn clueless snob, like she's some Southern belle looking down her nose at me like I'm a redneck."

Yeah, no, Tate wouldn't be telling her any of that. "But you are a redneck."

"And proud of it!"

"I know. I'll handle this, see if I can explain everything and get her to agree not to pursue charges."

"*Charges*? Jesus Ch—"

"I'll do my best, okay? If we need anything further from you, I'll let you know."

"You do that. In the meantime, I'm gonna go bang out some dents in your truck."

The line went dead before Tate could answer.

He hauled himself out of bed and stumbled into the bathroom to wash his face and brush his teeth, then grabbed clothes from his closet. At the brisk knock on his front door he hurried to answer it, wincing as he tugged his shirt over his head.

He pulled the door open to find Avery standing there with two coffee cups in hand. The sun was barely up, its rays casting a faint glow on the top of the roof across the street behind her, and the soaring peaks of the mountains beyond. "Morning," he muttered.

She winced in empathy. "Ooh. Rough night?"

"Sort of, yeah." Even with some extra-strength pain relievers before bed, he still hadn't slept well. He was surprised how sore he was from the impact.

She thrust one of the cups at him, along with two pills. "Here. Let's go."

"Thanks." He followed her out to her vehicle, inhaling the rich scent of the coffee to push the lingering fatigue from his brain.

"How sore are you?" Avery asked as she pulled out of his driveway.

He took the pills with a swallow of coffee. "I'm okay." He just needed another few hours of sleep and a long, hot soak in the hot tub after. "They seriously couldn't find anyone else to deal with this?"

"Nope. A lot of people are still away for summer vacation, so we're still short-staffed."

He grunted and sipped at his coffee. "What's her story?"

"She says Curt shot at her dog and chickens."

Tate shook his head. "He didn't. And this bullshit has been going on for weeks." Mrs. Engleman's constant stream of complaints ranged from annoying to ridiculous, but this was the first time Tate had been directly involved in an official capacity. Usually he just got a frustrated run-down from Curt across the fence.

"Nope. She was pissed right off, demanded the office send someone out first thing this morning. So, here we are. Lucky us." Avery shot him a fake smile and turned the corner to take them past the length of Curt's property.

Tate groaned. "This is why I stopped being a beat cop the second I could."

"Oh, stop whining. It's Rifle Creek, not the mean streets of inner-city Chicago. We'll go, hear her out, do our job, then I'll drive you home and you can crawl back into bed."

He'd never be able to get back to sleep now. Part of his military training that would never go away. Once he was up, that was it.

Two minutes later, Avery pulled into Mrs. Engleman's driveway and parked in front of the tidy little yellow bungalow. Multicolored flowers burst from hanging baskets and window boxes all around the front of the house. The emerald green lawn was so perfect it looked like the height had been measured with a ruler.

Tate rapped on the front door as Avery came up beside him on the front porch. Brisk footsteps came toward them, then the door swung open. Mrs. Engleman stood there dressed in slacks and a blouse with her gray hair and makeup done to elegant perfection, looking like she'd been up for hours.

"Good morning, officers." The hint of a drawl colored her voice.

Tate didn't bother correcting her that they were detectives. "Morning, ma'am. We understand you filed a complaint about a disturbance last night?"

"Yes. Please come in." She abruptly turned away and led them into the house. Tate and Avery followed after her, the scent of baking wafting from the kitchen. Everything in sight sparkled and gleamed, not a single item out of place. "I made banana bread this morning if anyone would like some, and maybe some coffee?"

He'd love some homemade banana bread, but this wasn't a social call and he didn't want to stay any longer than necessary. "No, thank you. Can we sit so you can tell us what happened?"

"Of course." She led them into her neat-as-a-pin living room and waited for them to be seated on the sofa.

The little white powder puff of a dog Curt had mentioned was perched on the love seat across from them and immediately scrambled into Mrs. Engleman's lap when she sat. It had a pink collar studded with jewels.

"You're aware that the rear of my property adjoins Mr. Larsen's?" she began.

"Yes. I live next door to him," Tate said, taking out a notepad to jot things down for the official report.

Mrs. Engleman's perfectly-shaped eyebrows rose. "Do you? Well, then you know what a menace that man is."

"I—"

"In spite of my polite requests that he refrain from doing so, he repeatedly patrols his property at night with a rifle and takes potshots at things. Last night when I took

38

Bella out to do her business before bedtime, he shot at her."

"Mrs. Engleman, what makes you think he was targeting Bella?"

"He absolutely did," she said indignantly, her pale eyes flashing as she cuddled her dog to her. "Scared us both half to death. Now Bella's afraid to go outside. She had an accident this morning by the sliding door for the first time since we've been here, because she refused to go into the yard. She's traumatized, and frankly, so am I. No one has taken my complaints seriously yet, but now that man needs to be dealt with. I demand y'all do something about this. It's unacceptable."

Tate shot Avery a look to tell her to take over, trying to be patient. Mrs. Engleman was brand new to country and mountain life. This was an alien environment for her, and he could understand why she was so upset about this. But while Curt was a lot of things, and a little eccentric, he wouldn't terrorize an old woman and her pet.

"We've already talked with Mr. Larsen about the incident," Avery told her. "He says he was shooting at some coyotes he saw wander onto your property last night, and the times match."

Mrs. Engleman's gaze cooled. "He can claim whatever he wants. But I believe that shot was a warning to both of us. Sometimes when Bella goes outside, she barks. He shot when she barked last night. And he's shot at my chickens before too. Now they won't lay."

"Mrs. Engleman," Tate said, unsure how to convince her that she had this all wrong. "I've only lived in the neighborhood for a few months longer than you. I know living next to Mr. Larsen takes some getting used to. You're aware that he owns a hobby farm of sorts?"

"Yes. What of it?"

"And that he's really protective of his goats?"

She blinked. "Goats?"

"Fainting goats."

Her eyebrows hiked up toward her hairline. "I beg your pardon?"

Okay, fainting goats weren't all that common, even out here in the mountains. Tate drew a breath and explained what they were, and that they tended to stiffen and even fall over when startled.

When he finished, Mrs. Engleman stared at him in disbelief. "Yet he goes around shooting at things in the middle of the night, making all his precious pets topple over and therefore even more vulnerable to predators?"

She had a point. "It's exactly because they're so vulnerable that he takes their safety so seriously."

"Even so, he can't run around with a weapon like a maniac, shooting at every threat he thinks he sees. This is a community, not the wilderness."

"I understand your concern. But let me add that Mr. Larsen isn't breaking any laws by protecting his property—and yours. We're outside of the city limits, so what he's done isn't a violation of any firearms laws. He's also an expert shot and served three tours in Vietnam in an elite special operations regiment."

Tate had hoped the intel would make Mrs. Engleman feel better, but she didn't react.

Avery nudged his thigh with hers, urging him to continue. "I understand how hearing nearby gunshots in the middle of the night would be unsettling for you, especially if you thought your dog was the target. But I know Mr. Larsen well. He's an animal lover, and I can assure you if he'd been aiming at Bella, you wouldn't be holding her right now."

Rather than comfort her, Tate's words made Mrs. Engleman gather Bella tighter to her. "Is that…supposed to reassure me?"

Yes. Yes, it is. "I just meant that you and your animals are actually *safer* with Mr. Larsen on patrol at night.

He's watching out for you and your property because you're his neighbor."

Avery nodded. "He's right, ma'am. And to err on the side of caution, I don't think you should let Bella outside at night at all without you having her on a leash. It's really not safe. There are all kinds of predators out in these hills, especially this time of year."

Mrs. Engleman clutched her dog to her chest, her expression full of alarm.

"Would it help if you met him on neutral ground with me there to make the official introductions?" Tate offered. "It might make you feel better if you got to know him a bit."

"I'll think about it. Thank you," Mrs. Engleman murmured, far more subdued now as she continued to clutch her dog to her.

She was uncharacteristically quiet as they took their leave a few minutes later. Driving away in Avery's car, Tate shook his head. "I almost feel sorry for her. Talk about a fish out of water."

Avery raised a strawberry-blond eyebrow at him. "Like you didn't wonder about Larsen's sanity when you first moved in next door?"

"Only for a day or two. Now I like the quirky old bastard."

"Yeah, because you're both Corps brothers. And speaking of fish out of water, what did you think of Nina?"

He'd thought *too* much about her. Including a lot of hot, dirty things last night in the shower before he'd crawled into bed. "She seems nice."

Avery shot him a censuring look. "Nice? That's it?"
"What?"

"She's my best friend. I want you to like her."

"I do like her." Probably too much.

"I just don't want things to be weird between you

guys. She's awesome and moving here is a huge change for her. So be nice."

"I am nice," he grumbled. "But what's her story?"

"What do you mean?"

"She seems a little…" He circled his wrist, searching for the right words and trying to be tactful. "I dunno, naive about life."

Avery laughed and slowed as they came to a stop sign. "You only think that because the military and being a cop has warped your world view."

Okay, maybe he was more jaded than he used to be. Between losing his mom and breaking up with Erica last year, on top of the things he'd seen overseas and the things he dealt with every day on the job, that wasn't a surprise.

"It just seems weird to me. I mean, the woman's a scientist. Aren't scientists supposed to be all about facts and evidence and math or whatever? Yet it's like she's got this dreamy look in her eyes when she talks about relationship stuff."

"I love that about her," Avery said with a fond smile.

Tate looked at her sharply, frowning. "Why?"

"That she has such a sense of wonder and an optimistic outlook on life. It's refreshing. And kind of infectious, to be honest." She eyed him. "Who knows, maybe some of that will rub off on us. Re-inflate our shriveled, blackened hearts."

"Yeah, doubt it," he said on a brusque chuckle. As she turned the corner onto his street he immediately spotted the red Jeep parked in his driveway.

"There, see? Your company wasn't gonna let you sleep in this morning anyway."

Mason. Tate hadn't expected him so early, but was glad his buddy was here. "Yeah. You wanna come in for a bit and say hi?"

"Nope. I'm going home to pick up Nina and show

her around town."

"Tell her not to blink on the tour."

"Ha, smartass."

"Maybe Mase and I'll see you later." The second he got out, his front door opened to reveal Mason standing there, wearing a black cowboy hat and a wide grin on his dark-bearded face.

"Hey, man," Mason called out. "Thought for sure I'd catch you sleeping. Was looking forward to waking you up." A medium-sized white, black and brown dog appeared at his side, and he absently reached down to stroke its head.

"You would." He loped up the steps and caught Mason in a back-slapping hug even though it made his shoulders ache more. They hadn't seen each other in over four months. "Great to see you, man." He looked down at Mason's service dog. "So this is Ric."

"Yep. Short for Ricochet. He's my wingman."

Tate let the dog sniff his hand, then stroked its fuzzy head. Ric gazed up at him with mismatched eyes, one blue, one brown. Cute, especially the brown eyebrows that gave his face such expression. "What kind is he?" He petted Ric's ears, scratched under the dog's chin.

"Border collie and Aussie shepherd, mostly, but I'm not sure exactly. Now. When can we check out this property you dragged me down here to see?"

"*Dragged* you?"

Mason's pale blue eyes twinkled with the promise of mischief. "Yeah."

Excitement stirred in his gut. "Right now, I guess. We can stop and grab a bite in town after." He wouldn't mind bumping into Nina and Avery.

They headed for Mason's Jeep. "Where's your truck?" he asked Tate.

"In the shop." Currently bearing the brunt of Curt's

frustrations with his new neighbor. "Got rear-ended yesterday." The instant he opened the passenger door, Ric jumped into the front seat and sat there staring at Tate, as if telling him the seat was claimed. "Yeah, sorry, buddy. I'm not getting in the backseat for you."

"Ric, get in the back, you doofus," Mason said, snapping his fingers toward the rear seats.

The dog's ears fell. He turned around, head down, tail between his legs and slunk his way into the backseat as though he'd been banished to the ends of the earth.

"He's so sensitive," Mason said with a chuckle. "Big sucky baby." He reached back to ruffle the dog's ears and received a feeble tail wag in reply, then Ric rested his chin on Mason's shoulder to stare out the windshield.

It was a twenty-minute drive up to the property for sale. Tate unlocked the small shed at the edge of the property line to reveal the ATVs parked inside. A large barn that had seen better days lay in the center of the clearing ahead.

"You up for this?" He wasn't sure he was. His muscles ached like a bitch and after this he was going to need a soak in the hot tub and a few beers to ease the pain.

Mason grinned. "Yeah, man. Come on, Ric." The dog bounded up beside him on the front seat of the ATV, ears perked.

Tate climbed on his, started it up, and led the way up the trail that wound through the nearly two-hundred-acre parcel. It had come up for sale a couple months ago, and after he'd mentioned it to Mason, his friend had thrown out the idea of opening up the business together with Braxton.

With every day that passed, Tate wanted it more and more, his mind filled with plans. There was so much they could do with it. Thick forest covered most of the property. If they were going to use it for training various groups, they'd have to clear certain sections to make it useable. They'd also need to build a lodge of sorts to house everyone.

"How far's the river from here?" Mason asked as he drove beside Tate. Ric was still perched in place, ears perked, nose quivering as he sniffed at whatever scents he caught.

"Just over a mile." He turned and headed for it.

Rifle Creek ran right through the southeastern edge of the property, and fed into a river system that was perfect for kayaking and white water rafting. The mountains themselves offered endless possibilities for training scenarios, including winter conditions. Getting permits for a shooting range up here shouldn't be a problem. There was so much potential for their business with this parcel of land.

He stopped at an overlook above a section of class three rapids, the banks covered with craggy rocks and tall evergreens. Mason grinned, eyes gleaming. "Awesome. We can do some gnarly shit with this."

Tate watched the water froth and churn around the rocks below, excitement firing his blood. He could almost feel the cold water sluicing over him as they traversed the rapids in a kayak or raft. Or the sun-warmed rock beneath his hands as they climbed and rappelled down a cliff face.

While he loved certain aspects of being a detective, like problem solving and helping others, parts of it sucked too. It would be refreshing not to have to deal with criminals and accidents on a daily basis. To work outdoors a lot instead of being stuck behind a desk.

He craved freedom. Flexibility. Being able to make his own hours, use the skill set he'd learned in the Corps to teach others. Working with his two closest friends, guys he trusted with his life, was the cherry on top of the sundae.

The place felt right. And all three of them were looking for a change.

"Got a site in mind for the lodge?" Mason asked, pulling him from his thoughts.

"Quarter mile east of here." He led the way, turning everything over in his mind. Mason had come a long way since his recovery, but Tate still worried about his buddy. After being forced out of JTF2 and then the military due to medical discharge, Mason had struggled to make the transition from elite military service back into the civilian world.

"Hey, how's the local female scene here?" Mason asked him on the way to the site Tate had short-listed for the lodge.

"In Rifle Creek?" It was a small town of less than twelve thousand people, including the immediate surrounding area, and a large percentage of the population was elderly. "There isn't one." Even as he said it, he thought of Nina.

Damned if he knew what to make of her. Or of his attraction to her.

He definitely wasn't looking for anything serious anymore. He wasn't looking, period. When he decided to date again it would be short and sweet with no strings attached. It was all he was comfortable with right now.

Nina didn't seem like she'd ever be interested in that kind of arrangement. She was all about soulmates and happily ever after, and he hated to be the one to tell her, but those things just didn't exist in the real world.

Avery was right about one thing, however—Nina seemed like an eternal optimist. He'd never met anyone with such an idealistic, romantic view of the world. And damned if it didn't make him feel old and cynical by comparison.

CHAPTER SIX

For the first time in months, it truly felt like Nina had a chance for a fresh start. Like she could finally leave the shadows from her past behind here in Rifle Creek.

Nina spotted the basket sitting on her doorstep the moment she turned the corner of the house on the brick walkway to the back. Smiling, she propped her grocery bag on one hip as she unlocked the door to her suite.

Crouching down, she bent to inspect the little bundle covered in a red-and-white gingham cloth. A jar of homemade blueberry jam and a loaf of homemade bread, along with a little handwritten note.

Welcome to the neighborhood. We hope you enjoy this little housewarming gift. Hope to meet you soon. Bev and Pat (across the street).

Ohhh, wasn't that the most charming, thoughtful thing ever?

Nina carried her gift into the kitchen, the smile still stretching her mouth. So far, small-town living was even more wonderful than she ever could have imagined.

Avery had taken her into downtown today to show her around all the historic brick and painted-wood buildings that lined Main Street and the surrounding area.

She'd asked a few questions about Tate, but not so much that it would make Avery suspicious that Nina was interested, and found out he'd broken up with his long-time girlfriend last fall, around the same time he lost his mother. Nina's heart went out to him. No wonder he hadn't dated much since. That was a lot of grief to deal with.

In the space of an hour during the tour, Nina had met the local café owner, the regulars at the coffee shop Avery frequented, opened up a bank account at the local branch, and received a brief history lesson about the town. Rifle Creek had once been a booming lumber town, and now the old sawmill had been refurbished as shops and restaurants. Now it was her home.

A tap came on the door connecting her suite to the stairs leading to Avery's. "Knock-knock," her friend called from the other side.

Nina hurried to answer it. "Look, the neighbors across the street sent me jam and bread," she gushed, grabbing Avery's hand and towing her into the kitchen.

"What kind of jam? Blueberry?"

"Yes, how'd you know?"

A half-smile formed on Avery's lips. "Because I dropped them off a huge box of blueberries yesterday."

"Oh, that was so nice of them to make us jam. You want some?"

"Sure. Everything Bev makes is delicious."

Nina sliced them each some bread, then set out some butter and the jar of jam. "I'm going to go introduce myself."

"Want me to come?"

"No, I'm okay going by myself. Are they right across the street?"

"Yep, the blue-and-purple Victorian."

Nina slathered butter and jam on her piece of bread. Oh, man, it was still warm. Carb kryptonite. "Are they a couple?"

"No, they're sisters. Never married, they both stayed here to look after their aging parents before they died. They've lived here forever."

"That's so sweet." She took a bite, closed her eyes and hummed in her throat. "Ohmygod. So *good*."

Avery hummed in agreement and savored her own slice of heaven.

"I think I'll take over some of the cherries we bought at the farmer's market." The last of the season.

"Sure, just save me some to make the sauce for the pork tenderloins later."

"Okay. Are Tate and his friend coming for sure?" she asked casually. Or, she hoped it came out that way. He'd been on her mind since he left last night. She was curious about him. Not to mention insanely attracted to him.

"Yeah, around six. You cool with that?"

"Of course." It was Avery's house, she could have anyone she wanted over. But knowing Tate was coming set off a little burst of excitement inside her. Nina was looking forward to seeing him again.

Avery headed back upstairs. Nina tidied up, gathered the cherries and packed them in the basket. The warm sun felt blissful on her skin as she made the short walk across the street to the pretty Victorian where the two sisters lived.

One of them was working in the front garden, bent over near the fence as she tied some sunflower stalks to the black, wrought iron fence. "Hello," Nina called out.

The woman straightened just as another popped up from behind some shrubs ten feet from her. They both wore matching Tilley hats, the brims shading their faces.

"Hi, I'm Nina. Just moved into the suite across the

street." She smiled at them. "Thank you so much for your thoughtful gift, it was delicious. I brought you some fresh cherries from the farmer's market in town."

"Oh, how lovely," one sister said, walking to the wrought iron gate to receive her. "Come in, dear, come in. I'm Pat. This is Bev. People around here think we're twins, but we're not. I'm older by thirteen months."

"Nice to meet you." Nina shook their hands and handed over the cherries, then shaded her eyes with her hand and gazed around at the house and yard. Clearly these women took a great deal of pride in caring for their home. "This is such a beautiful property."

"Thanks," Pat said. "Been in our family for four generations now. Inherited it through our father's side. You want some coffee or iced tea?"

"Oh, no, I—"

"It's no trouble, Bev always has both ready to go at a moment's notice in case we have company drop by."

Nina was starting to get the sense that Pat was the spokeswoman. Bev had yet to utter a single word. "Well, if it's no trouble…"

"It's not. Come on." Pat hooked her arm through Nina's and chattered away as she led them around the side of the house and onto the back porch, Bev hurrying ahead of them. "Did you know Avery's house was built by one of Rifle Creek's founding citizens? He was a lumber baron. Very wealthy." Pat frowned, her silver eyebrows drawing together over a pair of shrewd blue eyes. "Had more money than he ever needed, but as we all know, money can't buy happiness."

Nina nodded and made a sound of agreement as they walked across the porch into what looked like a sunroom. The kitchen lay beyond it, the heavenly smells of freshly baked bread and coffee wafting from it.

"His wife was a delicate little thing," Pat continued. "Eldest girl from a wealthy family in California. He brought her out here from San Francisco soon after they married. He'd built this house for her, you see, in the Victorian style so common in San Francisco at the time. So she wouldn't be homesick."

"Oh, that's so romantic," Nina said. "Maybe that's why I feel so at home here. That's where I'm from."

"Are you? Well, I don't believe in coincidences. You coming here was meant to be."

Nina beamed at her, recognizing a kindred spirit. "I think so too."

Pat patted Nina's arm. "Well, back to my story. The wife I mentioned was frail. Gave birth to their son and she never regained her strength. She died less than a year later, and so did the baby."

Nina's smile vanished. "That's terrible."

"Yes, very sad. People say her ghost haunts the house still."

Nina stared at her, her imagination taking off. "Really?"

Pat nodded. "Though I'm sure you're used to ghosts, coming from a place as haunted as San Francisco. So just don't be surprised if you feel a cold chill from time to time, or hear bumps in the night. Her name was Charlotte, by the way." She patted Nina's hand. "But don't worry, she's not a malevolent spirit." She gazed up at the ceiling with a dark look. "Not like the one that lives with us."

Nina opened her mouth to ask more, a tiny part of her that was buried beneath the scientist wondering if it just might be possible, but Pat brightened and squeezed Nina's hand. "It's so wonderful to have such friendly young people as neighbors. Now, here we go. Bev's got your tea ready."

By the time Nina left an hour later, it felt like she'd been through a whirlwind. She knew all about Lucille, the angry ghost living in Pat and Bev's attic. Legend said Lucille had been poisoned by her controlling, abusive and philandering husband, and she had vowed to haunt the place until she got her revenge.

Pat had also told Nina about the most important and influential people in town—which included her and Bev, as they were on both the historical preservation and home-owners' society.

She spent the early afternoon unpacking the rest of her things and playing with the furniture layout until she was happy with it. Then she texted Avery for a grocery list, hopped in her SUV and headed into town to buy the ingredients for dinner.

Arriving home with everything they needed, she found another basket waiting on her doorstep. She put it on the kitchen counter along with the rest of the groceries. Opening it, she found a cake caddy inside with another note.

Seemed like a good use of the fresh cherries. Enjoy! Love, Pat and Bev. Xo

Nina pulled off the lid to find a homemade black forest cake sitting on the tray. Three layers of decadent, dark chocolate cake sandwiched between whipped cream and cherry filling.

Nina frowned. First the blueberries into jam—which Avery had seemed unsurprised and amused by. Now this. And she was too quick a study to miss the pattern.

"Ahh, so it's like *that*," she murmured. Seemed Pat—because Nina couldn't imagine this was Bev's idea—had a bit of a competitive edge, with a penchant for one-upmanship. Well, Nina was up for the challenge.

She smiled to herself, delighted by the prospect of such an ongoing friendly rivalry in this quirky little town she now called home. "Game on, neighbor. Game *on*."

Forty minutes later she carried the fruits of her labor upstairs in a glass punchbowl. Avery was already in the kitchen prepping dinner. "Hey, is there room for this left-over cake in your fridge?"

Avery glanced at her. "Sure. You made cake?"

"Nope. Pat did. Well, I'm now assuming it was actually Bev, on Pat's orders." She slid the remaining cake into the fridge and shut the door.

When she turned around, Avery was staring at the bowl on the counter. "And what's that?"

"*That*, is black forest cake trifle. Made by yours truly. I'm going to take it over to their place right now. Like to see them top this."

A slow smile spread across Avery's face. "Ohh, I like this."

Nina chuckled. "Me too. Should be fun." She picked up the trifle.

"Wait, I'm coming with you." Avery hurriedly untied her apron and tossed it on the counter, grinning like a maniac. "I can't wait to see Pat's face when you give it to her."

They crossed the road together and stood on the front porch as Avery rang the bell. Pat answered it with a startled smile. "Well, isn't this a nice surprise."

"Yes. Thank you so much for the gorgeous cake, that was so thoughtful," Nina said.

"We're having a dinner party, so perfect timing. Can't wait to try it," Avery added.

Nina held out the bowl with a sweet smile. "I thought it would be perfect in a trifle, so I whipped this up just for you two."

Pat blinked at it, her smile fading. "My, that... That was so thoughtful of you." She took it, seemed at a loss for words for a moment before she spoke over her shoulder. "Look, Bev. Nina made us trifle with your cake."

Bev appeared behind her sister's shoulder an instant later, staring at the trifle with disbelieving eyes magnified by a pair of reading glasses.

"Only some of it," Nina said. "I kept most of it for us

and our dinner guests, because it looked too delicious. Anyway, thanks again and I hope you enjoy it. Have a good night!"

She and Avery breezed off the porch and down the wooden steps, grinning from ear to ear.

Avery laughed when they finally rounded the side of their house, out of earshot from their neighbors. "Did you see her *face*? That was so awesome." She cackled as she headed up the steps, Nina right behind her. "I knew you moving in here was a great idea. I've had more fun with you today than I've had in forever. Sad as that sounds."

"Me too. Wonder what she'll do next."

Avery tossed her a mischievous grin. "Bet we'll find out soon enough."

****

"Tate's friend is bringing a dog with him?" Nina asked her as they set the table on the back deck later.

It was a beautiful night out and Avery wanted to enjoy the warmth while it lasted because fall would be here soon. "Yeah, it's Mason's therapy dog."

"Is he disabled?"

"Not physically anymore, as far as I know." But everyone who went to war came home with injuries. Some of the worst ones were invisible. Veterans were suffering all over the country, and made up a disproportionate percentage of the homeless population. "Can you check the pasta?"

"Sure." Nina headed inside.

Avery finished laying the table and then paused to smooth the front of her dress. After seeing Nina in her cute little black sundress with cherries on it—which Avery was sure was no coincidence after the black forest cake incident—she'd put on a dress too.

The violet-sprigged material was soft and heavy enough that it hung nicely on her tall frame. It wasn't fancy or as cute as Nina's, but it felt nice to dress up a bit

54

into something feminine for a change.

"Ding-dong," Tate's voice called out from beyond the kitchen.

"Come on in," she answered, and went inside to greet them.

A white, brown and black dog came trotting in wearing a red bandana around its neck. When it saw her, it lowered its ears and head in a submissive posture, swishy tail wagging softly. "Well, hi there," Avery said, bending to hold out a hand for it to sniff.

"That's Ric," Tate said, his gaze sweeping right past her to Nina, who stood at the stove. He stared at her a moment, either unsure what to say or stunned into silence by the sight of Nina in her sundress. "Hi."

"Hi." Nina gave him a disarming smile, then completely dismissed him and knelt down to greet Ric. "Oh, aren't you just so handsome. Huh? Aren't you the handsomest dog ever?"

Ric's back end wagged almost as much as his tail as he rushed for Nina, head down.

"Ric," his shadowy owner said from in the hallway. "How do we say hello to ladies?"

The dog instantly plopped hit butt down in front of Nina and raised his right paw.

"Oh!" The joy on Nina's face was downright infectious, and when Avery glanced up from having her turn at shaking Ric's paw, she noticed something very interesting.

As Nina fussed over the dog, Avery's gruff and standoffish partner's full attention was on Nina. Glued to her, actually.

Well, well. Maybe she'd misread Tate's take on her friend completely. And If Nina couldn't shave off some of his rough edges, no one could.

Avery smothered a laugh and turned toward the tall

silhouette coming up behind Tate. "And this must be Mason."

"That's me." The man stepped past Tate, revealing himself in the light streaming into the kitchen.

She was tall, but he was taller than her by several inches, and a little broader through the chest and shoulders than Tate. He had short dark hair and a neatly-trimmed beard, and stunning ice blue eyes.

He held out a hand. "Avery. Nice to meet you finally. I've heard a lot about you."

She didn't miss the way his gaze swept over her as she shook his hand. A spurt of annoyance hit her, brought on by his player reputation Tate had hinted at. She'd invited him into her home and didn't appreciate being sized up just because she was a single, available female.

She gave his hand a perfunctory shake and let go immediately. "Likewise. Come on in, get a drink and make yourselves comfortable."

Mason walked past her to meet Nina. Avery caught Tate by the arm, waiting for him to look at her before speaking. "Remember, be nice," she murmured, too low for the others to hear.

He shot her an annoyed look. "I *am* nice."

Everyone helped carry something to the table to eat. When they were all seated, Avery raised her wineglass for a toast. "To good friends, good food, and great strategy." She winked at Nina.

"Cheers," the others said.

"Tate, how are you feeling now?" Nina asked as she passed him the chopped salad.

"Not bad, thanks. How was your first sleep in your new digs?"

"Awesome. I got woken up a few times because of noises I heard. Pipes banging and stuff like that. But now I wonder if it was Charlotte." Her eyes simmered with silent laughter.

Everyone looked at her. "Who?" Avery said.

Nina glanced at her, a mischievous smile tugging at her lips. "Charlotte, the ghost who lives upstairs here."

Avery's eyebrows went up. "What?"

"You didn't know your house was haunted?" Nina teased, becoming animated as she relayed the tale Pat had told her earlier. "But apparently she's not a mean ghost. Just a sad one." She shrugged. "I mean, if you believe in that kind of thing."

Tate was eyeing Nina from across the table with open skepticism. "And do you?"

Avery kicked his foot under the table. He shot her an irritated glance before focusing back on Nina.

"Not really," Nina answered.

"So…somewhat?" he asked, clearly trying to get a read on her.

"Well, who am I to say if it's real or not? I only just got here. I think a longtime resident would know better about that kind of thing than me."

"But you're a scientist." He was frowning now. Avery nudged his foot again but he ignored her.

"If there's enough evidence to support it, why not? There are lots of unsolved mysteries in our universe," Nina said with an easy shrug.

Avery could tell her friend was deliberately baiting Tate, and decided it was time to change the subject. "Well, as long as we've got a friendly ghost, I'm okay with it." She turned to Mason. Ric was politely lying beneath the table at his master's feet, not making a sound or trying to beg. "He's really well behaved."

"Yeah, he's a good boy." Mason's hard features softened in a fond smile as he glanced down at his dog. "Been through a lot together. Same as this guy and me," he said, nodding at Tate.

"How did you two meet?" Nina asked, propping her chin in one hand, elbow on the table. Innate curiosity and kindness shone from her warm brown eyes, a little smile on her lips.

One of the things Avery loved best about Nina was her sense of wonder about the world. Her friend found pleasure in the tiniest little things. Avery could stand to make an effort in that department. Nina was a good influence on her.

"Yeah, Tate, tell 'em how we first met," Mason said, his eyes twinkling.

"Afghanistan," Tate answered, a reluctant grin tugging at his mouth. "There was an issue with our barracks at base. Came back from a mission to find all our gear was dumped outside, and a big Canadian flag hanging above the doorway. I went in to ask what the hell was going on, and this dipshit announced we had to find new sleeping quarters." He jerked his chin at Mason.

"It was a match made in heaven," Mason went on. "We were sent out on a joint mission the next day, and Tate and I got to know each other pretty well over the next few days. First time he'd ever worked with Canadian forces."

"Never thought Canadians could be such assholes," Tate joked.

"What?" Mason feigned shock, putting a hand to his chest. "I'll have you know that my fellow countrymen are known as some of the most polite and respectful people on earth."

"Maybe, but none of the polite ones got deployed on that tour."

Mason grinned and helped himself to some pasta. "Come on, you know you loved me right from the start."

"You wore me down over the next eight months."

"So much that he called me up after I left the military and begged me to take a contracting job with him," Mason said.

Tate grunted. "I didn't beg. Figured you needed

something to do with your sorry ass after you got out."

"What made you decide to leave the military?" Nina asked Mason.

A second of awkward silence answered. Avery internally winced as Mason's smirk vanished. Nina had no clue that she'd just stepped into some very personal territory. But thankfully Mason was gracious enough to answer her.

"Medical discharge after the helo we were in went down."

Nina's face filled with alarm. "Oh, I'm so sorry, I wouldn't have asked if—"

"It's fine, no worries." The smile he shot her seemed genuine enough, but Avery caught the flash of pain in his eyes.

There was a ghost in the house tonight for sure, but it lived inside this man.

"Anyway, contracting wasn't for me," he continued. "Then Tate called me up a few months ago to tell me about this property that had just come up for sale. Starting up an adventure/training ranch sounded intriguing, and for some damn reason I just can't get enough of this guy, so here I am."

"Well, we're glad you came," Nina said with a soft smile. "And Ric, too." She bent a little to hold out her hand to the dog. Ric's tail thumped on the wooden deck at the mention of his name, then he shuffled closer to sniff and lick at Nina's fingers.

"Thanks, happy to be here," Mason said, any tension gone now. "And as usual, my dog has stolen the ladies' hearts."

"Because he's adorable," Avery said, petting Ric when he nudged her for attention. "Where did you get him?"

Those piercing blue eyes shot to her. And she'd have had to be blind not to notice the frank male interest in them. Interest she intended to firmly shut down right away. She had no interest in being used and discarded by a man ever again.

"From a program that has inmates train service dogs for vets. This guy washed out partway through the program, but they thought he'd still make a great service dog. And they were right," he said to Ric, who gazed up at him with adoring eyes.

Nina beamed at Mason. "That's so great." She leaned over to peer under the table, and Avery noticed the way Tate's stare dropped to the revealing glimpse of her friend's cleavage. "Ric, what a good boy you are," she crooned.

Ric scooted closer to Nina and leaned against her leg to gaze up at her, his tail thumping harder.

"Ric," Mason warned.

The dog stopped wagging and crept back under the table to lie at Mason's feet.

"He was searching for the weakest link in terms of treat-seeking potential," Mason explained, smiling at Nina. "And I think he found it."

It was true. Ric was poised in place at Mason's feet, gazing hopefully up at Nina from beneath the table.

"Guilty," Nina confessed with a grin. "I can't help it, look at him. Ack! Quick, let's eat. I can't stand those sad puppy eyes looking up at me."

The rest of the meal passed with entertaining stories about Tate from Mason and Avery. After dinner Nina and Tate cleared the table, leaving Mason and Avery outside.

Mason leaned back in his chair to regard her, and Avery would have to be dead not to notice all that blatant male power stretched out across from her.

Mason might have hard edges, but he wasn't hard on the eyes. "So, Avery. How is it being stuck with that guy day in and day out on the job? Be honest. I've been there, done that, so I know what he's like."

"Honestly? Tate's the best thing about my job."

Mason raised his dark eyebrows, his head dipping in approval. "Really? Do tell."

"He's solid, steady, dependable, and with his military service he can handle himself when things go south. Not that they do very often around here. But yeah, I love having him around all the time."

And it was going to suck so bad if Tate decided to start up this business with Mason and Braxton and give his notice at the sheriff's department. She wanted Tate to be happy, but being a detective here without him wouldn't be the same.

Nina came out carrying the remainder of the black forest cake. "Who wants dessert?"

"Me," Mason said, aiming a sexy half-grin at Avery. "I like sweet things."

Well then, you won't like me. Sweet wasn't in the list of words she would use to describe herself.

She gave him a warning look, earning a deep chuckle she liked the sound of far too much. Tate had told her enough about Mason to know he was popular with the ladies. That and his personal baggage was more than enough reason for her to make it clear she wasn't interested.

The doorbell rang, breaking the subtle tension between them. "Excuse me," Avery said, and left the table.

She walked through the kitchen and down the stairs to answer it. A large, checkered cloth-covered basket sat on the doorstep.

She grinned. Glancing up, she thought she spotted the top of a curly white head poking just above the boxwood hedges across the street.

"Nina," she called out as she carried the basket inside and shut the door. "Come check this out. Round five just arrived."

Her friend met her in the kitchen, her eyes gleaming

with anticipation when she saw the basket. "No way."

"Way." She set it on the counter. "Let's see what they did."

Whisking back the cloth, they both gaped at the contents. Blueberry muffins. Blueberry syrup in a jar. Blueberry cobbler. Cherry bars. Chocolate bark with cherries and pistachios.

Nina burst out laughing and Avery couldn't help but join in. "This is so ridiculous, and I love it."

"What's so funny?" Tate stood in the patio doorway, beer in hand as he watched them.

"We just have the best neighbors, that's all," Avery said, and carried the basket out to the table. "Hope you guys still have some room left."

The guys stayed long enough to demolish most of the basket's contents. Then Tate and Mason said goodbye to Nina, and Avery followed them to the door.

"Thanks, Ave. Great meal as usual," Tate said, giving her a squeeze on the way past.

"Welcome, but don't get used to it. You can cook for me next time, freeloader. And Nina, too."

A smile tugged at his mouth at the mention of her friend. "Deal."

She tensed a tiny bit when Mason paused at the door to look at her. She put on a smile. "It was nice to meet you and Ric." She petted the dog's head and the back of its neck, unable to not smile at him. He was too freaking adorable with his silky soft fur and mismatched eyes. Plus, this way she was spared from the intensity of the awareness that hummed along her nerve endings when Mason was close.

"You too. But maybe next time I'll leave him at home so you'll pay more attention to me."

She glanced up, a swarm of stupid butterflies fluttering around in her belly at that direct, pale blue stare. "I don't think you're hurting for female attention."

Interest lit his gaze. "Why do you think that?"

Because I know your type. "Let's just say I've got an inside source on you I consider to be credible."

A rueful grin tugged at his mouth. "Don't believe everything you hear about me, angel eyes." She started to frown at the pet name but he gave her a respectful nod. "Good night."

"Good night." It was almost a relief to close the door and block out the sight of him.

The man rubbed her the wrong way and she wasn't sure why. Since he was Tate's best friend and might be moving here, she'd better find a way past that, because it looked like she'd be seeing a lot more of him.

Lying in bed later that night, she thought about dinner. About how Nina was clearly attracted to Tate, and that Tate was into Nina too. Would that be weird and awkward if they got together and broke up? Whatever. They were adults, they'd figure it out.

It made Avery think about her own life. About how Mason had flirted with her subtly throughout the night, testing the waters and trying to figure out where the boundaries lay. She'd made sure he couldn't misunderstand that she wasn't interested, because there was no way she was touching that one with a ten-foot pole.

Angel eyes? She snorted to herself.

Mason was ruggedly good-looking, a wonderful friend to Tate and apparently the kind of guy you'd want at your back in a crisis. He also had major baggage, and might be moving here permanently. After barely surviving her divorce, she couldn't offer anything more than a fling, and that certainly wasn't happening with Tate's best friend. She wasn't an idiot.

Not anymore.

Her eyes flew open in the darkness at a soft thud overhead. The only light was the faint glow of the digital numbers of her bedside clock.

A series of quiet creaks came from above the ceiling overhead.

Her room was in the turret on the northeast side of the house. The only thing above her was a tiny attic space that had been sealed off by the people Avery had bought the place from. So how come it sounded like definite footsteps up there?

It could be a raccoon. Or maybe an opossum.

More creaks. Moving slowly. Tracking across the floor above her. Like someone pacing…

Avery snorted and rolled her eyes at herself. Damn Nina, putting stories in her head.

But as she pulled the covers up to her chin, she stared at the ceiling with an uncertain frown, feeling stupid. *Charlotte? Is that you?*

CHAPTER SEVEN

Now that Tate had decided for sure he wanted to go ahead with the business, everything was taking too damn long and his current job sucked.

"Hello? Earth to Tate."

Frowning, Tate looked up to find Avery standing in front of his desk with her arms folded. They'd been in the office since seven, getting a few files and reports finished up. Mostly theft cases, a few breaking and entering. Boring shit that threatened to put him in a coma. Not that he *wanted* murders or other violent crimes to solve here. He was just done with being in law enforcement.

He blinked at his partner. "Sorry?"

She frowned at him. "Didn't sleep last night, or what? You've been spaced out all afternoon. Your headache worse?"

"No, I'm good." The stiffness and soreness was much better now, and Curt had delivered his truck home last night, looking good as new. "What did you say?"

"I asked if you were still coming to the festival with me. Because I'm starving, and if I don't eat something in the next hour, I might die."

If he didn't get out of here and do something more exciting for a while, he might die too. "Well, we can't have that." He shut off his computer and closed the file folder sitting on his desk. "Where do you want to go?"

"Mini donuts for sure. But I was thinking Poultrygeist first. We can grab food to go and eat it in the park where the festival's set up. I promised Nina I'd meet her."

His pulse jumped at the thought of seeing her again, which was damn annoying. "Sure."

She narrowed her eyes a bit. "You hesitated."

"No I didn't. I'll invite Mason too."

Her expression tensed ever so slightly. If he hadn't known her so well, he would have missed it. "Fine. Let's go."

It only took two minutes for him to drive into town, but everything was packed. They wound up parking in front of Poultrygeist, situated in a two-story brick building right in the center of the main strip of downtown Rifle Creek. They specialized in chicken of all sorts, but it was their fried chicken they were famous for.

"I'll go grab us some takeout if you wanna stake out a spot for us in the park," Avery said.

"Sure. By the way, I took Curt over to introduce him to Mrs. Engleman last night after he brought my truck home," Tate said.

"Really? How'd *that* go?"

"It was awkward. Civil, though. Curt was on his best behavior."

"I'll bet he was."

"At least they've officially met. Can't hurt, right?"

"Let's hope not." She got out and headed into the restaurant while Tate walked to the park one block over, the warm air carrying the scent of cinnamon and deep-fried goodness from the mini donut stand and the kettle corn vendor. There were already lineups at both, as well as the lemonade stand run by two kids and their moms.

The park was filled with families. Looked like half the town had turned out to enjoy the sunshine and festivities. Various carnival game booths were set up, with street performers playing music or performing magic tricks. Tate chose a spot in the shade of a big aspen and spread out a blanket beneath it.

His whole body tensed when Nina breezed up a minute later. She was wearing another little sundress that left her lightly bronzed arms and calves bare. This one was deep blue and flowed over her curves, and her sunny smile when she spotted them hit him straight in the chest like a simunition round.

"Hey," she said with a bright smile, her sweet scent carrying to him.

He stood. "Hi. Have a good first day of classes?" He'd checked on Rylee earlier. She said her day had gone well, and that her roommate was nice, but more outgoing than her.

"Great." She glanced around, taking in the ambiance of the festival with obvious pleasure. "This is so neat. Where's Avery?"

"Getting us some fried chicken."

"I *love* the name of the restaurant. Is there a story behind it?"

"Yeah. They serve great chicken, and it's supposedly haunted." His tone was bland.

Her eyes widened a little. "No way. How many ghosts are there in this town?"

"A lot," Avery said with a laugh as she came up behind them. "Draws the tourists."

"And the gullible," Tate added. He was saved from making another smartass remark when his phone vibrated in his pocket. He fished it out and read the message. "Mase can't join us. He's across town hiking with Ric."

"Well, more chicken for us," Nina said.

While she accepted her box of fried chicken from Avery, Tate studied her. She was gorgeous, but he couldn't figure her out. Or the pull he felt to her. Hot and nice as she was, she wasn't his type. At all.

She was an academic and an astrophysicist looking for romance. He was a cop who didn't believe in romance anymore. Didn't seem to matter, though, because in spite of all that, he was drawn to her anyway.

Nina focused those intelligent brown eyes on him, and he swore for a moment he was being drawn into them. "Your niece is in my first-year astronomy class, by the way."

"She is?" That was news to him.

"Yes. She seems very quiet and studious so far."

He liked the idea of Rylee in Nina's class, listening to her lectures, learning from her. He'd love to see Nina teach. He'd bet she would light up the classroom with her enthusiasm. "She's a great kid."

"I told her I'd met you, and that I'd just moved in with Avery. She seemed to think that was pretty great. I offered to show her some things with my telescope next time she comes back here for a visit. You'd be welcome too, of course. Maybe I could teach you a thing or two."

He couldn't quite smother a grin. "Maybe you could." And then he could teach her a few things of his own.

Things that would make her moan and twist beneath his body and mouth. Because if she brought half the enthusiasm to sex that she seemed to bring to everything else, it would be one hell of a memorable night. But he couldn't hook up with his partner's roommate. And he wasn't ready to put himself out there again, no matter how interested he was.

"Anything new on the dating front?" Avery asked as they sat on the blanket together and began eating.

Nina half-smiled and lowered her gaze to her lap.

"Yes, as a matter of fact."

Tate hid a frown as Avery gasped. "What? Tell, tell," Avery demanded.

"It's the accountant from the other week. I thought our first date was kind of a bust because he didn't really seem that into me, but apparently I was wrong."

For some reason Tate didn't like hearing that she was going out on a second date, let alone with a guy who hadn't seemed into her the first time. "Were you into him?" he asked before he could stop himself.

"He was nice. I didn't get a bad vibe from him, so I thought another date was in order to see how things go."

"Was he romantic?" Okay, that had just slipped out. But after everything he'd learned about Nina so far, that had to be an important point to her.

Her soft laugh didn't bode well. "Well, he did buy me flowers."

"Do you want flowers?" He was curious as to what kind of romance she wanted. Couldn't be flowers. Too superficial for someone with such deep and dreamy ideals.

"It's the thought behind a gesture that matters to me." She shrugged, her long brown hair rippling over her shoulder. "I guess I'm kind of old fashioned that way. I just like knowing a guy is trying. That I matter enough to him to put in the effort. You know what I mean?"

Yeah, he did know. Effort definitely mattered, and so did little things like flowers if they were important to your partner. But he also knew how it felt to be on the other side of that equation, and to never measure up no matter what he did.

"And what about the chemistry?" Avery asked, looking skeptical. "Is it there?"

Nina frowned as she thought about it.

"So, no," Tate said with a stab of triumph. Both

women looked at him questioningly and he hid his reaction with an easy shrug. "If you'd felt it, you wouldn't have to think about it."

Her lips curved upward, and he noticed the bottom one was a little fuller than the top. He imagined kissing the top one, then the lower. Sucking on it gently. "I guess so. Sometimes that can grow over time, though."

No way. Chemistry is either there or it isn't.

He bit the words back. He'd already said too much as it was. If he said much more, he'd make it obvious that he was into her. He didn't want that, especially in front of Avery.

"Anyway, it's just dinner," she finished, and picked up her drink.

Tate watched the way those pretty pink lips closed around the straw, thinking of what they'd feel like wrapped around a part of him. But when he thought of her going out with another guy she wasn't really attracted to, it annoyed the shit out of him.

Also, she was dead wrong about romance mattering so much. When it came down to it, flowers and grand gestures didn't mean shit in a relationship compared to the rest of it.

What truly mattered was commitment, loyalty, and respect. A commitment between two people who loved each other enough to work through whatever life threw at them.

Because when those things were missing, all the hearts and flowers in the world couldn't fix it.

It hadn't mattered what he'd said or done, Erica had always wanted more, or something different. Eventually it had felt like she'd never trusted him. He'd always had to prove his love for her, and getting nothing back in return.

He'd mistakenly thought her deeply-buried insecurities about him leaving her would diminish over time, once she'd seen that he was committed to sticking it out. But it hadn't, and it had been an exhausting experience.

Not that he thought Nina was the same as Erica. They were totally different in almost every way. It was just that Nina's views on relationships hit his hot buttons.

He expelled a breath and finished his chicken, ordering himself to calm down and get over himself. Nina was a grown woman, and she could date whoever she wanted. Even if the asshole didn't appreciate her. Or deserve her.

His hackles rose at the thought.

The meal passed quickly as Avery and Nina chatted. Tate didn't say much, only answering when spoken to, otherwise not offering his opinion. It was hard not to stare at Nina. She was gorgeous, but that wasn't why.

She had a special kind of charisma. A genuine inner warmth, and an infectious sense of enthusiasm and joy in everything she did. Being around her made him realize just how cold and empty he'd started to feel inside.

Nina set her box down and wiped her hands. "You guys wanna play some of the games?"

Tate and Avery both made identical faces.

Nina laughed. "Oh, come on. It's my first time at the festival, I have to play some games." She popped up and grabbed their hands. "Come on. Up."

Tate shared a look of dread with Avery and suppressed a groan as he got to his feet. "What kind of games?" he asked.

"I dunno, let's go see." Nina tugged them after her. She stopped in front of a row of tables set out, each one hosting a different activity or game to raise money for various charities around town. "Trivia! I love trivia." She glanced at them. "You guys in?"

When they didn't answer right away Nina turned back to the woman running the table and handed her some money. "All three of us are in." She wrote their names down on the list. "When does it start?"

"You just fill out this sheet as a team and turn it back in," the woman told her. "And no cheating. You can't look stuff up on your phone. We'll announce the winner in an hour."

Nina took the sheet and moved to the next table where a huge glass jar of marbles was on display. "Oh, math, *yes*," she said almost to herself, throwing down some money and grabbing a pencil from the little basket.

Avery groaned. "I'm gonna get some donuts."

Nina hummed in reply and glanced over her shoulder at him, her eyes bright with excitement. "You wanna have a guess?"

He couldn't say no to that face, and he didn't want to seem like a killjoy. "Sure."

She handed a pencil and slip of paper to him, then immediately began studying the jar, mumbling to herself about volume of cylinders and spheres. Pi and radiuses.

Tate examined the jar, made his best stab at a calculation, and jotted down his number. Nina was still writing down precise math equations on hers, her lips moving as she worked. She filled the front of the page, flipped it over, and nearly filled that side too before finally coming to her answer.

She wrote it down and turned to glance at Tate's. "What did you get?"

He pulled the paper to his chest and turned away so she couldn't see it. "Never you mind."

She grinned. "Fine. Be that way." They slid their answers into the slot in the top of the box, then Tate followed her down the sidewalk to where Avery was still in line for the donuts.

He spotted a shooting gallery set up down the row of carnival games. Finally, something he was good at. "Can you shoot?" he asked Nina.

She frowned, watching the people at the shooting gallery. "No, but I'll try."

Good enough for him. "Let's go." He started toward it.

He set a ten-dollar bill on the counter and handed her a BB gun. She looked at it uncertainly. "It's already loaded for you. Just aim and pull the trigger," he told her.

She edged up to the counter, put the stock to her shoulder and leaned down on one elbow. Tate eyed her rear and shapely legs, only dragging his gaze back up once she started firing. She missed every shot except two, which pinged off the background.

"Shoot," she muttered, straightening. "I suck."

He grinned. "It's your first time."

"Let's see you do it."

Tate picked up his weapon, positioned himself a few yards back from the counter, and got ready. As soon as the kid manning the gallery started the mechanism, the targets began popping up. Tate missed the first one, immediately adjusted his aim, and began firing in rapid succession. He hit all but the second-to-last one.

Lowering the gun, he looked at Nina. Her mouth was open. "*Wow*."

He laughed. "I've had a little more practice than you."

The kid manning the booth pointed at the row of stuffed animals hanging from the awning. "Any one you like."

Tate raised an eyebrow at Nina. "You pick."

She brightened. "Okay, I'll pick one for Rylee." She studied the prizes, then pointed to a big, brown teddy bear with floppy ears. "That one." The kid handed it to her. She hugged it to her chest, so damn adorable Tate couldn't help but smile. "He's so squishy."

Avery walked up chewing on a donut, and held out the bag to Tate to help himself. "You won that?" she said to Nina in surprise.

"No, Tate did. It's for Rylee." She snuck a donut,

then tucked the bear under her arm and dusted off her hands. "Okay, trivia time."

She took the folded paper from her purse and clicked on the end of her pen. "First question. When was Rifle Creek founded?" She looked at them.

"1881," Tate answered.

She wrote it down. "Who was the founding father?"

"Cornelius Davenport."

Her pen moved on the page. "What kind of rock is Rifle Creek built on?"

Tate glanced at Avery. "I dunno. Probably granite."

"Okay, so, igneous." She wrote that down.

They wound up answering all the questions but one, and finally guessed at it. Tate had known Nina was smart, but seeing her mind work with the marbles and trivia made him admire her even more.

She turned in their answers and stopped to buy them all lemonades on the way back. "Cheers, guys," she said, toasting them with her plastic cup.

Before he knew it, the hour was up, and the mayor took the microphone on the little stage to announce the winners. They won the trivia, and Nina won the marble count. She went up to collect their prizes, and returned with a triumphant smile, carrying a huge bag of kettle corn and a bottle of wine. "Score!"

A surge of longing swept through him. Tate shook it off. He needed to go and do something to occupy himself and not think about her for a while. She'd taken up too much of his headspace over the past couple days as it was.

He glanced at his watch. "I should get going." Avery would drive back with her.

"Oh, but aren't you going to have any kettle corn?" Nina asked.

"No, I'm good."

"Okay." She handed him the bear. "Thanks for coming."

74

It was still warm from being held against her body. "You're welcome." It came out gruffer than he'd intended, but he was way too wrapped up in her and annoyed about it.

He walked the ladies to Nina's car. Nina was directly in front of him, giving him a perfect view of the way her hips swayed in her dress and her gorgeous, bare calves flexed with each stride.

Her scent trailed back to him, something fruity and light designed to torture a man with fantasies of burying his face in her hair and neck just to breathe it in deeper.

"Thanks again for dinner," Tate said to Avery.

"Yes, thanks again," Nina echoed, then flashed him a smile that had him squeezing his fingers into his palms to keep from reaching out to stop her from leaving. Talk some sense into her about this guy she was planning to go on another date with. For her own sake.

"No problem," he said instead. "Have a good night."

"You too."

It felt wrong to just let her go, turn away from her and head for his truck. He sat behind the wheel while she drove off with Avery, both of them laughing at something as they did.

Tate felt strangely empty inside all of a sudden. Alone.

He turned out of the parking lot and started for home, in the opposite direction of Avery's place. In his rearview he watched Nina's taillights disappear around the corner behind him, a sense of urgency growing inside him.

He hit the brakes without thinking, stopping there in the middle of the street. Seconds passed, the sense of urgency expanding in his chest until it ached.

"*No*, dammit," he muttered, and cranked the wheel around.

He turned the truck and drove after Nina. He had no

plan, wasn't even sure what the fuck he was doing or going to say, just that he couldn't let her go out with some asshole who didn't deserve her time.

She was already out of her vehicle and around the corner of the house just as he pulled up in front. If Avery saw him parked there, she'd wonder why he was here, but he didn't care.

He got out and strode along the brick path that led around back to Nina's suite. Without giving himself time to second-guess what he was doing, he rapped on her door.

She pulled it open moments later, a startled smile on her face. "Hey."

Damn, she was pretty. He felt less cold inside just seeing her. "Hi."

She raised her eyebrows. "Did you…want to talk to me about something?"

"Yes," he said, unable to keep the irritation from his voice.

"Okay." She looked at him expectantly.

"Don't go out with that guy again."

Her face went blank with surprise. "What? Why not?"

"Because he's not gonna give you what you're looking for, and I don't want you to get hurt." He couldn't stand the thought of someone so kind and full of joy getting her heart bruised.

Her face softened, her eyes filling with a tenderness he wanted to drink in. "You're worried about me."

"Yeah, I'm worried." Frustration pulsed through him. "I know you won't think so, but romance is overrated. And besides, you even said you're not attracted to the guy."

Her expression cooled. "I said that might grow with time."

He shook his head sharply. "It won't."

She folded her arms, annoying him more with the way it pushed her breasts up and together. Making it harder to keep his eyes on her face. "No? And you're an expert on these things, even though you haven't dated in what, a year?"

Touché. Maybe he deserved that. His face heated. "I'm just saying, you should be more realistic."

"Yeah?" She studied him a moment, her physicist brain performing calculations about him and coming up with her own answers. Probably that he was being an overbearing asshole. "Well, you're lonely and don't even realize it."

He faltered, becoming flustered as her words hit home. Okay, yeah, maybe he was a bit lonely. But that wasn't the point here. Stopping her from making a mistake, from getting hurt, was.

"This isn't about me. And sorry to break it to you, but life isn't a fairy-tale. There's way more important things in a relationship than flowers and romantic gestures."

She cocked an eyebrow at him, the gesture somehow condescending. Almost like she was giving him enough rope to hang himself. "Like what?"

His frustration hit critical mass, her challenge triggering something territorial in him. "Like *this*," he answered, stepping forward to wrap a hand around her nape and covering those tempting lips with his own.

She stiffened for a split second, her hands flying up to the front of his shoulders. But she didn't stop him or push him away, so Tate didn't let go. Instead he wrapped his free arm around her back, hauling her in close.

The feel of her softness pressed against him lit his blood on fire. He slanted his mouth across hers, captured her tiny gasp on his tongue as he drank her in, his entire body going hard as he tasted her.

Nina moaned softly, her hands curling into his shoulders. The kiss had started out dominant and forceful, but now it slowed and softened. Becoming something more than he'd intended, shocking him with its brutal honesty. The raw need it exposed.

He drew back, stunned that she'd broken his control so easily. Nina gazed up at him uncertainly, her big brown eyes searching his.

Shit. He hadn't meant to kiss her. He just hadn't been able to stop himself from touching her, tasting her, driven by the primal need to wipe the thought of any other guy out of her pretty head.

What the hell had he done?

His jaw tightened. "Just...don't go out with that guy." He started to turn away.

She laughed. He stopped dead, whipping around to stare at her. He was dead serious, thinking of her best interest, and she'd *laughed*.

She folded her arms, and he had to wrench his focus up to her face. "You don't get a say in who I can and can't go out with."

The reprimand hit home, making him wince inside. Fuck, he was acting like a damn caveman. If any guy had spoken to Tala or Rylee like he just had, Tate would be tempted to punch him in the face. "I know," he bit out. "But I don't want you to get hurt."

She softened, gazing at him equal parts amusement and sympathy. "Say I consider canceling my date on Friday. What's in it for me?"

His mind had stopped functioning. She'd short-circuited his fucking brain. "Sorry?"

"You gonna take me out instead?"

The idea was a lot more appealing than he wanted it to be. "Maybe I will."

Her eyes sparkled with silent laughter. "So you're a closet romantic after all."

What? No. He opened his mouth to refute it, but that soft look in her eyes and his actions made denying it pointless. He huffed out a quiet chuckle. "Cancel your date. I'll pick you up Friday after your last class."

She nodded once. "All right. I'm looking forward to it."

Damn, he was too, God help him. "Okay. Good night."

"Good night." She shot him one last smile that warmed him all the way to his bones before shutting the door.

Tate walked back to his truck in a sort of daze, still not sure what had just happened. Was this a bad idea?

Yeah. It was definitely a bad idea.

He wasn't the kind of romantic she was looking for, but damned if she didn't suddenly have him wanting to put aside his cynical views and make the effort for her.

CHAPTER EIGHT

"**R**ead that article I recommended, then try the practice problems. And if things are still as clear as mud on Monday, I have more office hours that afternoon. All right?" Nina gave the first-year student an encouraging smile.

She had always loved physics. Physics was logic and math, while still being exciting and interesting. But she recognized that not everyone felt that way. Some of her students were going to struggle, for various reasons. It was her job to help them through their course and try different angles to get the light bulb to go on for them.

The young man expelled a breath and nodded, still looking frustrated and overwhelmed. "Yeah, okay. Have a good weekend, Dr. Benitez."

"You too."

As soon as he left, she took her phone from the top desk drawer and called Tate. It was Friday afternoon and the first week back teaching had passed in a blur. She and Tate had been texting back and forth all week. Earlier today he'd left her a message but she'd been too busy seeing students to respond until now.

"Hey, how's your day been?" he answered.

Just the sound of that deep voice on the other end of the line made her toes curl in her sandals. He'd been on her mind constantly this entire week, ever since that sexy, molten kiss in her doorway.

If the man could turn her inside out with one kiss, she was looking forward to finding out what else he could do with the rest of him. She liked sex. She missed sex, and something told her with him it would be unlike any sex she'd ever had.

"Busy. I had to squeeze one more student into my office hours schedule since he was desperate. Is it too late for you to come out this way now? I still have one last appointment to go before I can leave, but I can be ready within an hour."

"I'll pick you up in an hour, then." He named a location on campus near her building where he could park.

Her insides fluttered at knowing she was going to see him in just sixty short minutes. She understood that him taking her out was big. He'd been hurt and was gun shy. She would be patient with him. "Okay. Do you want to see Rylee before you meet me?"

"No, she texted that she's out with friends tonight. What did you do to your students in the first week that has them so worked up, anyway?"

Picturing him wearing snug dress pants and a button-down shirt that stretched across the muscular plane of his chest and shoulders as he talked to her sent warmth pooling low in her abdomen. Tate Baldwin was pure male sex appeal and she couldn't wait to see him again.

"I was as gentle as I could be, but astrophysics is a pretty steep learning curve for the majority of students in their first year."

He chuckled, a low, sexy sound that had her pulse tripping. "I'll bet. Okay, I'll head out in the next few minutes and drive down to get you. See you soon."

"Looking forward to it."

She couldn't wipe the grin off her face as her final student walked in. The meeting went better than the one before, and she had just enough time after to tidy up her desk before throwing her light sweater on over her dress and heading to the spot where Tate was supposed to pick her up.

Her mind wandered as she waited, and the unpleasant thoughts she tried to keep buried started to surface. She shifted her stance, resisting the urge to glance around, the sense of unease expanding in her stomach. She was safe here, and Tate was coming.

Butterflies danced in her belly when his truck came into view, banishing the dark memory like matter sucked into a black hole. He pulled up to the curb and leaned over to open her door for her, wearing a silvery-gray button-down that hugged his sculpted chest and shoulders.

The welcoming smile he gave her almost melted her insides, the few days' growth on his face tempting her to rub her cheek against it. "Hi."

"Thanks for coming to get me," she said, climbing into the passenger seat. The scent of leather and his tangy cologne wrapped around her, clean and masculine. *Yum.*

"Of course. You hungry?"

"Yes. I had some thoughts about tonight. You game?"

He gave her an interested look, his gaze so full of banked heat it made her mouth go dry. "I might be. Why, what've you got in mind?"

She'd thought of a few ideas for tonight. But one stood apart from the others. "Let's park in the lot at the end of the street. I've got something I want to show you."

One side of his mouth lifted, the heat still there as his gaze dropped to her mouth. "Here in my truck?" His meaning was clear from the teasing light in his eyes.

"No," she said on a laugh. "And for the record, I'm not into exhibitionism."

"That's a shame." He steered them around to the nearest lot and parked the truck.

"How was your week at work?" she asked him.

"Good. Nothing major came up. It's a big change of pace from the departments I worked with before moving to Rifle Creek," he said.

"How long did you work in Missoula?"

"Three years, two in Billings before that. I don't miss it. I paid my dues, made detective in Missoula, then left for Rifle Creek seven months ago." He glanced at her as he took the keys from the ignition. "What do you think of Rifle Creek so far?"

"I think it's everything I'd hoped it would be and more. Except it doesn't have any Mexican food."

One side of his mouth kicked up. That half-grin was crazy sexy on him. And when he full-out smiled, he damn near made her breath stop. "Small-town living isn't for everyone."

He got out and rounded the back of the truck to meet her as she got out from the passenger seat. He took her hand to help her down, the strength and confidence of his grip making her heart skip, had her imagining what his hands would feel like moving over her naked body.

"So, where to?"

She tossed him a mischievous smile, hoping he couldn't tell how much he affected her. She didn't want to spook him. "This way." In three short blocks they reached their destination.

"You're kidding," he said when they got there. "You want to eat in a cafeteria?"

"I'll grant you that the food isn't the greatest, but it's cheap and close to our next stop." She glanced at her watch. "Which we need to be at in twenty-three minutes."

His expression was equal parts amusement and curiosity. "Not gonna tell me what you've got planned?"

"What fun would that be?"

He chuckled and followed her inside to the counter to get a tray. They each ordered different meals. He slid into the seat opposite her at a table for two, giving her a rueful grin that made her want to lean over and kiss him. "I'll admit, I didn't expect you to be such a cheap date." A teasing gleam lit his eyes. They were gorgeous, a mix of green and gold and caramel.

"Contrary to what you might think based on previous conversations, I'm actually a pretty low-maintenance kinda gal when it comes to relationships." She popped a chicken nugget into her mouth and fought not to smile. He thought she was unrealistic about matters of the heart?

Nina couldn't wait to prove him wrong on every count. "Now. Tell me what you like to do for fun."

He cut himself a bite of roast turkey. "I like to get outside. Love to shoot, hike, camp, hunt. That sort of thing." His eyes were warm as he regarded her. "What about you?"

"I like having adventures. Big ones or small ones, it doesn't really matter. Sometimes that might mean traveling to a place I've never been before, or maybe hearing a lecture I'm interested in, or going to a museum or gallery exhibit I've been wanting to see. It just depends. But I'm guessing you're not much of a museum or gallery guy?"

He lifted a broad shoulder, and she couldn't help but remember how hard and warm his muscles had been under her palms when he'd kissed her the other night. How hard and warm he'd been all over. "I like some museums."

History and military, she was betting. "Are you open to expanding your horizons a bit?" She took a sip of her tea, watching him.

"I feel like this is a test of some kind."

"What's your answer, then?"

His eyes glinted with humor. "I might be."

She winked at him. "Good answer. Now eat up, I don't want to be late."

When they were done, he took their trays and dishes over to the corresponding bins. On the way to the door, he placed a hand at the small of her back to guide her through the crowd gathered for the end of the dinner rush.

Tingles spread outward across her skin, igniting deep in her belly and settling between her thighs. His touch was light yet protective, the heat of his palm and fingers sinking through the fabric of her dress and sweater.

Mercy... What would it feel like to have those delicious hands moving all over her bare skin?

Outside, the sun had just disappeared behind the buildings on the western edge of campus. Tate surprised her by reaching down to take her hand.

She paused on the sidewalk, smiling up at him as she twined her fingers with his. Hand-holding was incredibly romantic, even if he didn't seem to realize it. "Ready for the next part of this adventure?"

He nodded, the intensity of his gaze making her mouth go dry and her heart thud. "Ready."

She tugged on his hand, turning them to the right. "Can I ask you some questions while we walk?" She wanted to know him better, and chatting would at least take her mind off the constant arousal pulsing through her.

"Sure."

"What made you want to join the Marines?"

"My sister."

Nina glanced at him in surprise. "Really?" She hadn't expected that answer.

He nodded. "Tala. Technically she's my half-sister, but I hate that shit. She's my sister, period. We share a dad."

Nina smiled, loving that he was so fiercely protective

85

of his sister. "Are you older?"

"No, I'm younger by eighteen months. We lived together when we were little, and stayed as close as we could after my mom moved me down here to Montana."

That must have been hard. "How old were you when your parents split?"

"Ten. Tala joined Cadets when she was thirteen and I thought it was the coolest thing ever. Our dad's dad had served in the Canadian Forces and saw action in the Korean War. I'd also heard stories on my mom's side about an uncle who served with the Marines in Vietnam."

"It's in your blood, then."

"Definitely. I hated school, it was way too boring and most of what they were teaching seemed irrelevant to me. I didn't know what the hell I wanted to do after I graduated, but I admired what Tala was doing in the military, so I went to see a recruiter and the rest is history." He squeezed her hand gently. "What about you? Did you always know you wanted to study astronomy and astrophysics?"

"Ever since I can remember. I was such a nerd, I read all the books about the solar system I could get my hands on as a kid. My parents bought me a cheap telescope for my eighth birthday, and one night that summer I saw Saturn through it. It was love at first sight. Of course, back then I thought I'd be an astronaut, or at the very least head of NASA." She laughed. "Reality eventually dictated I pick something a little less lofty. I'm glad, though, because I love what I do. And speaking of that… Here we are."

She stopped where the sidewalk intersected with another path and turned Tate to face the building at the end of it.

"What is it?" he asked.

"A planetarium."

He looked down at her, laughter in his eyes. "You

brought me here for our date? Seriously?"

"Yes. Now come on. You'll love it, promise."

Inside she got them tickets with her faculty pass and they went to the theater to watch a show about the wonders of the universe, followed by a presentation on star formation by a fellow faculty member. Seeing the film on the dome screen above still gave Nina a thrill.

The talk afterward was engaging and interesting, with good audience participation. She glanced at Tate a few times to gauge his reaction, and to her delight he seemed at least intrigued by it all.

Nina leaned closer to Tate as the speaker wrapped up, breathing in his scent as she whispered in his ear. She was looking forward to being alone with him after this. "You can wait and ask me questions later if you're shy."

He turned his head to look at her, only inches separating them. His gaze dropped to her lips before returning to her eyes. "I'm not shy when it comes to getting something I want."

A shiver sped through her, heat igniting in her core. Damn, she was in her favorite building on campus while a colleague gave an incredibly interesting talk, and all she could think about was getting Tate alone so she could kiss him again. Savor the feel of all those hard muscles as she ran her hands over him, lose herself in the masterful way he'd held her and transported her to another place.

He returned his attention to the presenter before she could gather her thoughts enough to respond, his fingers still wrapped securely around hers. Teasing her with the promise of what would happen when they left and found somewhere more private.

"That was actually totally fascinating," he said as they left the theater a few minutes later.

"You sound surprised."

"I am."

She laughed, energized by his interest and just being

with him. "Isn't it incredible? Just think." She tipped her head back and looked up at the stars now appearing in the purple sky. "Everything we see, everything on earth, came from supernovas. So in actuality, we're all made of stardust."

"It's amazing," he agreed, then let go of her hand to wrap a steely arm around her shoulders instead, drawing her closer.

Nina leaned into him, savoring his warmth and strength. She felt petite next to him. Protected. And turned on.

"What's your favorite planet?" he asked.

"Saturn, of course. It's everyone's favorite."

His lips quirked. "Why is it your favorite?"

"Because it's the coolest. Started out as a rocky planet and became a gas giant. Its rings are made up of rock and ice, and check this out—it even rains diamonds in its atmosphere."

He glanced down at her. "Get out."

"No, swear to God, it does. It happens on a few others planets in our solar system as well, but basically the atmospheric pressure is so great, it turns carbon in the atmosphere into freaking *diamonds*."

"Hell, someone needs to figure out how to capture them and transport them back here."

She playfully poked his shoulder. "Stop. So mercenary."

He let out a low laugh and tugged her closer to press a kiss to the top of her head. Nina's insides squeezed, her heart fluttering. "I don't think I've been to a planetarium since I was in elementary school, and I don't remember it being half that interesting," he said. "I loved it, thank you."

She smiled up at him, thrilled. "You're welcome."

Tate suddenly stopped and drew her off the path. He turned her to face him and settled his hands on her hips, his fingers squeezing gently, making her insides heat. The hunger on his face made the breath back up in her lungs.

He reached out to push a lock of hair away from her face, his fingers trailing ever so gently across her cheek and down the side of her neck. Raising goosebumps along her skin. "You are such a surprise."

Her heart was beating so fast. "A good one?"

His mouth curved into a sexy grin. "I think so."

Nina curled her hands around the tops of his shoulders, her fingers sinking into the hard ridges of muscle there. Oh God, she was going to melt.

Those gorgeous eyes dropped to her mouth again and he leaned in…

A ring tone went off.

Nina stopped, her eyes popping open. His phone. "Go ahead."

"No," he murmured, ignoring it as he cupped the side of her face in one big hand and covered her mouth with his.

Nina forgot how to think. Or breathe. All she could do was hold onto him, lean into that hard, lean body while his lips moved across hers.

This was so different from the last time. This time was deliberate, like he was savoring her. Teasing her. Seducing her with varying pressure of his lips, the subtle brush of his tongue across her lower lip.

She moaned and opened for him but he made a low sound and sucked on her lip instead, stroking it with his tongue before going back to caressing her lips with his.

At some point his phone must have stopped ringing because it started up again, the sound startling her. She groaned and lowered her heels back to the ground. "It sounds important."

Tate kept hold of her with one hand while he took his phone from his pocket with the other. "I'd better answer, it's Rylee." He put it to his ear. "Hey, little girl. What's up?"

Whatever his niece said must have been bad, because he went rigid and sucked in a breath. "What?" he said in a low, dangerous voice.

Nina's insides tightened. *Oh, no*... What was wrong?

He grabbed Nina's hand and immediately strode for the sidewalk. Nina hurried alongside him as he spoke to Rylee, her stomach tightening. Whatever had happened, it wasn't good.

"Are you in a safe place right now? Is there someone with you?" He listened tensely. "Okay, stay there. I'm on campus right now and I'm coming to get you. I'll be there in ten minutes. Rylee, do you understand? Don't move." Another pause. "Good girl. Just hang tight. I'll be there soon." He ended the call.

"What's wrong?" Nina asked, worried.

"She was drugged at a club. Passed out, and when she woke up, her friend was gone."

Nina's insides congealed. Flashes of ugly memories bombarded her but she forced the fragmented, disjointed images aside. This was about Rylee, not her. And Rylee was safe. She was going to be fine. "Is she all right?"

"I'm going to get her right now."

"I'll come with you. If you want," she added hastily, not wanting to overstep.

His eyes burned with banked rage as he glanced down at her, then they softened with gratitude. "I'd like that," he said, and escorted her to his truck.

CHAPTER NINE

Tate shoved down the fear and anger coiling inside him as he and Nina pulled up to the coffee shop where Rylee was waiting for them.

"Want me to stay here and wait?" Nina asked softly.

"No, come in. She'll be glad to see you. She told me after the first day that she could already tell you were going to be her favorite professor."

"Really? Aww."

He helped her out of the truck and strode for the entrance. Nina hung back as he pushed through the door and immediately scanned the place for his niece.

Rylee was seated at a table on the far left side, her elbows on the table and her head in her hands.

"Ry."

She looked up at him and the mingled relief and shame on her face hit him hard. She got out of her chair and met him partway in an unsteady gait, walking right into his embrace when he reached for her.

Tate closed his arms around her, his cheek pressed to her hair. "You okay?" he said in a low voice.

"I still don't know where S-Samantha is," she choked out. "I didn't call the p-police yet because I'm still not sure what h-happened."

"All right. We'll handle it." He eased his grip enough for her to move back a few inches.

She nodded and sniffed, wiping at her eyes with the bottom of her sleeve. Her makeup was smeared, her hair mussed. She looked so damn young and broken, and the thought of what could have happened to her tonight twisted his insides. "Can we go somewhere else?" she whispered.

People were watching them, sensing something was wrong. "Yeah. Come on." He turned her around, kept an arm locked around her shoulders as he steered her to the door. She definitely was still under the influence of whatever she'd ingested. He needed to find out what she'd been given and alert the cops. "Professor Benitez is here."

Rylee lifted her head, looking around. "She is?"

"Waiting by the front door. She was with me when you called, so I asked her to come. That okay?"

"Yes." She managed a wan smile for Nina when they stepped outside. "Hi, Dr. Benitez."

"Nina, please. Dr. Benitez for class only," Nina said with a gentle smile that faded into concern. "Are you all right?"

"I think so. Don't feel so great, and my roommate's missing."

Nina nodded, her eyes full of sympathy. "I heard. I'm so sorry."

"Thanks," Rylee mumbled, wiping at her eyes again.

Nina glanced from her to Tate. "Listen, if you two want to talk alone, I can go—"

"No, it's fine," Rylee said, leaning into him again. "I just wanted away from here because it felt like everyone in there was staring at me."

"Let's get you into the truck," Tate said, steering her

toward it. He put Rylee in the front seat while Nina got into the back.

Once he was behind the wheel, he turned to face his niece, cataloguing everything he saw. She looked shaken and miserable and her pupils were slightly dilated. "Are you dizzy?"

"Yes, and weak, and kinda sick to my stomach."

Wanting to reassure her, Tate reached out and curled his hand around hers. "Ry, listen to me. We have to report this, and I need to get you checked out. I'm going to call a contact of mine on the Missoula PD and set up a meeting, have him meet us at the clinic I want to take you to. All right?" Minutes mattered if Samantha had been taken.

"Okay."

He fired up the truck and made two calls as he pulled onto the road. One to a doctor he liked there, and the other to an old colleague on the Missoula force.

As soon as he was done, he glanced at Rylee. "Can you tell me what happened?"

She blew out a breath and ran a shaky hand through her hair. "I...I was with my roommate at a club she wanted to check out," she blurted, flushing and avoiding his gaze. "I only had one drink—a martini."

Tate refrained from asking her how she'd gotten in and served, since she was only eighteen. How she'd managed to get a fake ID wasn't what mattered right now. "Go on."

"I left it with her when I went to the bathroom. When I came out, she was talking to these guys. She still had my drink in her hand, so I didn't think anything of it and drank the rest."

"Tell me about the guys," Tate said, trying to keep his tone level while every cop instinct he had clanged in warning.

She paused, frowning. "I remember finishing the drink and putting the glass on the bar. My roommate was dancing with one of the guys. He brought her back a minute later saying she wasn't feeling well, and took her to the bathroom. I knew something was wrong and got up to follow her, but then I started feeling woozy too. The guys all seemed worried about us. One of them catching me before I fell off the stool. When I woke up there was a crowd around me. The guys were still there and Samantha was gone. Someone went to find her and couldn't."

"Was the guy who escorted her to the bathroom gone too?"

"No, he came back and said she was sick in the bathroom."

"Didn't anyone call for an ambulance?" Tate asked, getting more agitated by the minute. Sounded like classic Rohypnol drugging. Someone should have fucking called for help.

"No, I told them not to, asked them to take me outside to get air. I was so embarrassed, and just worried about Samantha." She looked over at him, her eyes filled with torment. "What if someone took her?"

Yeah, he didn't like the feel of this at all. Seemed likely that Samantha had been kidnapped, and Rylee was damn lucky to have escaped that same fate as well.

Tate glanced at Nina in the rearview mirror. She was still and quiet in the backseat, a sad, almost haunted look in her eyes.

Doctor Whitaker met them at the clinic. Tate and Nina stayed in the waiting area while the doctor examined Rylee and took blood and urine samples. By the time she was done, Tate's contact Greg and his partner had arrived. Doctor Whitaker told them that while they needed to wait for the lab results to be sure, she was confident it was Rohypnol.

Tate set his jaw and wrapped an arm around Rylee when she dropped into the seat next to him.

He and Nina flanked her while Greg and his partner

questioned Rylee about what had happened. "If your friend was distracted, any of those men she was talking to could have slipped a crushed pill or a liquid into both your drinks without her noticing," Greg said.

Rylee shook her head, adamant. "I know that, but it doesn't make sense. They were so nice, and they all stayed to make sure I was okay. Two of them searched for Samantha after she didn't come back from the bathroom. If they were guilty of drugging us, they would have just taken off."

Maybe. But Rylee had been pretty out of it and might not have realized what was really going on. Totally possible the guys had just hung around to cover their asses.

Greg turned to Tate. "We'll review the security footage and interview everyone we can find. For right now, our priority is finding Samantha."

"Of course."

Greg's partner made a note on her pad. "Where is your roommate from?" she asked Rylee.

"A little town in South Dakota. Can't remember the name of it off the top of my head."

"Does she have any family or close friends here?"

"Not that I know of." Rylee rubbed her face, her expression crumpling. "I was her only friend here. I should have looked out for her better."

"Hey." Tate wrapped his arm around her and pulled her into him. "This isn't your fault. And the police will find her, I promise."

Rylee sniffed, her shoulders hitching as she forced a nod. "What do I do now?"

"You're coming home with me," he said. "There's nothing more you can do right now, and I don't want you worrying about anything else tonight."

She seemed to sag with relief, still looking miserable. "All right, thank you."

He kissed the top of her head and looked at Greg.

"Can I take her home now?"

"Of course. I'll be in touch."

Rylee seemed steadier on her feet as he and Nina walked her out to his truck, but she was quiet. Tate settled her in the back seat. "You want to call your mom, or should I?"

Rylee groaned. "You, please. She'll just freak out if I do it."

Tate nodded, shut the door and turned to find Nina standing behind him on the sidewalk, her arms wrapped around her waist. She seemed a little pale, her usual sunny personality dimmed. "I'll just catch a lift back to my car," she said. "It's twenty minutes in the opposite direction, and you need to get Rylee straight home."

"No way." She seriously thought he'd leave her here to find her own way back after what had happened, and after she'd stayed to help? "I'll drive you to your car. Or, just come with us now and I can drive you back in the morning if you want."

She hesitated for a moment, then glanced at Rylee and nodded. "All right, if you're sure I won't be impos-ing."

"No, not at all." It was also an excuse to spend more time with her, and he was all for that.

Nina got into the front beside him. Tate liked having her there.

He called his sister as soon as he pulled away from the curb. Tala stayed admiringly calm while he relayed everything that had happened. "She's okay, Tal," Tate emphasized. "I took her to get checked out. Everything's fine, and I'm taking her home with me until we get to the bottom of this. She's just really worried about her room-mate." And so was Tate.

"All right, thank you. Can I talk to her?"

He glanced in the rearview and found Rylee fast asleep, her head resting against the window. "Sorry, she's already out."

Tala expelled a heavy sigh. "All right. Tell her I love her and that I'm glad she's safe. And that yes, she has to call me as soon as she wakes up. And you'll update me if you get any news about the situation?"

"Absolutely. Don't worry about Ry, I've got this. Love you."

"Love you too, Tater."

Nina was staring at him, a soft smile on her face as he ended the call. "What?" he asked.

"I love seeing the bond you have with your niece and sister, that's all."

He lifted a shoulder. "They're my family."

"Have you always been close?"

He nodded, glad to talk and get out of his head for a while. "Pretty sure she thought I was a living doll when I was first born. My mom said Tala carried me around everywhere, even took me to school for show and tell one day."

"Adorable." Her grin faded. "Was it hard for you when you moved away?"

"I hated it. Hated my mom for it for a long time, too." He shifted his grip on the wheel, forcing his muscles to relax. "Going from seeing Tala every day down to a couple times a year, sucked. She'd always looked out for me."

"And now you look out for her and her daughter."

He inclined his head. *Damn right.* "Tala's been through a lot. She became a single mom while she was still in high school."

"That must have been hard. Is Rylee's dad in the picture?"

"No. He and his family refused to take responsibility, so they up and moved him back east somewhere before graduation. Tala's raised Rylee all on her own, with support from my dad and stepmom. Especially while she was deployed and after she was wounded."

Nina looked at him sharply. "She was wounded?"

"In Afghanistan, four years ago. Her convoy was hit by multiple IEDs. She jumped out to take a defensive position and stepped on an anti-personnel mine. She lost her lower leg and foot." Thank God Braxton had been there, or she might have bled out while the rest of her team was engaged in the ensuing firefight.

"Oh, I'm so sorry."

"Thanks. She's tough, though. Fought through it like a warrior and now she's training to become a Paralympic biathlete."

"Wow, biathlon? She must train like crazy. And she's obviously an amazing mom, because Rylee's fantastic."

A grin tugged at his mouth. "Yeah, to both those things. I always kind of worshipped her, growing up. But if you ever meet her, you can't ever tell her I said that."

"Wouldn't dream of it." She reached for his hand, her fingers slender and soft as they curled into his palm. The way she'd reached for him, so natural, and her touch eased the lingering anger and anxiety swirling inside him. "How are you doing, anyway?"

Her concern filled him with warmth. "Fine now that I know Ry's okay."

Nina glanced back at Rylee as if to make sure she was still asleep before continuing. "Do you think someone took her friend?" she murmured.

He nodded. "Yeah. Just hoping the cops find her within the next hour or two." He'd been a cop long enough to dread what the alternative likely meant.

Nina lapsed into silence after that. Tate focused on the feel of her fingers wrapped around his, grateful for her kind, gentle presence. They passed the rest of the drive without speaking, only the country music on the radio playing softly in the background. Tate liked that they didn't have to talk. That Nina didn't feel obligated to fill the silence.

"Want to come in while I get Rylee settled?" he asked quietly as they took the turn off the main highway to Rifle Creek. "I'll drop you at home after."

"Sure, that's fine."

Mason's Jeep was gone when Tate pulled into the driveway a few minutes later, his buddy out somewhere. Rylee was still fast asleep in the back, barely stirred when Tate tried to wake her. He bundled her up in his arms and carried her inside, straight down the upstairs hallway past his door to her room at the end. He'd left it exactly as it had been the day he'd moved her out.

She curled onto her side with a sigh when he laid her on the double bed. Tate pulled the covers over her and stood there a moment, staring down at her in the dimness.

A fierce wave of protectiveness surged through him. Some fucking bastard had drugged her tonight. In the hopes of raping her or worse, who knew.

Stop. She's safe now. Let that shit go.

He shut the door without a sound and walked back down the hall to find Nina. She was in the kitchen, sitting on a stool at the counter, her long dark hair spilling over one slender shoulder. It shone in the overhead kitchen lights, so silky and shiny his fingers itched to slide through it. "She still asleep?" she asked.

"Yeah, never opened her eyes. She'll be back to normal in the morning."

Nina studied him, an unreadable expression in her gaze. "And you? Will you be fine in the morning too?"

He paused next to her, close enough to breathe in her sweet scent and see the flecks of caramel in her warm brown eyes. She'd been there for him and Rylee tonight. That meant a lot to him, enough that he wanted to be honest with her now. "I want to find the asshole who did this to her and rip him apart."

She nodded and slid off the stool to wind her arms

around his waist, resting her cheek on his shoulder. "That's what I thought."

Tate heaved a sigh and returned the embrace, soaking up her warmth and concern. It didn't bode well that the cops hadn't found Samantha yet. He didn't want to think about what might have happened to her, but he couldn't stop himself. He'd seen too much on the job to assume everything would be fine. "Sorry our date ended like this."

"Don't apologize. I'm just glad Rylee's okay."

"Me too." He kissed the top of her head, nuzzling her hair. "Want something to drink? I think Avery left a bottle of wine last time she was over."

Nina shook her head. "No. Just you."

His heart squeezed. She made him want to wrap her up in his arms and never let go. And it shook him.

He led her out to the back deck and tucked her into his lap on the porch swing. Cuddling her close, he ran his fingers through the cool silk of her hair as he pushed the swing back with his foot. The quiet creak of the chains anchoring the swing to the ceiling blended with the chirp of the crickets singing in the grass.

"It's so peaceful and quiet out here," she whispered.

He loved the feel of her, all warm and cuddly against him. Trusting and relaxed.

He was in big damn trouble where she was concerned. He'd made up his mind not to risk his heart again, but she was already winding around it. "Thanks for being there tonight." He appreciated the way Nina had handled things. She had a big heart and a sense of empathy he hadn't come across too often.

Everything tonight had changed his mind about her. From dinner in the cafeteria and the planetarium show to the situation with Rylee. Nina wasn't naïve, she was a dreamer.

He admired that, even as it made him crazy protective of her. Dreamers were vulnerable and he didn't want anyone or anything to hurt her. Ever.

She tipped her head back on his shoulder to peer up at the sky beyond the porch roof. "Look at all the stars out here. Crazy how many are visible without light pollution obscuring them."

Tate studied them with her. There were a lot of them up there, and he'd never thought to care or appreciate it before. For him they were a tool, nothing more. "I've only ever used them for navigation. Maybe you can expand my horizons a little."

Her soft laugh rippled through him, touching places he'd thought he'd walled off a long time ago. "Never say that to an astronomy freak unless you're prepared for the consequences."

"What kind of consequences?"

She sat up and turned toward him more, her pretty face bathed in moon and starlight. "Like a fanatical lecture about the galaxy or the meteor shower happening Sunday night."

"I can take it. Go ahead." Tate gazed down at her, stroking his fingers through her hair. Unexpected and incredible as it was, she made him believe in hope again. "Show me the stars, Nina," he murmured.

Her sexy lips curved into a smile as she leaned up to meet him halfway. Tate took her head in his hands as they kissed, learning the shape and feel of her, exploring. Varying pressure, tender glides until the hunger took hold. He was hard and aching for her already, just from this gentle kiss.

Needing closer, he lowered one arm to lock around her hips, lifting her until he settled her astride his lap, facing him. He barely smothered a groan as her core settled against his erection. She shifted her knees on the thick cushion and threaded her hands into his hair to hold him close while he delved his tongue into her mouth to taste her.

Nina moaned low in her throat and met the caress with her own, shifting her weight until her core pressed tight to the ridge of his erection. Tate made a low sound of approval and pleasure and palmed her ass to pull her closer, his fingers sinking in, squeezing her softness.

The sound of a vehicle pulling into his driveway alerted him that they were no longer alone. Mason would be inside within a minute. Hello, mood killer.

Cursing his buddy's timing, Tate took one last taste, paused to suck on her plump lower lip, then gently released her mouth and eased back to see her face. Nina's breathing was uneven, her eyes heavy-lidded with need, that sultry mouth swollen.

He couldn't look away, felt himself getting lost in those gorgeous eyes. Damn. She had such passion and a sense of wonder for life. He hadn't realized that's exactly what he'd been lacking until she'd acted like a mirror held up in front of him.

"Mason's timing sucks," she whispered.

Tate laughed softly. "What else is new." He cupped her face in his hands, his heart thudding against his ribs. This woman held the power to turn him inside out with a single smile. He wanted to do something romantic and meaningful for her. "Before I take you home, what are you doing tomorrow night?"

Amusement and anticipation gleamed in her eyes. "That depends. You got something in mind?"

"Yeah." The kitchen light came on behind them, alerting him to Mason's impending arrival, but he kissed her one more time anyway, because he couldn't help himself. He was already addicted, God help him. "Matter of fact, I do."

CHAPTER TEN

Vince crept through the garage door into the mudroom just before midnight. The house was dark and still, his wife and daughters all fast asleep upstairs.

He'd thought coming home would help, but the sudden quiet made the agitation inside him ten times worse.

He paced the length of the kitchen and back, scrubbing a hand over his jaw. The scrapes on his face and neck stung like hell. He had to lie low until they healed.

Tonight was supposed to have been the best hunt yet. His epic finale in Missoula, with a big payoff at the end for all the risk involved.

Instead, the thrill had turned into a nightmare.

Everything had gone wrong, almost right from the start. He'd barely made it out of the club with the one girl undetected. Then things had gone from bad to worse.

The girl had come to unexpectedly. She'd fought him. Terrified someone would hear or see them, he'd quickly shut her up.

He'd crossed a line. Panicked. Bolted without sticking around to find out what happened, or take steps to mitigate any DNA traces he'd left behind.

The entire drive home he'd half-expected the cops to come after him. She'd fucking seen him. Up close.

"Oh, shit," he breathed, stopping to lean against the kitchen counter. His heartbeat drummed in his head, nausea swirling in the pit of his stomach. What had he done?

She might be able to ID him. And maybe even her friend, too. Vince wasn't certain, but he'd thought the other brunette had seen him as he approached them at the bar while they'd been talking to those college guys. He'd waited for one girl to leave and made sure the other was distracted before dosing their drinks. No one had noticed it. But it hadn't mattered.

Now what?

He'd been careful to avoid the security cameras inside the club, having scoped them out a few nights ago, after he'd overheard the brunettes talking about going there tonight. Except the camera above the bar would have caught him. He'd worn a ball cap and kept his head down so it wouldn't pick up his face, but…

"Vince?"

He almost jumped out of his skin when his wife stepped into the kitchen, lit up by faint moonlight coming through the sliders leading to the back patio. "Hey," he said, quickly turning to hide the marks on his face from her.

"What are you doing down here in the dark? Is everything okay?"

No. Not by a long shot. "Yeah, just a tough call at work tonight."

"Oh. Is that why you're home so late?" There was more than a little suspicion in her tone, and her expression was guarded. She still suspected he might be cheating on her. She wasn't wrong.

He forced an easy smile even though his heart was

racing and his insides were in knots. "Yeah. Everything's okay now, though."

She nodded once. "All right. You coming up to bed?"

The thought of crawling into bed beside her right now made him physically ill. Lying next to his wife after what he'd done? Even he couldn't stomach it. "Nah, I'm gonna shower, then probably stay up for a while." He often did that after an eventful shift, watching a movie or whatever. "You go on back to bed."

She lowered her gaze, her shoulders slumping, and it was just more proof that he'd become a monster. "See you in the morning. Don't forget Tammy's recital is at eight."

"I won't."

He waited until her footsteps retreated up the stairs and down the hallway above him. Dragging his hands over his face, he headed for the guest bathroom.

His mind wouldn't stop spinning. There were no answers or solutions, only questions, each one worse than the last.

Hands braced on the shower wall, he closed his eyes as the hot water poured over him for a few minutes before scrubbing every part of him down.

But no amount of soap and hot water could make him clean.

Everything was out of his control now. They would catch him, and it would be both a nightmare and a relief. He dreaded his wife's and daughters' reaction, the fallout afterward. But he couldn't see any way to hide it now.

His life was on a collision course with an immovable object. And that meant he had to be smarter than ever to avert disaster.

****

Mason jackknifed up in bed as gunshots echoed in his head, his heart pounding in the darkness.

It took him a second to realize he was in the bedroom

in Tate's basement suite. Not back overseas getting his ass shot at. Shit, he must have been dreaming.

Ric was over by the door, whining. And not a let-me-out-I-have-to-pee whine. A high-pitched, frightened one.

Normally when Mason had a nightmare Ric crawled up next to or even on top of him, instinctively recognizing something was wrong and trying to soothe him.

"It's okay," Mason said, swinging his legs over the side of the bed. "Hey, buddy, come—" He broke off, his head jerking up when the distinct sound of a rifle shot came from somewhere outside. "What the hell?" Yanking on his jeans, he lunged for the door and charged into the rest of the suite.

Tate had told him what happened earlier. Someone had targeted Rylee at a club. Had they come back here with a weapon?

Fuck that.

Ric was right beside him as he pushed through the door onto the stairs connecting him with the upper floor— just as another shot rang out from the backyard. His hands itched for a weapon. Tate had a gun safe in his den upstairs.

"Tate," he snapped as he neared his buddy's room. The door was shut. "What—"

"It's just Curt next door," came the muffled reply. "Go back to bed."

The hell he would. He flung the door open. Tate was sprawled out on his stomach, stark naked, and barely cracked an eye open at the sudden intrusion.

"Are you sure it's your neighbor?" Mason demanded, his heart still thudding erratically against his ribs.

"Yes. Good *night*, Mase," Tate muttered, sounding irritated. Well, more irritated. He hadn't been too happy when Mason had shown up while Nina was here earlier, either.

"Sorry, we should have warned you," a soft voice said from behind Mason.

He had never seen Tate move so fast. Hearing his niece's voice, Tate bolted upright and scrambled to cover himself just as Rylee stopped next to Mason in the doorway.

"Stay there, I'm not decent," Tate blurted in horror, blankets jerked up to his chin.

"It's not like I'm gonna come in there and crawl in bed next to you like when I was a little kid," Rylee said in exasperation, then looked up at Mason. "Curt likes to do night patrol to protect his goats, apparently."

"Fainting goats," Tate added, still clutching the covers under his chin.

"What. The *hell*," Mason muttered, glancing from one to the other and willing his heart to slow the fuck down. The damn thing had nearly stopped, waking up like that to unexpected gunfire in the middle of the night. For that split second before his brain had snapped into gear, he'd thought he was back in Afghanistan.

"I know. Scared the crap out of me the first time too. Well, I'm still not used to it, actually." Rylee patted his bare back, then cleared her throat and dropped her hand, wiping it on her jeans.

Shit, he was covered in a damp sweat. "What's he shooting at?" Mason demanded. What the hell kind of redneck town was this, anyway?

"Coyotes. Maybe a mountain lion or a wolf. He's a crack shot. Former Marine Raider."

"Yeah, but we all know those guys shoot like shit."

Tate grunted, apparently not amused by the wisecrack, and waved them both away with one hand. "Can you guys shut my door now?"

"Yeah." Mason jerked the door shut and turned to face Rylee. She was fully dressed, her hair all mussed from sleep. She looked okay, though. "How you feeling, young lady?"

"Better." Her gaze dropped to the hardwood floor. Ever prescient of human emotion, Ric went over to sit at her feet and look up at her with his chin pressed to her thigh. She reached down to stroke him. "Guess you heard about what happened?"

"Yeah." He was mad as hell that some asshole had drugged her and taken her friend.

She raised her eyes to his. "Did Uncle Tate say there was any news on Samantha when you talked to him?"

"No, I'm sorry."

She nodded, looked down again.

"Hey." He waited for her to meet his eyes. "Not your fault, all right?"

"I feel like it is, though. I'm really worried about her. And I keep thinking that it could've been me…"

Mason set his hand on her shoulder, wishing he could make it better. The world was a fucked-up place when a woman couldn't even go out with friends on a Friday night without fearing something like this. "Yeah, that had to have hit home hard. But thankfully you're here, safe and sound, and your uncle Tate and I will make sure you stay that way."

She gave him a sad smile. "Thanks. Think you can go back to sleep now?"

Smart cookie. She knew he was battling his demons and that the gunfire could trigger them. Maybe because she'd seen what her mom had gone through. "Please. After serving in the military for so long, I can drop off anywhere in seconds."

A total lie. He used to be able to. Not anymore. Not when every time he closed his eyes it transported him back to those final moments as they plunged toward the earth. Then the impact, followed by the hellish screams and images he couldn't forget.

"Good. See you in the morning?"

"Yeah. Get some sleep, kiddo. We'll take care of everything in the morning."

Rylee nodded. "Okay. Good night, Ric, you cutie pie." She went back to her room.

Mason went back to the basement, Ric at his heels. Back down in his room, he shut the door and sat on the edge of the bed. He let out a long breath, dragged a hand through his hair and realized it was trembling a little.

Shit. He'd hoped coming here would give him a fresh start. But it seemed he'd never be able to outrun his ghosts, no matter where he went.

He dropped back onto the covers and lay there staring up at the thin strips of moonlight on the ceiling coming through the slats in the blinds. Tried to clear his mind.

Another rifle shot echoed from outside.

Even though his brain understood there was no imminent threat, his body didn't. His heart rate jacked up, his skin cool and clammy with a light sheen of sweat as his mind transported him back to his recurring nightmare.

Screams. Firefight. Flames and smoke. *Trapped...*

He sucked in a deep breath, staring up at those strips of light as he sought something to push the awful memories away. A certain strawberry-blonde popped into his head.

Long, shapely legs. Golden eyes hiding things he wanted to know. Angel eyes.

His heart rate slowed, the sense of alarm receding as he thought of Avery. He'd heard a lot about her over the past few months from Tate, but Tate had never told him how hot his partner was. Or how distant.

She'd knocked his ego down a peg by not seeming the least bit interested when he'd flirted with her, blocking him out on the other side of an invisible wall she'd put up between them.

What she'd said earlier was true. He wasn't hurting for female attention—when he wanted it. But he wasn't quite the player she thought he was, either. And lately he'd been keeping to himself. Because nothing seemed to capture his interest anymore, even women.

Until Avery, who ironically seemed completely impervious to the charms that had never failed him before.

CHAPTER ELEVEN

She was starting to break through Tate's shell. Nina knew it in her gut.

That thought preoccupied her as she mixed the scone dough in the bowl at her kitchen counter on Sunday morning while she talked to her mom on speakerphone. She hadn't seen Tate yesterday as planned because he'd been busy with Rylee and following up with the investigation, so she'd spent the day getting things prepped for the coming week's classes. She missed him.

"I know, Mom. I miss you guys too, but it's beautiful here. You're gonna love it when you all come to visit me."

Though to be honest, as much as she loved her family, she was far more interested in spending time with Tate right now. It felt like things had shifted between them Friday night, but she wasn't sure where he was at in his head.

"And your roommate? She's nice?"

"The best. We've been having dinner together a lot, when she doesn't have to work late." She'd purposely kept the conversation light, not mentioning Tate or the incident last night with Rylee and her friend.

Nina was trying her best not to dwell on that. It reminded her too much of what had happened at the end of the last semester, and she'd worked too hard to try and put that all behind her.

"And are you seeing anyone?"

Nina had to smile. Her mom and sisters were constantly asking her about her romantic life and dating adventures. *Seeing someone* was code for more than two dates. And more than two dates meant that Nina saw serious relationship potential.

Given her dating history, that rarely happened. Tate, however, was another story. He oozed potential—although she wasn't sure if he was ready for a relationship, serious or otherwise. "Maybe."

Her mother gasped. "Really? Tell me!"

"Nothing to tell. We're just seeing each other." Although she hoped things with Tate would keep progressing more, because he was the kind of man she could definitely see herself committing to. Solid. Dependable. Trustworthy. Respectful.

And hot. So very, *very* hot. "He's a good person, he's a detective, and that's all I'm saying because there's nothing else to tell." Yet.

Her mom switched to rapid Spanish. "I hate it when you won't tell me details."

"And I love keeping you guessing."

Her mother made a frustrated sound. "Just wait until I tell your sisters, they'll be hounding you day and night for more info."

"Okay, but how about for now, we change the subject? Because there's nothing more to tell on that front."

"I don't believe that for a moment, but fine. Now. You mentioned your neighbors. You've made friends with them already?"

"More like...friendly rivals," Nina said with a smirk

as she finished patting the dough into a circle on the counter and began cutting it into triangles with a sharp knife. "I'm making them a double batch of blueberry-cinnamon scones right now. I'll take some across the street first, then give the rest to—"

"To your man."

Nina laughed. "Ever hopeful, Mom, that's why I love you." Although she sure liked the idea of Tate being her man. Coming home to him every night would be wonderful.

"I just want you to be happy, to see you settled down with someone who loves and respects you. For you to have what I found with your father."

"I know, and I want that too, but only with the right person." She hoped sooner than later, because she was pretty sure Tate could be that person. He had all the qualities she was looking for in a partner, and she'd never been so attracted to anyone.

But he was also gun shy since his breakup and she had to be careful not to get her hopes up this early on. Things could change between them at any time.

She didn't want to think about that either. "Anyway, I need to let you go because I'm just about to pop these in the oven and then I need to clean up and get ready to deliver the goods."

"All right. If you feel like sharing any details, call. I love you."

Nina laughed softly. "I will. Love you too, and say hi to Dad." She was more likely to share those kinds of details with her mom than her sisters. At least her mom could keep a secret. Sort of.

But there were some things she didn't even tell her mom.

The happy bubble she preferred to live in popped as that night last spring intruded again. She shoved it aside and restored her happy mental place as she brushed the scones with an egg wash and slid the pan into the oven. Then she scrubbed the kitchen to keep busy. In spite of her efforts to not think about it, the incident with Rylee was weighing heavy on her mind.

She quickly showered and dressed. When the scones were done, she texted Avery. *About to take some scones over to Rylee, Tate and Mason as a surprise. Wanna come?*

Sure. Gimme five minutes.

Nina nestled the warm scones in baskets lined with linen napkins and went out front to wait for Avery. Nina still hadn't said anything about her and Tate, it was so new. But if things progressed, she or Tate would have to tell Avery.

Her roommate came out a moment later wearing snug, dark jeans and a gorgeous sleeveless, floral top. The teal was incredible against Avery's strawberry-blond hair. "You look amazing."

Avery flashed her a smile. "Thanks, you do too. How many summer dresses do you have, anyway?"

"A lot. They're my favorite, no worrying about what goes with what, I just grab a dress from the hanger and I'm good to go." She gestured to the basket. "Let me drop these off, and I'll be right back."

She crossed the street to deliver the first basket. "Good morning," she said when Pat opened the door. Her neighbor had her Tilley hat on and looked ready to tackle more work in the garden. "Brought you some blueberry scones to go with a cup of coffee."

"Oh, that's lovely. Thank you so much. Bev," she called, and her sister's head appeared around the kitchen doorway a moment later. "Nina brought us homemade scones."

"Well, enjoy," Nina said, and turned to walk down the porch steps.

"How'd it go?" Avery asked as Nina climbed into the

114

front passenger seat of Avery's car. Nina's was still at campus. Tate was going to drive her and Rylee there tomorrow morning before class started.

"Hard to say. Might have stumped them with this one. Hard to make something out of scones."

"Good one. But you know they'll try."

Mason's and Tate's vehicles were both in Tate's driveway when they arrived a few minutes later. His house was beautiful, a log home nestled into a large, neatly kept yard with huge mature trees. "It's such a gorgeous house." She'd only seen a bit of it Friday night, and it had been dark.

"Yeah, he's done it up nice. The inside's cozy, with tons of character. The backyard's twice this size, and he's got a fire pit and a woodshop out there too."

Nina walked with her to the front door and smoothed the skirt of her green polka-dot dress as she waited on the doorstep, nerves and anticipation buzzing inside her.

Tate answered it a minute later, a startled smile lighting his handsome face when he saw her, the sunlight catching on the bronze whiskers he hadn't yet shaved. "Well, this is a nice surprise."

She held out the basket, her heart fluttering all over the place as she remembered how much he'd enjoyed the planetarium, the way he'd kissed her after, and then again at his place later on. "I thought you guys might like a treat for breakfast."

"Thanks. Come on in." He stepped back out of the way, his eyes on her, and swirls of heat replaced the tingle of nerves.

"How's Rylee?" Avery asked, finally drawing his attention away.

"Still sleeping. But I think you guys and this basket could tempt her out of bed." He gave Nina another smile and pulled her aside when Avery continued into the kitchen, disappearing from view around the edge of a stone countertop. "You still free tonight?"

Oh, he smelled good, and looked even better. "I might be. Why?"

"I want to take you out."

She liked where this was going. "Where?"

"Dinner, then I thought I could drive us out to a special spot that would be a great viewing point for the meteor shower."

Nina stifled a gasp and resisted the urge to put a hand to her heart. "Tate Baldwin, are you trying to seduce me?"

His eyes glowed with humor and arousal. "If I was, is it working?"

"Yes."

He laughed, then his expression slowly sobered, his gaze becoming intense. Reaching out, he tucked a lock of her hair behind her ear, his fingers sliding through the strands in a caress that sent warmth pooling between her legs. "I want to take you out into the hills to watch the sunrise."

Nina internally swooned all over the place, and couldn't help the sappy grin curving her lips. "Oh, wow." He was seducing her, all right. And doing a hell of a good job at it. Watching the meteor shower and then watching the sun come up together, just the two of them? Yes, please.

He drew his thumb across her cheek, his eyes full of sensual promise it made her pulse skip. "I know it's not ideal timing, because it's a Sunday night and that means you won't get much sleep before you need to leave for work, but—"

She caught his hand and nuzzled her cheek into it. Staying up all night with him would be worth losing any amount of sleep. Especially if part of the night involved getting naked together. "I'd love to watch the sun rise with you."

A slow, sexy smile curved his mouth. "Then it's a

date. I'll pick you up at seven."

She lifted on tiptoe to brush a teasing kiss across his mouth, her insides sizzling at the molten heat in his eyes. "I'm looking forward to it already."

****

Tate loaded the last of the gear into the bed of his truck and headed out to pick up Nina, his whole body buzzing with anticipation. Her reaction when he'd asked her to watch the sunrise with him was all he'd been able to think about all day.

Other than getting her naked and finding out what sounds she made when she came. That had kept him up at night lately. He was betting she wouldn't be shy in bed, and wouldn't hold back about what she liked and what felt good. He couldn't wait to find out.

She was waiting on the curb with a folded blanket in her arms when he arrived, her dark hair swept over the front of one shoulder. He leaned over to pop her door open, then froze when he took in the sight of her in a calf-length, form-fitting coral dress that hugged every sexy curve to perfection.

Tate's tongue stuck to the roof of his mouth. *Holy hell...*

"Hi. I wasn't sure what proper sunrise-watching attire was, so I brought a blanket in case it got too cold later," she said, setting the blanket inside to climb into the passenger seat.

"You look beautiful." So sexy he couldn't stop staring.

The instant she pulled her door shut and straightened, he reached up to cup the back of her neck with one hand and slid his thumb over the pulse point in her neck. A hot thrill raced through him at the way her pupils dilated. "You won't need the blanket, though. I'm going to keep you plenty warm."

A light blush colored her cheeks and a sassy smile

curved her lips. Her glossy, kissable lips. "I like the sound of that."

"Me too." He dropped a light kiss on her mouth and straightened before he could get carried away and start making out with her in plain view of Avery's house and anyone passing by who cared to watch.

Not how he wanted Avery to find out about them. "How do you feel about barbecue?" he asked Nina.

"I feel like it's damn tasty."

He chuckled. "Good." Turning the truck around, he headed for the center of town.

"How's Rylee holding up?"

"Physically she's fine, but she's really shaken up by the whole thing."

"Any word on her roommate from your contact in Missoula?"

"No. No sign of her yet, and Greg said there was no further information about the case."

"Damn."

"I know." He reached for her hand, curled his fingers around it and squeezed. "We just have to hope for the best. Mason's hanging out with Rylee tonight, so she won't be alone."

She nodded. "That's good." After a moment she glanced over at him. "Can I ask you something?"

Despite himself, he tensed a little, unsure what she was going to say. "Sure, shoot."

"I haven't said anything to her, but pretty sure Avery knows or at least guesses something's up between us. How do you want to handle it?" She waved her hands in front of her, palms out. "Not trying to push you into any-thing or whatever, I just… What do we tell her?"

He wasn't surprised that Avery had figured out something was happening. His partner was a damn good detective, first because she was good with people, and second because she noticed things most others didn't.

What *did* surprise him was that the idea of being in a relationship with Nina wasn't off-putting. Not that he was ready for anything serious yet. "I'll talk to her about it." She was his partner, and he'd known her longer. It should come from him. "But if she asks you in the meantime, just say we're seeing each other."

He didn't want to hurt Nina's feelings. However, given what he knew about her romantic tendencies, he was a little worried that she might be jumping ahead in her mind, envisioning them in a place he wasn't ready to go yet.

"Okay." She kept watching him, and he could feel her intimidatingly brilliant scientist brain searching for parameters, a way to file their status into the appropriate category in her head.

He didn't want to lie to her or give her false hope, but he also didn't want to stop seeing her, either. "I like you, Nina. A lot. Enough that I want to keep seeing you, but I want to be up front that I'm not ready for a serious commitment." He needed time. "If that's not enough for you, I understand. It's your call."

"No, I'm okay with it. For now," she added with an impish little smile that made him want to pull over and kiss her until she was gasping for breath, even as a tendril of unease curled inside him.

Get out of your head and enjoy the night.

He drove them to the barbecue joint just outside of downtown. The scent of hickory smoke perfumed the air outside it. "Best brisket and beans in Montana right here," he told her, setting a hand on her waist as he led her inside. She felt incredible, all soft and curvy.

"Smells fantastic."

He wound up ordering a sampler platter so she could try a bit of everything. He fed her a bite of the beans from his own fork, hunger tightening low in his gut at the way she held his gaze as her lips closed around the tines.

119

"Good?"

"Mmmm, amazing," she murmured, watching him in a way that made it hard for him not to slide in beside her and do something completely inappropriate in public.

They started with ribs, then moved onto the brisket, pulled pork and chicken. She didn't bring up their relationship status again, and he was relieved. It was too early to make promises or put a label on what they were. No matter how great she was, or how comfortable he felt with her, he would have resented any pressure from her about it.

"I know you haven't dated in a long while, but I just thought you should know that so far, this is already the best and least awkward date I've been on in… ever," she told him as she helped herself to another rib.

He couldn't help but grin. "Even better than the other night?"

"The other night was great too. What about for you? So far, so good?" Her lips twitched in a teasing smile. "You're not ready to bolt out the door on me?"

"No." She was so damn adorable, even when she was giving him a hard time. He liked that she was comfortable teasing him. Tala would love her. No wonder Avery did. "Did that guy you ditched to go out with me Friday night ever contact you again, by the way?" He'd been curious.

She looked up, a mischievous gleam in her eyes. "He might have."

Tate lowered his fork, hiding a frown. He'd just told her he wasn't ready for anything serious, and here he was, annoyed by the thought of another guy sniffing around. "What did you tell him?"

She laughed. "I told him thanks but no thanks. Wow, Tate, for a guy who professes to only want something casual, that was awfully territorial of you."

His face heated, because it was true, and he needed to be careful not to give her mixed signals. "Yeah. Guess it was." He couldn't help it with her.

She tilted her head to study him, curiosity bright in her eyes. "Can I ask what happened with your ex?"

Ah, damn. He didn't like talking about Erica, let alone on a date. Hadn't planned on talking about her with Nina, but it felt like there was something real happening between them, and she deserved to know why he was so leery about getting into another serious relationship. "Let's just say I couldn't meet her expectations."

"What expectations?"

"Pretty much all of them," he muttered.

When she kept watching him, he sighed and gave a brief rundown about his relationship with Erica. "I was with her for four years, lived together for over three of those. I thought eventually she'd feel solid about us, and then stop being so critical. But that never happened, and one day I came to the realization that it didn't matter what I did, it would never be enough to make her happy."

"See, you just said the magic words right there," Nina said, setting a rib down.

He frowned. "What do you mean?"

"You said 'to make her happy.' That's a major red flag—no one should ever be expected to make someone else happy, in any kind of relationship, romantic or otherwise. That's not fair. Everyone's responsible for their *own* happiness. A partner can add or detract from that, true, but happiness is a personal choice. And it also sounds like she had major insecurity issues."

Tate blinked at her, taken aback by her accurate and concise summation. "Yeah. Yeah, to all of that."

Nina nodded. "I know."

He laughed. "Is that why you have such a rosy outlook on life? You just decide to be happy, and go with it?"

Something shifted in her eyes, a brief shadow, then she gave him a lopsided smile that made something catch in his chest. "Pretty much." She shrugged. "I know that probably seems weird to you. And I know you think I have unrealistic views about love and relationships, but I come by them honestly."

"Because of your family."

She inclined her head and helped herself to a bite of barbecued chicken. "I also come from a stable home with two parents and have never served in the military or been to war. Given all that, your parents splitting up and your past experience with your last relationship, it's not surprising that you have a more cynical view of the world."

"I'm not that bad," he protested. Nina softened that part of him whenever she was around. He was powerless to stop it.

She smiled, her eyes twinkling. "No, you're not. And any man who would suggest a date to watch the sun rise has a romantic soul."

He made a face. "I dunno about *that*."

"I do. Because forms of romance are just like the universe—infinite. Anything can be qualified as romantic if the sentiment is there. It doesn't have to be words or gifts. It can be as simple as a look. A touch. Filling up your partner's gas tank when their vehicle is low on fuel. A text to say you're thinking of them. As long as it's genuine and comes from the heart, then it's romantic."

He gave her a skeptical look, wondering if she was being totally honest with him. "Really?"

"Really. Now tell me all about this business idea you and your friends are considering."

Glad for the change in subject, Tate outlined the idea, the possible services they could offer. "Anything from private civilian groups to private security and military contractors. We can tailor everything to meet each specific group's needs." He was getting excited just thinking about it.

"What role would you take on?"

"Bit of everything, but mostly operations management. Mase is our numbers guy, so he'd handle the books and finances. Brax can instruct on a million different things that might be of interest to clients, and fill in the gaps."

"And how does he fit into your group?"

"He served with Mason in Canada's most elite unit."

"How did you meet him?"

"He and Mase's unit was doing mountain training near my hometown of Kelowna. I happened to be in town visiting Tala, Rylee and my dad, so we all got together, and Mase brought Brax with him."

"Where is he now?"

"Overseas somewhere. He's still active duty, but his contract finishes next year. We're trying to convince him to come down here and join us instead of re-upping. He's a sniper."

"Wow, you guys sure have impressive CVs."

"Our backgrounds give us a lot of breadth in terms of what we can offer. We're all SOF-qualified, and we all have combat experience. Weapons, tactics, medical training, rappelling, water ops, mountaineering, climbing. Personal protection, CQB—"

"What?"

"Sorry, close quarter battle. And we're also trained in hostage rescue."

Her eyes widened. "That's incredible. Makes me want to sign up for a week at this place."

Tate laughed. God, she was cute. And sweet. And so damn sexy. For damn sure he'd never met anyone as brilliant as her. Her mind never stopped.

He could probably spend years with her and learn something new from her every day. He also liked getting glimpses of her view of the world, so different from his own. "I'd train you for free."

She beamed at him. "You would?"

"Yes, ma'am. What do you wanna learn?"

Her eyes sparkled with excitement and desire. "*Everything.*"

"Just say when, sunshine," he murmured, the word coming out without any effort or forethought.

She stopped and raised her eyebrows. "Sunshine?"

He shrugged. "That's what you're like. Bright, sunny. Warm."

She shook her head, a bemused smile on her face. "Lord, Tate, the things you say when I least expect them. And in answer to your earlier thought… Tonight. We'll start teaching each other tonight."

His blood heated, that hum of arousal buzzing through him at the thought of all the things they could teach each other in the hours ahead.

As they finished eating, Tate couldn't stop thinking about what she'd said before.

Hell. Maybe he was a romantic deep down after all.

CHAPTER TWELVE

" **A**re you about done there?" Tate asked dryly from the bed of his truck as he watched Nina.

It had been ten minutes and she still wasn't done setting up. They'd gone for a walk after dinner, wandering around downtown and along the creek for a bit until twilight before returning to his truck for the drive up here.

She stood ten yards away with her back to him in the middle of the small clearing he'd parked in, fiddling with her telescope. She'd declared the moonless night perfect for stargazing. "Just about."

It wasn't a hardship to watch her, because the view was incredible. That stretchy dress hugged her hips and ass in a way that was impossible to look away from. He wanted to trace every curve with his hands, mouth and tongue. Find every sweet spot on her body and linger there. Get her so worked up that she trembled and clung to him, desperate to come.

She looked at him over her shoulder, an excited smile on her face that had nothing to do with sex. "Okay, we're ready. Come here."

He climbed out of the bed and walked up behind her, closing his hands around her hips. He'd wanted to do it since that first night at Avery's place, when she'd walked down the stairs in front of him. She felt incredible. "What are we looking at?" he murmured, nuzzling the side of her neck, inhaling her addictive scent.

She let out a tiny gasp and reached back to slide a hand into the back of his hair. "I forget. Do that again."

He ran his nose down her neck, following the way it curved into her shoulder, and paused at the edge of the neckline of her dress to give her a slow, damp kiss there. "That?"

"Oh, yeah," she breathed, and tipped her head to the side, her hand tightening in his hair.

Tate moved in closer, pressing his swelling cock to the soft curve of her ass and wrapped his arms around her waist as he reversed the path of his lips and lingered on the sensitive spot at the side of her neck that made her shiver and squirm.

He loved how responsive and genuine she was. Couldn't wait to lay her down in the bed of his pickup and explore her the way he'd been fantasizing about this past week. But first…

"What did you want to show me?" he whispered.

"Hmmm?"

He laughed softly and shifted his grip, bringing her flush against him. "You were going to show me something about the stars. And after you're done, I'm going to take you to them."

"Oh, God." She let out a breathless laugh and quickly turned them so that he was standing behind the telescope. "You'll have to adjust the focus slightly for your eyes using this wheel here." She set his hand on the right one. "But go ahead. Take a look."

Tate paused to wrap an arm around her waist and

lean in for a slow, seductive kiss. When she moaned and melted against him, he sucked on her lower lip, stroked his tongue across it and lifted his head. Her eyes were hazy, her cheeks flushed.

Biting back a groan, he released her and bent to put his eye to the eyepiece.

At first all he saw was a blur of light. He tightened the focus, slowly bringing the patch of sky she'd selected into sharp relief.

Stars. Incredible numbers of them, packed into that one field of view. And different colors in the background. Purples and blues melting into the black. "It's beautiful. But what am I looking at?"

"The Milky Way. But ignore all of that and focus on the bright dot near the center."

He did. And then suddenly the dot became something more. A round object with rings. He grabbed the telescope, pressed his eye harder against the eyepiece, suddenly captivated. The image was unmistakable. "Wait. Is that Saturn?"

Her soft laugh caressed him. "Yes."

"Damn, that's unreal. I can see the rings," he said in amazement.

"I know, right? How awesome is it?"

He could literally see individual rings, and tiny dark lines between them. "I can't believe it."

Nina draped herself along his back and slid her arms around him, her palms resting on his pecs. "I knew you'd appreciate it." She sounded so happy.

"I do." He stared for a few more moments, awed. Then he straightened and turned to face her, his arms going around her hips. "But I like looking at you even more."

Her smile tugged at his heart. "If I beat Saturn, I'll take that as a compliment." She glanced past him at the truck, and her face filled with surprise. "Oh! Did you do all that while I was setting up?"

"Yep." He caught her hand, tugged her toward his truck. He'd spread out rolls of foam in the bed and covered them with open sleeping bags and a few pillows, with a couple of quilts standing by for them to cuddle up under.

"Up you go." He lifted her, smiled at the startled little yelp she made, and climbed in after her.

She crawled up toward the front of the bed, giving him an awesome view of her round ass before stretching out on her back with her head resting on one of the pillows. Her delighted smile made his earlier efforts worth it.

When he stretched out beside her, she turned toward him and ran a finger down the side of his face. "Thank you for doing this."

"It's my pleasure." And hopefully hers too, soon.

Tate reached for her, drawing her close and tucking her head into the curve of his shoulder. He held her, stroked a hand through her hair as they gazed up at the stars, enjoying himself even more than he'd thought he would.

"Isn't it spectacular?" she murmured.

"Yeah, it is." Only he'd never appreciated it fully until now. And he loved the feel of her snuggled up next to him like this, all warm and soft and trusting.

After a few minutes she lifted her head to look at him. "I feel so safe with you," she said quietly. "Safe, but also really damn aroused."

He grinned at her honesty. Shifting to lay facing her, he curved his hand around the rise of her hip, squeezing gently. "That's good to hear." He leaned in to claim that tempting mouth.

She met the kiss eagerly, threading both hands into his hair and pressing flush against him, her softness melding with the harder planes of his body. Tate angled his head and plunged his tongue inside to taste her, drinking in the soft sound of need she made. He stroked her tongue, ran his hands over her, mapping every curve and hollow.

Nina wiggled closer, her fingers digging into his back as she wrapped her leg around his.

Tate rolled her onto her back and stretched out on top of her, swallowing a groan at the way she arched beneath him, his cock nestled against her mound. He cradled her head in his hands and rocked into her, battling the frantic need she ignited in him.

The ache between his legs was getting worse by the second, but he didn't want a fast fuck with her. He wanted to slow down, savor this, make her crave him with every cell in her being.

He kissed his way down her jaw to her neck, lifted up on his elbows as he blazed a path down to where the neckline dipped just above her cleavage. Nina reached down and impatiently tugged the fabric down, revealing the swells of her breasts cradled by the creamy pink lace bra. He nuzzled the valley between them, smiled at the way she grabbed his head to hold her to him.

Don't worry, sunshine, I'm gonna give you as much as you want.

The significance of giving her a pet name didn't escape him. But it felt right, so he wasn't going to question it, cynical bastard or not.

His tongue darted out to flick against the skin at the edge of one lace cup. He could see the hard point of her nipple pressing against the fabric.

"Tate," she whispered, lifting toward his mouth. Chasing it.

He tugged the lace cup down, a low sound coming from his gut at the sight of her bare breast and tight nipple awaiting him. He flicked his tongue across it, reveled in her sharp intake of breath, then slowly sucked it into his mouth. Nina mewled softly and dropped her head back, her fingers digging into his scalp.

Tate stayed exactly where he was, sucking the sensitive bud, rubbing it with his tongue. Nina shoved the dress down more and arched to reach back and undo her bra. He pulled it off her and cupped her other breast, zeroing in on its center with the same attention as he'd just given the other.

Easing his weight off her, he ran a hand down her back to her rear, cradling her to him. She rolled her hips, rubbing against his erection until the need burned like fire up his spine.

Nina grabbed the hem of his shirt and started pulling upward. Tate lifted enough for her to get it to his chin, then reluctantly released her nipple to yank it over his head. As soon as it was gone, he went right back to what he'd been doing, his fingers gliding up and down the backs of her thighs now while her hands roved over his back, chest and shoulders.

"Wait," she whispered, pushing at his shoulder. "Let me—" She ducked down and rubbed her face against his bare chest, hands curling around his shoulders, squeezing his muscles. "Oh, Tate, look at you," she breathed, her mouth driving him crazy as she kissed and licked at his suddenly over-sensitized skin.

He'd thought he was turned on before, but the way she looked at him, the hungry way her mouth and hands moved over his body, her tongue darting out to tease him as she kissed her way down his stomach toward his waistband—made every one of his muscles tighten and his heart pound.

When her hand cupped him through his jeans, he sucked in a ragged breath and caught her wrist, allowing himself just one stroke against her palm as he rolled his hips. Then he pulled her hand away and settled it back on his head as he bent to her breasts and eased his hand under the hem of her dress.

Nina caught her breath and stilled as his hand

skimmed up her bare thigh, pausing just at the edge of the lace covering her mound. With a sweet, soft moan, she parted her legs.

Tate rewarded her by brushing his fingers against the center of the lace.

She twisted against him, her hands locking in his hair. "Tate…"

"Shhh." He wanted to make this memorable. So she'd never forget him or this night together. He took his time, teasing and stroking her through the lace, switching his mouth to her other breast.

A long, liquid moan bubbled out of her, the muscles in her thighs quivering.

Finally, he tugged her panties down and eased his fingers into the soft, wet heat that awaited him. They both moaned. Tate caressed her slick folds, gliding up to tenderly brush against the hard bud at the top of her sex.

"Oh God, don't stop," she begged, her voice a breathless, desperate plea, her body rigid with need.

"I won't," he promised, circling her clit, paying attention to every cue she gave him about location and pressure.

She quivered in his grasp, her breathing ragged, tiny whimpers spilling from her lips. Tate drank it all in, began kissing his way down her body, and eased one finger inside her just as his mouth settled over her core.

Nina moaned and rocked into his tongue, her tight grip on his hair only pushing his arousal higher. Every sound made the need burn hotter.

She was close now, he could feel it in the way she squeezed his finger and hear it in her ragged breathing. He licked her softly, closed his lips around the fragile bud to suck on it as he rubbed that secret spot inside her. She called out his name and shuddered as she came, holding him close.

Tate's heart slammed against his ribs as she relaxed

her grip on him and collapsed back with a broken moan. Gently easing his hand from between her legs, he kissed the top of her mound, then her lower belly, hard as a rock in his jeans but reluctant to stop pleasuring her.

"Tate. Come here," she whispered, tugging his shoulder.

He braced his weight on one hand to lift up and meet her kiss. When she pressed on his chest he didn't resist, immediately lying on his back for her. She crawled on top of him, that lithe, sexy body blanketing him.

He moaned into her mouth when she rocked against his erection, shuddered when she sucked at his tongue, knowing she was tasting herself.

Wrapping his hands in her hair, he watched, spell-bound, as she rubbed her cheek on his chest, over the ridges of his tensed abs. Her nimble fingers undid the top of his fly, and he held his breath as she tugged the denim down, then his underwear. The rigid length of his cock sprang free into her grip, and the feel of her hand wrapped around him sent shards of pleasure splintering through him.

With a soft, sexy hum, she stroked him, her tongue busy licking at his abs, torturously close to where he was dying for it. His heart thudded out of control, the breath halting in his throat when those soft, full lips closed around the head of his cock.

Fuck, oh, fuck…

He gripped handfuls of her hair, tried to keep his eyes open because he didn't want to miss a single second, but then she took him deep and he was lost. His eyes slammed shut, the pleasure so intense he couldn't breathe. She was so giving. Making him feel things he wasn't sure he was ready for.

Thankfully she didn't tease, didn't torture him by slowing down and reveling in her power over him. Instead she gripped him tight in her hand, using it and her mouth to drive him right to the edge of his control.

"Nina," he rasped out, swallowing. "You're gonna make me come soon."

In response she reached up her free hand to close around his fist and squeeze, asking him to hold her hair tighter.

Jesus. Tate gripped it harder and lifted his head, struggling for breath at the sight of her sucking him off.

His thigh muscles twitched, his whole body tightening, gathering for the moment she made him explode. Then she moaned, a soft sound of pure enjoyment, and he lost it.

Hands locked in her hair, he arched his lower back and cried out as he started coming. Nina froze and stayed absolutely still, taking everything he gave her.

It was the hottest goddamn experience of his life.

He finally had enough control to unclench his fists from her hair. He combed his fingers through it, swallowed as she raised her head to smile up at him. He swore his heart rolled over in his chest.

Oh, hell. He was in such trouble with her, and he didn't even care.

Not trusting himself to speak, he reached for her, tugging her up until he could cradle her in his arms. She sighed and snuggled into him, her face tucked into the side of his neck. He reached over for a quilt and carefully covered her with it, making sure every inch of her was protected from the chill or any mosquitoes out hunting.

Once she was all wrapped up, he held her like that, slowly gliding his fingers through her silky hair. He couldn't remember ever feeling this content. Or this protective. Against all odds she'd already partially wormed her way into his heart, and he'd do anything to keep her safe and spare her pain.

Damn, it would be way too easy to fall for her if he let himself. He needed to be careful.

He didn't realize he'd dozed off until later when his phone alarm woke them just after two in the morning. The sky was dark now, a black velvet canvas dotted by a million stars.

"It's almost show time," he whispered to Nina, gently turning her.

She rolled off him and settled up tight against his side, her head on his shoulder. "Did you know meteor showers are caused by debris from comets?" she murmured drowsily.

His lips curved up in the darkness. Sexy little scientist and her busy brain. "No. What else?"

He cuddled her close, warm and sated while she told him about more astrological trivia, enjoying her enthusiasm and the sound of her voice. Then she broke off in mid-sentence with a gasp, and he glanced up in time to see a trail of light streak across the sky.

"There! Did you see it?" She shook him gently, her excitement palpable.

He grinned. "Yeah." Another streak flashed across the sky. Then another. And another, until it was like watching a cosmic artillery barrage.

Eventually the meteors began to peter out. Nina came up on one elbow beside him, her smile contagious as she looked into his eyes. "This is the most romantic night of my entire life."

That surprised him. "Ever?"

"Literally *ever*. Thank you."

"You're welcome." He tugged her down for a kiss.

She hummed in appreciation, gave into him for a long moment before lifting her head. "So. By my calculations, we've got a little over three hours until the sun comes up. I wonder what we can do to pass the time until then?"

A low chuckle rumbled in his chest. "I'm sure we can think of something."

He rolled her to her back and cradled the back of her head in one hand as he kissed her. He'd wanted her to crave him, but now he craved her on a scale he hadn't bargained for.

He wanted to matter to her. For her to value him, appreciate him for who he was, look at his good qualities instead of his faults.

She was right. He had been lonely until she came along. He was tired of being lonely, and the thought of losing her now made him feel empty inside.

Every minute he spent with her, the link between them strengthened. He couldn't just treat this as a fling and then walk away. Didn't want her to date anyone else. But he couldn't hand his heart to her, either, so it wasn't fair to ask.

Tate didn't want to hurt her. But if he was honest, he was more afraid of getting hurt in turn.

CHAPTER THIRTEEN

"So to review… The dimmer an object appears to us, the higher the numerical value given to its magnitude, with a difference of five magnitudes corresponding to a brightness factor of one-hundred exactly."

Nina paused to make sure her second-year class seemed to be following her thus far before leading everyone through the example calculation step by step, explaining everything as she went.

"Therefore, we can say that the apparent magnitude of our sun as seen by us here on Earth is… -26.74." She finished writing the answer with a flourish of her digital pen and looked up from her podium. "And voilà. That's how easy it is to calculate apparent magnitude of a star. See? We did it."

She gave the class an enthusiastic smile and scanned the room. "Any questions?"

No one raised a hand. Several students were looking at her blankly. One off to the left side looked deeply concerned. She was betting he would show up during her office hours that afternoon.

"No? You sure?" she prompted.

Still nothing.

"All right, give the practice problems at the end of the chapter your best effort for next class, then review everything we've covered so far. Because next time we meet we'll be starting on my personal favorite topic of the whole course—dark matter, dark energy, and black holes."

Several faces brightened at the news, making Nina grin. The math was going to increase in difficulty from here on out, but it was just so damn cool. They could do it, though some would need more help than others. She didn't mind. She actually liked it when students came to her for help. It meant they trusted her enough to approach her, and then she really felt like she was doing her job.

"Dismissed. See you all Wednesday." She packed up her bag as the students began filing out. No surprise, the alarmed student paused in front of her, looking slightly sheepish.

He glanced around as if to make sure no one could overhear, then said to her in a low voice, "Can I come see you this afternoon?"

"Of course. Don't worry, we'll get that light bulb to go on yet. I have total faith that it'll click for you eventually."

He gave her a relieved smile. "Thanks, Professor Benitez."

"No problem. Have a good day and I'll see you later."

She left the classroom and headed up to her office, feeling like she was floating on air. After getting only three hours' sleep last night she should be exhausted, but instead her entire body was energized and still on an endorphin high.

Being with Tate last night had been completely magical. She still couldn't get over it. They were opposite in so many ways, but clicked where it mattered. After more stargazing and a second round of orgasms they'd lain in the bed of his pickup together, tucked under the quilts while the sky gradually lightened, the mountains rising behind them.

A sense of awe had enveloped her as the first golden rays of sunlight crept into the valley below them. Cuddled up with a thermos of coffee he'd brought that was still hot, they'd watched the sun appear over the edge of the eastern horizon, bathing Missoula in its light.

After that Tate had driven her home, waited while she showered and changed, then driven her into Missoula. Rylee had decided to stay with him for now, not comfortable going back to campus while her roommate was still missing, and Nina totally understood that.

They'd stopped for breakfast at a cute little diner she'd never been in before, then he'd driven her to campus. The way he'd kissed her goodbye before she got out of his truck, with those strong hands gently cupping her face as if she was the most precious thing in the world to him, had made her belly flip and her heart catch.

See you later, sunshine. Go reveal the secrets of the universe.

A shiver sped through her just thinking about the look in his eyes. Hot. Full of the things he wanted to do to her the next time they were alone. And also pride.

He was proud of her and what she did. That felt incredible.

She couldn't wait to see him again, hopefully tonight. They hadn't technically had sex yet, and she was looking forward to it. Except she was already falling for him, even if it wasn't smart. And once they crossed that line, for her there would be no stopping the rest of the fall.

If Tate wasn't ready to catch her…

Her phone rang. She grabbed it off her desk, went all gooey inside when she saw his number. "Hey, I was just thinking about you," she answered, her body tingling in anticipation of seeing him later.

"Can you talk right now?"

Her smile faded at his grim tone, and her stomach tightened. "Yes, I'm in my office. Is something wrong?"

"Yes."

Nina braced herself and took a breath, trying not to jump to conclusions. Was he pulling back because of last night? Had something about their connection scared him into pushing her away? "What's going on?"

"I got word on Rylee's friend. Samantha's dead."

Nina gasped and sank into the chair behind her desk, reeling from shock. "Oh my God. Oh, I'm so sorry." That poor girl. "What happened?"

"I can't go into too much detail, but she was found dead on the south bank of the Clark Fork about a mile-and-a-half east of campus. Looks like she was out there since Friday night or early Saturday morning. Whoever took her killed her and left her there."

Ice slid through Nina's veins. She swallowed, her pulse thudding in her ears, the past slamming into the present. "Was she...raped?"

"Pretty sure, yeah."

Nina closed her eyes, the cold growing inside her. No. This was a nightmare. A horrible nightmare.

What if it's connected?

"Anyway, Rylee's pretty torn up about it. I'm at home with her right now. I don't want to leave her alone, and she's scared because this guy is still out there somewhere."

Fear crawled up Nina's spine, filling her until she couldn't breathe. Oh, God. The druggings. The location where Samantha had been found. Being here on campus prior to the attacks.

They were more than linked. It might be the same damn attacker. And she'd said *nothing*.

"Nina? You still there?"

"Yes. Sorry." She rubbed her forehead, trying and failing to push the fear away. "Tate, I gotta go."

A taut, split-second of silence followed. "What's wrong?"

"I'm sorry. I gotta go," she mumbled, then ended the call and immediately got up to shut her office door. Her fingers were unsteady as she turned the lock home, that terrible crawling sensation moving up and down her spine.

Okay. Stop. Breathe.

She returned to her desk and sat in the chair, closed her eyes and forced in a couple of slow, choppy breaths. It didn't help. Her throat was already clogging, the backs of her eyes burning with the threat of tears as nausea swirled in her stomach like oil.

She should have reported it when it happened. But she hadn't, because she'd wanted to bury the whole thing and forget it. And now Rylee's friend might have been killed by the same man.

There was no way she could stay silent now. She had to come forward.

Avery.

Her hands shook as she dialed her friend's number. Her breaths were uneven, her jaw trembling. All her muscles were locked. Jerky and uncoordinated.

"Avery Dahl."

"Av-Avery," she managed, grief spearing her.

"Nina? What's the matter?"

She struggled to pull in a breath. Her teeth were chattering. "Sam-mantha's k-killer. I…"

"Whoa, sweetie, slow down and take a breath."

She tried. The air wheezed into her lungs and shuddered out. Oh, God, she was going to be sick.

"I'm guessing Tate told you the news?" Avery said.

"Y-yes. But—" She sucked in another breath. "The attacker. I…I think…"

"Hey, it's all right. Take a minute and get your breath back, and then you can talk. I'm here, okay? Not going anywhere. Whatever you need to tell me, I'll listen. But let's get you calmed down first."

Her friend's calm, reassuring tone helped a little. Nina closed her eyes and took several slow breaths until she no longer felt like she was choking or about to throw up.

Finally she was in control enough to haltingly begin her story. Fear, guilt and shame swamped her as she told Avery everything she remembered. Her body was alternately cold and then numb, little tremors ripping through her.

"I don't… D-don't remember m-much of it. Just flashes. I d-didn't think I'd be able to p-prove anything, so—" Her throat closed up.

"It's all right. I understand."

She gasped out the main details she could remember about that night. Mostly it came out in a jumble of apologies and excuses. "It just s-seems too s-similar," she finished, then babbled for another minute.

At last she fell silent. And waited. Dreading Avery's response. Fearing a lecture or even condemnation for her earlier silence that might have contributed to this unspeakable tragedy.

"Nina, you have to report this to the Missoula PD. Now." Avery's tone was quiet but firm.

"I know," she whispered, stricken. If she could have prevented this tragedy, if she'd known what would happen, she would have done things so differently.

"I'll meet you at the department. I don't want you to be alone when you talk to the detectives."

That almost pushed her into the tears she'd managed

to hold back so far. "Thank you." Her voice was barely audible. She felt so small and helpless, the sense of violation as strong as it had been the first time. "Just promise me you w-won't tell T-Tate."

Avery sighed. "Sweetie, he's gonna find out almost as soon as you file the report, because he worked on two other cases like this when he was in Missoula. From what you've just told me it sounds like there's a good possibility they're connected, and so they're going to want to consult with him immediately."

"Oh, shit," she breathed, closing her eyes again. She hadn't wanted him to know. Hadn't wanted anyone to ever find out. But especially not Tate. It was humiliating.

Avery was quiet a moment. "You guys are seeing each other, right?"

No point in tiptoeing around it now. "Yes."

"Then you have to tell him." A pause. "Do you want me to call him for you?"

"No," she blurted, a burst of panic spurting through her. They were just starting to build something that could be incredible, and this could blow it all up. Once he found out what had happened, he might not want to touch her ever again.

But even she could see that him finding out was inevitable. She'd rather it come from her, as hard as it would be to tell him face to face and watch his reaction. She had no choice. "I'll—I'll tell him." Her stomach pitched at the thought.

"Would you rather have him or me with you when you talk to the detectives?"

She cringed. "I…"

"If you want him there, I can just tell him you need him. Simple as that, no details. I'll stay with Rylee, and have him meet you at the station there. You can have either him or me there, I just don't want you to go through this alone."

There was no help for it. She'd stayed silent for too long as it was, and an innocent victim had paid the ultimate price for it. "Okay, then Tate." He would want to talk to her about it once he heard anyway. She'd rather tell him up front.

"All right. Now I'm going to call a contact I have on the Missoula PD. She'll come pick you up and take you in to make your official statement. I'll make it clear they're not to start anything until Tate gets there. All right?"

"Yes. Thank you."

"Sweetie, don't mention it. I'm proud of you for coming forward, and so damn sorry it happened at all. I'll be here to support you every step of the way, no matter what. Love you."

"I love you too," she choked out. After ending the call Nina curled up in her chair and drew up her knees to rest her forehead on them, filled with dread and shame.

She should have done this a long time ago. Now she would have to do it in front of the man who held the power to crush her heart with his reaction.

CHAPTER FOURTEEN

Avery walked into Tate's kitchen and eyed the display in front of her dubiously. "What's this?"

"Dungeons and dragons," Rylee answered, writing something down on a sheet of paper while Mason set out a tray and pouches of dice. "You said you'd play."

"I thought it was a board game." More like bored game. Avery would rather stab something sharp in her eye than be stuck playing a game right now, but Rylee still didn't know what had happened, and Avery was here to make sure she was okay.

"No, it's a role-playing game," Mason answered from the other side of the table.

She met his pale stare, felt a ripple of something deep inside her. He didn't know why Tate had raced out of here so fast, only that Nina had asked for him. But it was their job to occupy Rylee and keep her mind off everything for now. "How long does it take?"

"Hours for a good session," he said meaningfully.

Perfect. She'd suck it up and spend time with him if it meant distracting Rylee for a while. "What do I need to do?"

"You have to make a character. Here." Rylee slid a piece of paper and an open book over to her.

Avery listened while Rylee explained everything, secretly becoming less enthusiastic about this whole thing the more Rylee told her. Dragons and orks and trolls? Ugh.

She glanced up at Mason, squinted at his shirt. "What does that say?"

He grinned and sat up straighter so she could read it. A picture of a weird-shaped die sat beneath the words: *Beware the dungeon master who wears a smile.* "Dungeon master?" Was that some kind of BDSM thing?

Humor shone in his eyes. "It means I'm the master of this game."

Wait. "You have a dungeons and dragons T-shirt?"

"Hell yeah, I do," he said with pride, winking at Rylee. "I played it back in high school, and now it's having a resurgence."

"It's true, all my friends play it. It's awesome," Rylee said, still making notes.

Huh. Until now Avery had thought it was something nerds played in their parents' basements. "Okay then." Rylee helped her through the process of creating a character, then Mason began the game.

She'd expected to hate it, but in actuality, Avery found herself entranced by Mason's deep voice as he began to set the scene, his descriptions so vivid she could picture the medieval village in her mind. She followed Rylee's lead, asking questions and as they navigated their way through the adventure, rolling different weird-shaped dice that determined the outcome of various decisions.

By lunchtime they'd defeated a group of bandit assassins and killed the main villain responsible for holding the town hostage. She was so into it, she was surprised when her phone vibrated, and saw how much time had passed already.

But it wasn't Tate or Nina calling. She silenced it, then glanced up to meet Mason's questioning gaze with a subtle shake of her head.

"So, what do you think so far?" Rylee asked her eagerly. "You like it?"

"Yeah, I do." It was immersive, and sure made the time pass.

"Good." Smiling, she turned to Mason. "Carry on, dungeon master."

"As you wish, lady ranger."

Avery watched him, found herself drawn more and more to him while he continued the game. He was well aware that something bad had happened, but he didn't let on, and was doing a fantastic job of keeping Rylee distracted. She had to give him points for that, even if she didn't fully trust him. She'd already made the mistake of getting involved with a smooth operator, and had the divorce papers to prove it.

****

Tate still had no idea what the hell was going on when he arrived at the main police headquarters in Missoula.

Avery had shown up at his house forty-five minutes ago to say Nina needed him for something important, related to Samantha's case, and promised to stay with Rylee. She wouldn't tell him what it was about, only that Nina was okay and needed him.

That worried him, especially since she'd asked for him and not Avery, her best friend. Wondering what it was about had driven him insane the entire drive down here, his brain coming up with one awful scenario after another, each one worse than the last. He'd called Nina twice on the way to try and talk to her about whatever was happening, but she wouldn't pick up.

Worry churned in his gut. Had she seen or heard

something on campus that related to Samantha's case?

He jogged up the station's front steps and pushed the front door open. His friend Greg appeared from around the corner partway down the hall.

"Tate. This way."

Tate rushed toward him. "Is she all right?" His first concern was for Nina. The second, how she fit into Samantha's case.

"Yes. She's in here." Greg led him down another short hall and paused beside a closed door. "I'll just give you guys a while to talk alone before we start the interview." He opened the door for Tate.

Anxious to see her, Tate stepped inside. Nina rose from a chair across the room and gave him a wobbly smile that made his insides tighten in dread. She was pale. And her eyes were puffy, as though she'd been crying. His stomach muscles grabbed. "Nina, what's going on?"

Greg shut the door behind Tate, and Nina indicated the chair closest to him. "Can you sit?"

He sat, his muscles wound like springs as he tried to get a read on the situation. She was clearly upset. Whatever she was going to say had to be bad. "Are you okay?"

"Yes."

He relaxed only a fraction. "Avery said you wanted to talk to me about something connected with Samantha's murder."

She nodded. Started pacing in front of him, moving from Greg's desk to the far wall and back again while the tension in the room ratcheted higher. "When you told me about Samantha, about where she was found, and knowing that she and Rylee had been drugged at the bar the other night... I had to come forward. I'm just sorry I didn't come forward sooner, and that I'm telling you this way."

Telling him *what*? He held his frustration in check and watched her, waiting, his pulse drumming in his ears.

She blew out a breath, seemed to struggle with herself before stopping and facing him, the pain in her eyes stabbing him in the chest. "I was raped at the end of last semester."

The air rushed out of his lungs, his hands curling around the edge of his chair. *No...*

"It's why I spent the summer back home, to get away for a while. Anyway, I was drugged at a bar here in Missoula and woke up almost naked hours later in a similar spot to where Samantha was found." She fidgeted with the edge of her skirt. "I'm afraid it might be the same guy."

It felt like someone had slammed a sledgehammer into his gut. "Oh, sunshine, no," he breathed, his voice full of anguish. The thought of her going through something like that tore him up.

Nina glanced away. "I didn't report it. I was out with some faculty members. We'd had dinner, then out to a bar for drinks after. They eventually left and I stayed. I'd been drinking a lot. Flirting with a couple different guys. They bought me drinks. Danced with me. I only have flashes of memory after that."

Tate resisted the urge to drag a hand through his hair, making himself sit absolutely still as she continued, his heart sinking.

Nina resumed pacing, not looking at him. She was clearly agitated, her cheeks flushed, her breathing erratic and her voice tight as she tried to get through what she wanted to say. "I don't remember anything after the bar except getting into a pickup with a guy. I don't know who. Then flashes later inside it, when he..."

She trailed off, and it was all Tate could do to remain sitting in his chair while she suffered in front of him. But he didn't want to interrupt or stop her. Needed to at least let her vent all of this and listen.

"I woke up outside alone in the middle of the night, on the riverbank, and didn't know what had happened. I was mostly naked and had obviously been dumped there, so I figured I'd been…assaulted, plus I was tender. But I wasn't sure who I'd been with. Couldn't even remember his face to give a description, let alone a name. So I went straight to the hospital instead of the police and had a rape exam."

Oh, thank God. At least she'd told someone, and been checked out. "Were you injured? Physically?"

"No. And there was no DNA evidence. He'd used a condom. And I honestly couldn't say I hadn't given my consent, because I didn't remember any of it, but I don't think I did. They didn't find skin beneath my fingernails. No foreign hairs on me or my clothes, no defensive injuries that suggested I tried to fight him off. Thankfully I didn't get an STI or anything."

She swallowed, her pain and embarrassment difficult to witness. "The worst part is the not knowing. Not knowing who it was, or what had actually happened. I'd had a lot to drink, but not enough to make me black out. Did I agree to go with him from the bar? Clearly I didn't try to fight him off, because of whatever he'd given me. And because I don't remember any of it, it had to be because I was unconscious."

Tate ached to hold her. Pull her to him and try to absorb some of her pain. He hated to watch her hurting and not be able to stop it. Hated that she'd been violated and left to question whether it was partially her fault all this time.

Pausing to pull in a steadying breath, she wiped the heel of her hand under her eyes and continued. "I was new to town, and it was my first semester as a professor. Like I said, I'd been out with faculty, and they'd all seen me drinking and flirting. I didn't want them to find out what had happened. I was embarrassed and ashamed.

"I'd worn a sexy dress and heels that night, and I'd had way too much to drink. I was afraid that people would say it was my fault, or that no one would believe that it was rape, when I couldn't even be sure of it myself. I didn't want to be branded as a slut by my colleagues."

Tate closed his eyes for a second, he couldn't help it. He'd heard this same thing from so many women during his time as a cop. As a man and an officer of the law it sickened and shamed him, filled him with a helpless fury that victims were afraid to come forward for fear of not being believed, of even being blamed for their attack.

Opening his eyes, he focused on Nina and shook his head, wishing he could make this all go away for her. "I'm so sorry."

She dismissed his words with a tight frown and resumed pacing. "Anyway, Montana law states that if a victim chooses not to report the crime at the time of a medical exam, then the information obtained during it is classified as medical information. Which is protected by federal and state law. But given that my case might be linked with others, including Rylee and Samantha, I've changed my mind, and now that information will become confidential criminal justice information. I'm hoping there will be enough evidence in it—something—to help catch this guy."

She stopped and stared at him, the haunted look in her eyes making his entire chest hurt. "I wish I'd reported it initially."

A barrage of emotions hit him. Anger, grief, helplessness. He was desperate to touch her. To erase the distance between them and pull her into his arms so he could hold her tight against him. Comfort her. Protect her. Reassure her it wasn't her fault.

He also wanted to hunt down the son of a bitch who'd done this and beat him into a coma.

"You have nothing to be sorry for," Tate ground out, his voice like gravel as his mind spun, trying to digest everything. "It wasn't your fault."

It had to be the same guy Tate had been hunting two years ago here in Missoula. Those three other cases and the most recent ones had the same MO. All the victims were young, attractive brunettes in their late teens to early thirties who either attended or worked at the university. They'd all been drugged. Then dumped near the river.

Tate was betting there were more victims who hadn't come forward.

Rage built, burning through the pain in his chest. That bastard had drugged and raped Nina. Had drugged Rylee and her friend, then raped and killed Samantha. Might have done the same to Rylee if he'd managed to take her the other night as well.

Tate ran a hand over his mouth and chin, not knowing what else to say as he battled the rush of anger surging through his veins as he thought about what Nina had endured.

God dammit, he hadn't known. Hadn't had a clue about what she had gone through earlier this year, alone. Worse, he'd unfairly decided she was naïve and clueless about the harsher realities of the world, not realizing she'd experienced that brutality firsthand in the worst kind of violation a woman could experience.

Still standing across the room, Nina twisted her fingers, looking uncertain. "But if I'd come forward when it happened back in May, maybe he would have been caught. Now Samantha's dead, and he almost got Rylee, and I…"

There was no way in hell he would let her carry that burden on top of everything else.

"No." He stood and took a step toward her, unable to keep his distance an instant longer.

Nina retreated a step. Tate stopped, the shame in her eyes and the way she shrank from him slicing him up inside. "This isn't on you. None of it," he said in a low voice, needing her to hear him and believe it. If it was anyone's fault, it was his, for not catching the bastard before.

Her gaze dropped to the floor again. "But what if it is?" she whispered, her voice catching.

Tate swore his heart broke. He felt it crack, the quick, searing pain in the center of his chest. "Sunshine, please come here," he whispered, holding out a hand to her.

Nina looked up at him, her hesitation clear. As if she couldn't believe he would want to touch her now.

Tate wanted it more than he wanted air to breathe.

He kept his hand out, his heart thudding against his ribs. It seemed like a small eternity as she slowly reached for it. The instant her chilled fingers touched his, Tate held on and drew her close.

He wrapped his arms around her tight and squeezed his eyes shut, pressing his face into her hair, one hand cupping the back of her head. Trying to surround her.

A tiny shudder sped through her. She was rigid at first, but when he remained silent and just kept holding her tight, eventually she began to relax.

"I'm sorry I didn't tell you before. I didn't want anyone to know," she murmured.

"You have nothing to apologize for. I'm just so goddamn sorry you went through all that." And that he hadn't been able to take the motherfucker responsible off the street while he was still on the case.

Her arms crept around his waist and she leaned into him, making his heart clench. "Do you think it's the same guy?"

"I think there's a good chance the cases are all related." Fuck. If Tate had been able to ID the guy, he would have been able to put him away two goddamn years ago, and none of this would have happened. And that part about her being raped in a truck… "God, and then I took you up to that remote lookout point last night in my truck," he whispered, feeling sick.

Nina pushed away slightly to look up at him, shaking her head. "No, don't think that. I wanted to be there with you, it was the most incredible night of my life."

He wanted to believe her. "Did it trigger anything for you?"

"Not even once, I swear." She cupped the side of his face, her palm and fingers cold against his skin. "I meant what I said, I really do feel safe with you."

Thank God. He caught her hand and brought it to his mouth, pressed a gentle kiss to the back of it. "You *are* safe with me. Always."

The tremulous smile she gave him threatened to break his heart into more pieces. "I know." She stepped back and wiped under her eyes again. "Will you stay with me while I talk to your detective friend?"

"Of course I will." He wasn't budging from her side through any of this. She shouldn't have gone through any of it alone in the first place, and while he couldn't undo what had happened, he'd do everything he could to be there for her now. "And Nina."

She looked up at him.

"Thank you for telling me." That had taken a hell of a lot of guts, especially face to face and given that they were involved. He respected and admired that kind of bravery.

Her smile was wry. "You're welcome? Actually, I'm glad you know now. I'd wondered if what happened to Rylee and her friend might be related to what happened to me. I just hope there's enough collective evidence now to find the guy and put him behind bars so he can't hurt anyone else."

"It will." It had to.

The most frustrating part was, it was entirely out of Tate's hands now. This was no longer his case—all his old files and cases had been assigned to Greg.

All he could do now was take care of Nina and Rylee

and hope that the hand of justice captured the asshole responsible for their pain.

CHAPTER FIFTEEN

She *knew*.

Vince couldn't shake the terrifying thought as he left the parking lot and drove away as quickly as he could without drawing undue attention. The last thing he'd expected was to see Nina Benitez being led up the steps of the police station when he drove by.

She must have remembered something. Enough to ID him?

He took the first right, watching his mirrors for any signs of being followed. Paranoia rode him hard. He'd already lied and called in sick to work first thing this morning, because there was no way he could make it through his shift like this. But where the hell did he go now?

He couldn't go home. His wife would ask too many questions.

Nina was talking to the cops right now. She'd stayed silent about everything for so long. Maybe she'd come forward now because of Samantha.

This was bad. So bad. How much had she remembered?

He ran a hand over his sore face and headed east, toward home. He wouldn't go there, however. Not yet. Not until he was sure they weren't coming for him.

All weekend long he'd been on pins and needles. Waiting to see what happened with Samantha. So many times, he'd been tempted to go to the spot at the river to check. Just to drive by and see whether she was there or not, to ease the agony of suspense.

He'd thought things couldn't get any worse. He'd been wrong.

First the breaking news story on the morning news that Samantha was dead. Someone had found her body while out walking their dog.

Sweat slicked the base of his spine. He hadn't meant for it to go that far. He'd thought she'd been alive when he took off. And he'd left her in a secluded spot that was similar to the others, but in a different location. Because it had worked up 'til now.

Everything was so chaotic. He still didn't know how things had gone so wrong.

He'd given her a high enough dosage that she should have been unconscious until well after he'd finished and left her at the spot he'd chosen. Maybe she hadn't consumed enough of it, or maybe her body metabolized it faster than normal.

Whatever it was, she'd come to right in the middle of it, while he was inside her. He'd been on the verge of coming when she'd stirred and opened her eyes in confusion.

Vince swore his heart had stopped in those few seconds, horror freezing him in place. She'd ruined everything, taken away the rush he'd been craving and the orgasm he'd almost reached.

It had reminded him too much of the night with Nina. Except Nina had only surfaced briefly, and Samantha hadn't gone back under.

He'd known an instant after her eyes opened that she recognized him from campus. She'd said his name, then tried to fight him.

She'd screamed. Wouldn't stop, no matter what threats he'd hissed or how hard he'd clamped his hand over her nose and mouth to shut her up. At that time of night her screams and struggles would have carried on the air. Someone might have heard.

He hadn't had anything to gag her with, not without leaving something of his behind. In the end he'd been forced to wrap his hands around her throat to silence her. Squeeze until she stopped thrashing, her bulging eyes turning blank and her body going lax.

As soon as she'd gone limp, he got off her and raced back to his truck, leaving her as she was. He hadn't checked to be sure, but he thought he'd seen the pulse in her neck flutter.

He'd been wrong about that too. And now he was a murderer as well as a rapist.

The music coming from the speakers suddenly seemed irritating and high-pitched. He snapped off the radio with an angry punch of his finger and kept driving, his mind in turmoil. He didn't know what Nina remembered. She hadn't reported their encounter when it happened, he'd checked.

But she might have had a medical exam. He'd been careful not to leave any evidence behind with her, though it wasn't impossible that they'd found something of his on her. Hair, maybe clothing fibers. Which meant his DNA might already be in the system.

And now Samantha…

He glanced at his reflection in the rearview mirror, his jaw tightening even as fear curdled in the pit of his stomach. The scratches on his face and neck guaranteed she had his DNA beneath her nails. He hadn't had time to deal with it, so there might be even more evidence against him now.

The scratches and other marks on his face were impossible to hide, even with sunglasses and a ball cap. He needed to stay off the radar for another couple days until he could cover them with makeup at least.

His gaze caught on the pictures of his daughters attached to his sun visor. He snatched them down, shoving them into the center console so he didn't have to look at them. The guilt was killing him, the constant fear eating at his insides.

Why was he like this? Why couldn't he stop? Ignore the dark cravings inside him?

If Nina had identified him, a team would be coming to question him. Then his DNA would seal his fate.

If she hadn't and he ran, it would make him look way too suspicious. No matter how much he wanted to flee, running wasn't an option. He had to stay. Keep living the lie and put on the best act of his life to make the people closest to him think everything was normal.

He didn't want to give up his life because of what he'd done. There had to be a way out of this.

As a possible answer came to him, he slowed and turned into another parking lot. He pulled into the shade cast by a large delivery truck and thought it through.

Yeah, it could work.

Nina. He had to get rid of her to protect himself. Knew just how to make it happen.

But he had to do it as soon as possible, and then cover his tracks using every trick he'd ever learned on the job if he wanted to remain a free man.
****

"You sure you don't want to be with Rylee right now?" Nina asked him as Tate pulled up in front of Avery's house that evening.

"Avery and Mason are both there with her. I'll call her in a bit." There was no way he was leaving Nina alone right now. Not after what she'd gone through today.

He wanted to be the one to take care of her. Right now, he wanted to get her settled in her own safe space, make her as comfortable and relaxed as possible. She needed it.

But there was also another reason he was staying with Nina. One that stabbed him with needles of unease.

The bastard behind all this devastation was still at large. They didn't even have a decent description of him to go on. Only the vague details Tate had received back when he'd worked on the case. Thirty-something Caucasian male, dark hair, strong build.

Whoever he was, the monster was escalating. He'd made the jump from rape to killing a young woman. He was a predator and a killer and needed to be hunted down.

Tate knew that kind of profile well enough to know this asshole wasn't done. The guy had gotten away with it this long. If he wasn't brought in, it was only a matter of time before he struck again, and another innocent life taken. And if the perp was worried that either Nina or Rylee could ID him, he might get desperate and come after one of them again.

Which was why Tate wanted both Avery and Mason with Rylee tonight—a former JTF2 assaulter and a dedicated cop there to protect her.

Tate forced back the surge of anger that threatened to swamp him. He wanted that son of a bitch caught and punished for what he'd done. Wished he could be reinstated on the case but that wasn't possible, especially now that his own niece and the woman he was seeing were both victims of what all the evidence said was likely the same attacker.

Instead he'd been forced to watch everything from the other side of the desk. He'd stayed with Nina throughout the interview with Greg.

It had been hard to watch her relive everything in detail and only be able to hold her hand in support. She'd held it together admirably well, but reliving that terrible night step by step and not being able to leave anything out had taken a toll on her.

They'd spent hours going over everything, getting her records from the hospital and then getting her official statement, having her sign various forms and legal documents to file an official police report. She'd been quiet ever since leaving the station.

He kept a hand on her waist as he walked her around the back of the house to the entrance to her suite. There was a basket sitting on the doorstep.

She stopped, and at the way she stiffened he immediately stepped in front of her to intervene, his hand flashing back to grip the weapon he'd tucked into its holster. "What's wrong?" he asked, seeing no sign of danger.

"Nothing, it's fine." She pushed past him and marched toward the basket. "What on earth did they do this time?" she muttered under her breath.

Confused, Tate stood there watching her as she picked it up, lifted the cloth on top and sighed. "Blueberry scone bread pudding. Damn, they're good."

He didn't have a clue what was going on. She seemed torn somewhere between amusement and irritation. "You got something against bread pudding?"

"No." She looked up at him. "You like it?"

"I like pretty much anything that comes out of the oven."

"Good. You can have some with me." She reached into her purse for her keys and unlocked the back door.

She was handling everything well. So much so, he was actually a little worried about her. She'd told him she'd seen a therapist after the rape, but today had shaken her. Now she was acting like everything was normal.

"You hungry?" he asked as he shut and locked the

door behind them. "I can order us something." He wouldn't leave her alone, not even for the short drive to downtown to pick up dinner.

"I just want bad stuff. I've got ice cream in the freezer we can eat with the bread pudding. That okay?"

"It's fine." Whatever she wanted.

"I'm gonna go have a shower."

"Sure. Take your time." As soon as she left, he called Rylee. "How you doing, kiddo?" he asked her.

"I'm just really sad. I know I only knew her for a week, but I felt like I was all she had here. And then I think about how terrified she must have been before she died."

Tate winced. "I know, sweetheart, but it's likely that she was unconscious, too drugged to be frightened. Mase and Avery taking good care of you?"

"Yeah. I don't think he's Avery's favorite person, though."

"Really? What makes you say that?"

"I think his sense of humor rubs her the wrong way, that's all. He's been pulling out all the stops, trying to lighten the mood, including making Ric show off all his tricks."

"Yeah, Mase's sense of humor takes some getting used to. You okay there with them?"

"Yes. Is Nina all right?"

He paused. "Did Avery tell you what happened?"

"Yes, a little while ago." She sighed. "I feel so bad for her. You really think it could be the same guy?"

"Looks that way."

"How is she?"

"Wrung out but putting on a brave face. I'm going to stay with her at least for tonight, Ry. I don't want her to be alone."

"Me neither."

"Thanks for understanding. And you know I

161

wouldn't have left you with Mase and Avery unless I thought you'd be safe. I trust them both with my life."

"I know. Thanks for checking on me. Will you tell Nina I send her a big hug?"

"Absolutely. I'll call you in the morning. But if you need anything, you just call me, okay?"

"Okay. Love you, Uncle Tater."

"Love you too."

As soon as he ended the call, Avery phoned him. He told her as much as he could about what had happened without violating Nina's privacy, since he wasn't sure what level of detail Nina had given her about the rape, then changed the subject. "Is Mason driving you nuts already?"

She snorted. "I'm a big girl. I can handle him."

"Oh, I know you can," he said with a chuckle. Avery was more than capable of putting Mason—or any other man, himself included—in his place. "It's good for him."

"Doubt he thinks so, but I'm glad you approve. Call if you need anything."

"Will do. Bye."

Nina came out a minute later wearing a pair of pale pink pajamas and a fuzzy robe. Her hair was loose around her shoulders, the ends slightly damp still, and her face was scrubbed clean. "I know, I look like I'm fifteen right now," she said as she made her way to the kitchen.

She looked adorable, and in need of some comfort. "Twenty."

One side of her mouth turned up. "So you're saying I at least look legal, then."

"Exactly. I'm a law-abiding citizen and upholder of the law."

She snickered and went to work dishing them up some dessert.

"Feel any better?"

"A little." She scooped bread pudding into two

bowls. "Just tired."

"I'll bet." He watched while she heated them up in the microwave and then added big scoops of vanilla ice cream. "Does your family know?" he asked softly.

She stopped, her back to him. "No." She put the ice cream back in the freezer. "I need to call my parents later and tell them. But not right now."

He shifted on the couch when she came over and handed him a bowl, then settled into the opposite end, her feet tucked beneath her.

She took a bite of the dessert, made a soft humming sound. "Damn, this is good. How does she do it?"

"Who?" Tate took a bite. She was right, it was really good.

"My neighbor across the street. Bev. She and her sister live together in the big Victorian over there." She waved her spoon. "We've got this competitive rivalry thing going on. And I think they just won, because I can't think of a thing I can make out of this."

"French toast."

Nina looked up, blinked at him. "Yeah?"

He nodded. "Just cut it up and fry it on both sides in a little butter. It's already got the egg in there. Then sprinkle a little cinnamon on top and add some whipped cream if you want to get all fancy."

A slow, appreciative smile formed on her face. "Tate, that's brilliant."

He shrugged, intrigued by the friendly game and glad to see Nina smile. "I'll help you make it in the morning if you want."

Her smile faded, her expression turning serious. "In the morning. Are you coming back that early, or…?"

"I want to stay the night. On your sofa," he added. He hadn't asked her if she wanted him to stay, because her personality was to say no, not wanting to inconvenience him. "If that's okay with you."

She looked almost relieved. "It's more than okay with me. Only I don't want you on the sofa."

They stared at each other across the length of the sofa, and Tate was overcome with the need to touch her. He reached out to cup her cheek, ready to draw her close, when her phone rang on the coffee table.

She glanced at it and groaned. "It's my mom. I swear she's got a sixth sense for when I'm upset about something." She met his gaze. "Part of me wants to ignore it, but I really should talk to her and get this over with."

"Want me to step outside?"

"No, I'll just take it in my room." She picked it up and stood, flashing him a brave little smile that tugged at his heart. "Wish me luck." With that she answered in Spanish and retreated to her room to shut the door.

Tate hurt for her. Having to relive the horror of being raped was tough, but telling her family would be even harder.

While he waited, he made one final call to his neighbor Curt, briefly explaining the situation with the suspect and that they might have a potential security issue. "I'd appreciate it if you'd keep an eye out for anything suspicious, just in case."

"Done. Is your niece all right?"

"She's fine. But I'd consider it a personal favor if you could refrain from shooting anything for the next couple days."

A pause. "Copy that. I'll bring Reggie and his friends inside at night for the next while."

"I appreciate it."

"Don't mention it. And I think old lady Engleman will like the peace and quiet too. I'm going there for dinner shortly."

Tate's eyebrows lifted. "Yeah?"

Curt grunted. "Some kind of peace offering, I'd imagine. I was thinking of cutting some flowers from my garden for her. Do you think she'd prefer roses or dahlias?"

"Really couldn't say. I'm sure either would be fine."

"Well, have a good night. I'll keep an eye out here, don't you worry."

"I'll sleep better now, thanks," Tate said with a smile, and ended the call. Nina's door was still shut. He could imagine how upset her parents would be.

He watched TV for a while, then turned when her door opened. His heart clenched. Her eyes were puffy and red. She looked so lost, standing there in her pajamas and robe. "How'd it go?" he asked softly, absently shutting off the TV.

"It was hard."

He nodded, desperate to go to her but unsure of what she wanted. Right now he wanted to do everything in his power to protect her, help her heal, be there for her after she'd bared her soul and been forced to face her pain all over again.

"They want to get on the first flight here in the morning, but I told them no. That I'm okay, and I'm safe with you here. I just need time to decompress before I see them."

"I get it." And it warmed his heart that she'd told them she was safe with him here.

She ran a hand over her face. "I'm wiped. Gonna read for a bit in bed, then crash."

"Okay. I'll be here if you need anything."

She hesitated in the doorway. "Will you come sleep next to me?"

His heart almost imploded. "Yeah, of course." He was up and off the couch in a heartbeat, following her into her room.

She draped her robe across the foot of the bed, then crawled into the left side. Tate slid in the other and turned to face her on his side. Nina immediately snuggled into him. He rolled slightly to his back and wrapped his arms around her, bringing her cheek to the hollow of his shoulder.

Nina expelled a long sigh and rubbed a hand over his chest. "Thank you. I needed this."

"Me too." He kissed the top of her head and ran a soothing hand up and down her back, the flannel of her PJs soft beneath his palm. It felt good to hold her like this. Offer his comfort and protection. She smelled like toothpaste and shampoo.

"Tomorrow's going to be better," she murmured.

Even after all of this, she was still determined to be optimistic. She amazed him. "Yes. And every day going forward, it will get a little easier."

She made a humming sound and relaxed more into his hold. "Has to."

There was so much going on inside him, too much for him to look at all at once, but he had to tell her this or he'd burst. "I want you to know how much I admire your courage. How brave you are."

She groaned and tucked her face tighter into his shoulder. "I'm not brave. If I was brave, I would have done the right thing in the first place."

"No, you're wrong." How could she not see that? "You came forward after everything told you to stay silent and bury what happened to you before. You opened yourself up to a lot of pain and scrutiny in order to help find this bastard and stop him from hurting anyone else. That's fucking brave, Nina."

She cuddled in closer. "Thank you for being there for me today. And for staying now."

"I wouldn't want to be anywhere else." He meant every word. Even if he'd never expected to feel this way and didn't know what the hell to do with it.

CHAPTER SIXTEEN

"You sure you had enough? You didn't eat much."

Nina smiled at Tate's concern as she helped carry dishes into his kitchen two nights later. After taking yesterday off for a video appointment with her therapist and more phone calls with Tate's detective friend on the Missoula force, she'd made the decision to go back today for her Wednesday classes.

Tate had invited her back to his place for dinner so she'd driven straight here after work to find that he, Avery, Mason and Rylee had all pitched in to make the meal together. After the last frantic few days, unwinding with her friends was just what she'd needed.

"I had more than enough. It was just nice to be able to come home to you." As soon as she said it, she cursed herself for making him uncomfortable and turned her attention to loading up the sink. But damn, it was exhausting trying to censor herself to spare his feelings on top of everything she was already dealing with.

To her surprise Tate took her by the elbows, turned her to face him, and kissed her gently. "We'll handle the dishes tonight," he said, nodding at Mason, Avery and Rylee, who were also carrying things in from the dining room table. "Why don't you take a glass of wine out back and relax for a bit?"

He didn't seem bothered by her earlier comment, but she didn't want to read too much into it. "You sure?"

"Positive. Here." He picked up her empty wineglass, filled it, and handed it to her. "Meet you outside in a bit."

She wasn't going to argue. She'd slept badly the last two nights, even with Tate there beside her. Both nights she'd had nightmares. Tate had woken her, soothed her and lulled her back to sleep by holding her close. Even her subconscious trusted him, because she'd been able to go back to sleep with him holding her.

They still hadn't had sex yet. Hadn't even fooled around since the night in the bed of his pickup, and she was starting to worry that he might be reluctant to touch her that way now.

Not because he thought she was tainted in any way, but because he didn't want to trigger any painful memories for her with intimate contact. Their entire relationship —if it even was one—was confusing her now.

She smiled at Avery on the way out to the back deck. The sun had just set, and it wouldn't be long now before the sky darkened enough for the stars to appear. She'd promised Rylee a mini astronomy lesson, mapping the most visible stars and planets.

They were both heading back to campus in the morning. Rylee would stay with Tate for the time being and commute with Nina back and forth each day for school until the man responsible for the string of attacks was caught, but neither of them could afford to take time off right now.

Nina's bare feet tapped lightly on the wooden steps as she headed down to the backyard. A seven-foot-high privacy fence enclosed the large, neatly-trimmed lawn, bordered by shrubs and some trees at the back, the roof-line of Tate's woodshop just visible in the shadows. He'd told her that in his downtime he liked to work on little projects and carve things.

The sweet, green scent of cut grass wafted up as she walked across the lawn to the deck chairs arranged around a rock fire pit. A small fire burned in the middle of it, the cheery flames crackling yellow and orange as dusk settled over the yard.

She was just lowering herself into one of the chairs when movement to her right made her whip her head around.

She shot from her chair with a startled gasp at the sight of an animal thirty feet from her. The animal—a black-and-white goat—jerked its head up to stare at her, then went completely stiff and fell over onto its back, its legs standing straight up in the air.

Nina cried out in alarm and clapped a hand over her mouth as she took a step toward it.

Hurried footsteps came from the deck behind her. "Nina? What—"

"The goat. I didn't see it," she blurted, hurriedly setting her wine down. "I scared it and it fell over." Oh my God, it still wasn't moving. Had she killed it?

She glanced over her shoulder to see Tate walking across the grass toward her. He was grinning. Looked like he was trying not to laugh. "What's funny?" she demanded.

"He's fine." He continued past her toward the goat. "Come on, Reggie, shake it off, buddy. Up you get."

Nina stared in amazement as Tate walked up to the goat, rolled it right side up and placed it on its hooves once more. Reggie wobbled on his feet. Tate held him steady with one hand, then pulled out his phone with the other and called someone.

"Reggie got over the fence and scared my company

to death by fainting in front of her. Can you come get him? Thanks." He put the phone away, picked Reggie up and started toward her. "Wanna pet him?"

Nina eyed the goat and approached them slowly. "What's wrong with him? Is he sick?"

"No, he's a fainting goat. They do that whenever they get startled."

She held out a hand so Reggie could sniff at her palm. Did goats do that? Better safe than sorry, she didn't want to risk scaring him again. "Hi, Reggie. Don't faint on me again, okay?"

Reggie stared back at her through yellow eyes with weird, rectangular-shaped pupils, ears twitching.

"It's okay, you can pet him. He likes it," Tate said.

Nina gently stroked the goat's head as it sat contentedly in Tate's arms. She knew the feeling. Tate's arms were the best place to be in the entire world. "You scared me to death."

"You scared each other," Tate said with another grin.

The scramble of paws on the deck behind them was their only warning. Nina turned just in time to see Ric flying at them like a furry bullet over the grass.

Reggie saw the dog coming, jerked like he'd been electrocuted and tipped over in Tate's hold as Tate angled his body to protect him. "Ric, *no*. Mason, come and get your dog!" he shouted.

Poor Reggie was stiff as a poker. He looked like he'd been frozen solid.

Nina quickly intervened, whirling to catch Ric by the collar. "Ric, *no*," Nina said, firmly. Ric strained against her hold, quivering and whining as he locked onto Reggie with an unblinking stare.

"Ric! Leave it," came the firm command from up on the deck. Mason hurried down the stairs. "*Leave* it."

Ric whined and sat, trembling, his stare fixed on Reggie.

"He won't hurt him," Mason said, rushing over. "Wants to herd him, more like. Collie-shepherd thing." He dashed over and grabbed Ric. "I'll take him back inside. Doofus," he told the dog, then tugged him back toward the steps, ignoring Ric's whimpered protests and straining to get away.

Tate carried poor, frozen Reggie over toward the fence, the goat's little legs still poking straight out.

"Hey, sorry about that, neighbor," a voice said from the other side of the fence. "Guess I stacked the crates too close to the fence and he decided to go exploring." The top of a gray head appeared over the edge of the fence.

"He just thinks the grass is greener on the other side," Tate joked.

Nina laughed softly as a deep chuckle sounded from beyond the fence. A moment later the elderly man's bearded face and torso appeared over the top of it. He grinned at her. "Hi. I guess you met Reggie."

"He's very cute," Nina said. "But I thought I'd killed him for a minute there."

The man laughed. "I'll bet. I'm Curt, by the way."

"Nina."

"Nice to meet you. Sorry for the scare. Come on, Reggie. Time to come back and slum it in your own yard with the second-rate grass." He reached over the fence as Tate handed the goat up, and lifted him back over to the other side. "Enjoy your night."

"You too," Tate said. "Hey, how'd it go with Mrs. Engleman?"

The man made a face, still holding Reggie, who was finally starting to thaw out again. "That woman is a real piece of work. But it was okay. I don't think she wants to have me arrested anymore, at least."

"So you guys are on your way to being besties, then," Tate said cheerfully.

"Cold day in hell, Tate."

Grinning, Tate walked back toward Nina as Curt disappeared with Reggie.

She shook her head at him, fighting a smile. "So you rescue damsels in distress *and* goats. Be still my heart."

"All in a day's work, ma'am." He pulled her to him, kissed her just long enough that her body began to heat and tingle, then stopped and led her back to the fire with an arm around her shoulders. "So whaddya think of country living as opposed to being closer to downtown with Avery?"

"Both have their charms," she said in a dry voice. "But I think country living could take some getting used to."

"It was an adjustment for me too. We've got quite a few characters around here." He kissed the crown of her head. "Want to sit by the fire and finish your wine, or go home?"

Just looking at him made her heart beat faster. Being this close made her entire body hum with arousal and need. She'd enjoyed the meal and the visit, but she wanted to be alone with him now. She'd do the astronomy lesson with Rylee another time.

Alone and naked, with his hands and mouth all over her, and hers on him, banishing bad memories and replacing them with magical ones. "Home."

His slow grin melted her insides. "Was hoping you'd say that." He bent, plucked her wineglass from where she'd left it on the edge of the fire pit, and walked her back inside to say their goodbyes.

"We heading out?" Avery asked when they stepped inside. Tate had driven her home to his place after work.

"If that's okay with you," Nina said.

"Absolutely."

Based on Avery's somewhat stiff interaction with Mason throughout the meal, it seemed to Nina that her friend was glad for the excuse to leave. She'd have to ask

Avery what the story was later.

Nina said goodbye to him, fussed over Ric for a moment, who was lying on the floor pouting after being deprived of his chance at goat herding, then hugged Rylee. "I'll pick you up first thing in the morning. We can grab something for breakfast on the way out of town."

"Sounds good." Rylee looked between Nina and her uncle, a faint smile playing at the edges of her mouth. "Enjoy your night."

Tate ignored the innuendo and led Nina out to his truck with Avery behind them. "You sure you're ready to go back full time right now?"

She wasn't sure if he meant because of everything being dredged up on Monday, or because the attacker was still at large. "Yes. What happened to me was a long time ago. I need to put it behind me, and work is the best thing for that. I have bills to pay. Also, I care about my professional reputation and my students need me."

"Good for you," Avery said, coming up on Nina's other side. "You're in control of your life, not that asshole. And he's *going* to get caught."

"Yes, I am, and hell yes, he is." Nina fist-bumped her friend, determined to believe both those things were true.

CHAPTER SEVENTEEN

Once at Avery's house, Nina and Tate started to head around back, but Avery stopped her with a hand on Nina's arm. "Hey, can you come up and grab the leftover dessert from the other night?"

It was clear her friend was making an excuse to get her alone, and Nina was pretty sure why. "I'll be down in a sec," Nina said to Tate, and handed him her key.

He and Avery exchanged an unreadable look, some unspoken conversation happening between the two of them over the space of a few seconds. "Sure," he said, then started around the side of the house.

Nina followed Avery through the front entrance and into the kitchen. Her friend went straight to the fridge and pulled out the leftover cake. Placing it on the counter, Avery turned to face her. "I'm gonna make this quick."

Oh, good.

"Has Tate told you what happened with his ex?"

"Yes."

Avery nodded in approval. "He's seriously an amazing guy. But I don't want to see you get hurt. Either of you," she clarified. "So maybe…"

"Keep my expectations down to a dull roar where commitment from him is concerned, in case it doesn't work out?"

Avery looked relieved at not having to say it. "Yes."

"I will." Even as Nina said it, she knew it was already too late to heed her own advice. Tate was the most incredible man she'd ever met—outside of her dad—and in another galaxy compared to the other men she'd dated.

She was in for as long as she could handle him not committing. If he was never able to get past his fears and commit to her, then yeah, she would have to end it eventually, and it was gonna hurt. Bad.

Still, she'd been through a lot. She'd survived a lot. And right now, both her heart and her head were telling her not to hold back. "We good now?"

Avery grinned at her. "We were always good, and always will be. I'm just doing my due diligence and looking out for you. I take my best friend duties seriously."

"And I love you for it." Nina hugged her, then stepped back. "Sure you don't want to keep this cake?"

Avery made a face. "Take it before I eat it all. And have a good day tomorrow. Go kick some astronomy ass."

"I will. G'night."

A strange weight sat in the middle of her chest as she made her way back down to her suite. She couldn't stop thinking about what they'd just talked about.

"That all for us?" Tate asked, his eyebrows going up.

"Yep."

"You want some now?"

She put the cake in the fridge and crossed to him, then wound her arms around his neck. "No. I just want you."

His eyes heated. "Well, that's lucky."

"Isn't it?" Smiling, she lifted up to brush her lips across his.

Tate immediately drew her closer and deepened the kiss, one hand coming up to cup the back of her head. She loved it when he did that.

But he didn't take it further. Frustrated, she reached down for the bottom of his shirt and began peeling it upward. Tate broke the kiss and raised his arms, allowing her to strip it off him.

Just seeing all that raw male power and knowing she could touch him all over was enough to make her dizzy. She rubbed her nose against the center of his chest, following the deep line between the ridges of his pecs.

"Nina."

"Hmm?" She kept going, her hands busy exploring his back and working their way down to his muscled ass.

"Are you sure?"

Of course he would ask. He was too honorable not to. But Nina didn't want to be treated like a victim. She wanted to put the past aside and enjoy this to the fullest. She lifted her head to look into his eyes. "Yes. I trust you, and I know you'd never hurt me." Not physically, and never on purpose in any other way either.

"Never," he whispered, stealing another chunk of her heart.

"Then unless you don't want me—"

"I want you." He slid his hands into her hair, his gaze intense, full of hunger.

She held his gaze, her heart hammering. "Then don't stop."

With a low, rough growl he stepped into her and fused their mouths together. Nina opened immediately, a hot throb of desire settling between her thighs as his tongue danced with hers.

He bent to scoop her up in his arms and carry her toward her bedroom.

She giggled. "Now, this is romantic."

"Sunshine, you haven't seen anything yet."

A tiny shiver sped through her at the dark promise in his words. He laid her on the bed and came down on top of her, his weight pressing her into the mattress and his hips wedged between her thighs, adding pressure right where she throbbed so badly.

She helped him get her dress over her head, then lay back and enjoyed the way his molten gaze raked over the length of her in her bra and panties. Giving his hands plenty of bare skin to enjoy.

He stripped off her bra and panties, cupped her breasts together and held them there for his mouth. Nina gasped and shivered as his lips and tongue worshipped her aching flesh, sending streamers of sensation flooding throughout her body.

She was so wet, and getting wetter every moment until finally he eased to the side enough to dip his hand between her legs. A plaintive moan spilled free as he cupped her, then began rubbing subtly. When she moved restlessly against it, he switched to the other breast and turned his hand so he could caress her throbbing clit.

He reached for the condom on her nightstand, shifted to his knees. Nina stroked his thick length as he rolled it down, earning a rough groan, his abs tightening under her avid gaze.

Before she could enjoy him properly, he gripped her thighs and scooted down the bed until his face hovered directly above her slick, flushed folds, those gorgeous hazel eyes burning into hers.

Nina curled her fingers around his broad shoulders and waited, the delicious anticipation stretching out. Finally, he closed his eyes and lowered his head.

She cried out as his lips and tongue made contact exactly where she needed him. And when he eased a finger inside her while his tongue licked her most sensitive spot, that dark wave of pleasure began to crest.

"Tate. Tate, now," she gasped out. She needed him

inside her. Craved that complete connection, of holding him inside her.

Tate crawled up the length of her body to brace himself on one forearm and gaze down at her, the head of his cock lodged just inside her. Nina stared up at him, unable to look away, spellbound by the incredible, magical connection between them. But the need coiled tight in her core. She groaned, tried to lift up to push him in deeper.

Tate's grip tightened on her hip, then he surged forward.

Nina's eyes closed, her body arching as pleasure shot along her nerve endings. He was so hot and thick and hard, stretching her, filling her. Before she could adjust to the feel of him, he slipped his hand back between her legs to find her swollen clit and rub it.

She whimpered and dragged his mouth back to hers, tangling her tongue with his as he began to thrust. The way he stroked her inside and out was incredible.

She couldn't think. Could barely breathe, holding on for dear life as her hips churned, the hunger burning in her center. A soft, helpless sob broke free, her fingers clenching in his hair as the pleasure suddenly intensified.

Tate growled into her mouth and maintained the steady, inexorable rhythm of his thrusts, hitting the sweet spot just inside her while he stroked her clit.

Suddenly everything went supernova. She shattered, pulling her lips from his to cry out her pleasure into the thick silence. Every measured stroke of his cock kept it going, prolonging it as the shockwave rippled through her.

She was still drifting in the waves, gripping his shoulders tight when he abruptly drove deep with a throttled cry, his powerful body shuddering against her. Gradually the tension melted out of him. His weight settled on top of her, his face buried in her hair.

Nina wound her arms around him and ran her hands

through his hair, her chest and throat tightening. She closed her eyes as tears flooded them, a tiny hitch quivering through her.

Tate pushed up on one elbow to look down at her. Nina opened her eyes to stare up at him through her tears, unable to speak.

It wasn't until that moment that she realized how much of herself she'd held back with every other man she'd been with. Or how afraid she'd been that the rape had damaged her subconsciously.

Tate didn't look alarmed by her tears. Didn't say anything. He gently wiped her tears away before they could fall, and bent to cover her face with warm, tender kisses that made her heart clench.

She closed her eyes and absorbed it, feeling the broken parts she'd buried deep inside her slowly knitting back together again. Her heart felt swollen, ready to burst with everything she felt for him. Holding it inside was painful, but she didn't want to ruin this by blurting out something he wasn't ready to hear.

When she'd calmed completely, a sense of peace filled her like a warm tide rising inside her. Tate rolled off her and immediately got up to deal with the condom. He came back a minute later and pulled her into his arms, holding her close, his chin resting on the top of her head.

"It's never been like that for me," he said a minute later.

Joy and hope expanded her heart even more, until her whole chest hurt from the pressure. "For me either."

But he didn't say anything else, didn't give her the words she was dying to hear, so she closed her eyes and said them to him in her head.

I think I'm falling in love with you.

She pushed everything from her mind and focused on the here and now. Of being warm and sated and tucked into Tate's embrace, safe in her bed, and even safer in his arms. He cared about her. A lot. Maybe in time he would allow it to be more.

His big hands smoothed up and down her back, over her hips and bottom, his touch at once soothing and proprietary. "You tired?"

"Yes."

He drew the covers over them both and tucked the edges around her with care, just as he'd done that night in the bed of his pickup. "What time are you getting up in the morning?"

"Five-thirty."

"I'll get up with you." He stroked her hair. "You sure you don't want me to drive you and Rylee to campus?"

"I'm sure. But thanks."

"I know you've both got to get back to normal, but I still hate knowing I won't be there tomorrow."

Nina smiled softly. Always the protector. "We'll be just fine," Nina murmured sleepily, totally relaxed as she basked in the closeness they shared. "But I love that you want to watch over me."

When she was with him, she felt like nothing bad could ever happen to her again.

****

Vince kept the hood of his jacket pulled down low over his forehead to help obscure his face as he walked through campus. The scratches and bruising were still visible, even with the makeup he'd tried to cover them with.

Luckily it was dark now, and there was hardly anyone else out here at this time of night. Mostly maintenance and janitorial staff, and students who lived in residence. Nobody that would pay any attention to him as he carried out his mission.

This time he wasn't here to scope out a new target. He was here about an old one.

The building he'd come to see stood in front of him, only a few lights on in the windows. Someone was just coming out one of the doors in the side entrance when he came up the sidewalk. He moved aside to let them by, using the time to check above the doors.

It was easy to spot the cameras, and there weren't that many of them. He went inside, keeping his hands in his pockets and his face averted slightly downward while he studied the layout. He counted only two cameras along the length of the first-floor hallway. None in the stairwell.

But there was one place in particular he needed to know inside and out.

He made his way down another hallway, noting the positions of the only two cameras on the floor. Offices lined the exterior wall of the building, their doors facing a solid wall across the hallway where the classrooms were located.

His pulse accelerated with each step as he scanned the doors he passed. Until finally…

Dr. Nina Benitez.

He paused in front of it for only a moment, glancing through the window in the door. There might be a camera in there, but it wouldn't matter. He'd studied the campus emergency procedures and now had seen what he was dealing with up close.

He continued down the hall and exited the far door, anticipation stirring in his gut. Based on everything he'd just seen, his plan would work. All he had to do now was put it into action.

CHAPTER EIGHTEEN

"You want to maybe grab lunch together later?" Rylee asked Nina as they entered her office the next morning. They'd just arrived at campus after the drive in from Rifle Creek.

Nina smiled at Rylee. "I'd love that. We could go over some of the things you missed last lecture if you want."

"Or we could, you know, just eat and talk."

Nina laughed. "I know, I know, I get carried away with my enthusiasm for the subject matter. I'm determined to make an astronomy nerd out of you yet."

"I love learning about space. But I hate the math." She made a face and shuddered.

Nina's phone buzzed in her pocket. She pulled it out and grinned. "And there's your uncle, wanting to know we're still okay. Gotta love him."

She sent off a quick text. *Here safe and sound. Trying to force more astronomy down Rylee's throat before she heads to class.*

Good. Get our money's worth out of the tuition.

She showed Rylee his reply, and his niece rolled her eyes. "Uncle Tater. What a guy."

"He really is."

Rylee's eyes gleamed. "You guys seem really into each other."

Nina's cheeks flushed. "He's a wonderful man."

Rylee raised her eyebrows. "And?"

"And it's still new, because we just started seeing each other."

She scoffed. "Whatever, you're the first person he's dated since he broke up with what's-her-face. And from what I've seen, he's pretty damn into you, even if you guys are new."

"Well." Nina cleared her throat, not knowing what to say. "I should really go over some notes before I go to my first lecture."

Rylee chuckled. "All right, all right, I'll stop. But I'm just gonna say, I think you're exactly what he needs and I hope he realizes it."

Me too. "Thank you. I mean, I'm pretty awesome." They shared a grin.

"Meet you back here at twelve-forty-five?" Rylee asked.

"Perfect." And if they left campus by five, that would get them back to Rifle Creek by six at the latest, depending on traffic. Rylee wasn't going back to her dorm until the serial rapist/killer had been caught. "Have a good day."

"You too." Rylee walked out the door into the hallway.

Nina pulled out her tablet and booted it up to go over some lecture notes she'd prepared for her first lesson, but her mind was still on Tate. What if he never got over his baggage? What if he never fell in love with her?

She shook the thoughts away and focused on work. A minute later she was halfway through the first page of notes she'd compiled on dark matter and dark energy when her phone buzzed on the desk.

She ignored it, wanting to finish up the current section until she checked the message. Somewhere outside an announcement came over the outdoor speakers posted near the building entrance.

The sound of hurried footsteps a moment later made her look up. People were rushing past her office door, looking concerned. Several doors began closing farther down the hall.

Nina grabbed for her phone just as Rylee darted through the door, eyes wide and face pale. "The building's on lockdown," she blurted, and immediately shut the door.

Shock burst inside Nina. When she checked her phone, the message was there from the school's emergency notification system.

Lockdown in place. Seek shelter immediately.

Holy shit. She shot out of her chair and rounded the desk to grab Rylee's arm and push her toward the back of the room. "Get under my desk," she whispered, rushing for the door. There was no further information about what kind of threat it was, but Nina wasn't taking any chances.

The hallway was filled with a throng of fearful-looking students. Nina looked left and right, didn't see any imminent threat and started herding people into her office. Seven of them quickly scrambled past her, whispering amongst themselves, while others veered into the doorway closest to them.

Once the hall was empty, Nina shut and locked her door, fingers clumsy and her heart thudding in her ears. This didn't feel real. It felt like a bad dream. What was it? A bomb threat?

No, they would have evacuated the building for that. It must be an armed person or persons.

Cold prickled down her spine as she flicked the light

switch to off, going through her mental list of what to do. There was no blind or shade to pull down over the square-shaped window in the top of her door. "Phones on silent," she snapped in a low voice.

She whipped around to lunge toward her desk. Rylee and the seven others were all huddled either under or behind her desk, all crowded together. Nina held a finger to her lips to signal for absolute silence, then grabbed the full-size notebook on her desk and ripped both covers off. She ripped open a drawer and fumbled around for the roll of tape she kept there, then hurried back and taped the covers together over the window, obscuring them from view.

Eight pairs of eyes fastened on her as she turned to grab the fire extinguisher off the wall and then positioned herself in front of the others, lowering herself to the floor. There was nowhere else to hide, and this was as far away from the door as she could get. If someone shot through the door or hallway wall, she would be one of the first ones hit.

Don't think about it. Just be ready to react.

She detached the extinguisher nozzle end and held it at the ready with one hand, her fingers clamped around the trigger. If whoever was out there tried to come in, she would blast them straight in the face.

She wasn't sure how much time passed as she sat poised there. At least ten minutes.

No one said anything. Nothing moved out in the hall.

Nina finally pulled out her phone to start checking social media. Someone shoved their phone at her. She turned to see Rylee crouched behind her right shoulder, her face pinched with worry.

"We're okay," Nina whispered as quietly as she could, and forced a reassuring smile before checking the site Rylee had pulled up. Students were all commenting about the situation unfolding in Nina's building. Speculating whether it was an active shooter or a group of them.

Nina's blood chilled even more. She scrolled through the feed, trying to see if there was anything of use, but it was all fear and wild speculation.

She handed it back to Rylee and shook her head, aware of everyone else watching her. "It's all speculation," she whispered, giving Rylee's hand a squeeze. "We'll be fine." She turned right and left to look at the others, gave them a nod.

A door opened and closed somewhere down the hall.

Nina snapped around to face forward as the tension in the room went up a thousand percent. She gripped the extinguisher and waited, straining to make out any more sounds down the hall over the roar of the blood whooshing in her ears.

The distant door opened and closed again. Nina swallowed, waiting.

Footsteps. Sounded like more than one person. Slowly moving toward her office.

Heart pounding, she laid on her side to get as close to the ground as possible in case someone started shooting through the door, and aimed the extinguisher at it.

The footsteps came closer. Closer still.

Nina held her breath, her fingers curled around the trigger, her attention riveted to the door.

They slowed.

Someone behind her sucked in a breath and started to scuttle away. Nina pulled in a deep breath and braced herself, gearing up for the possible moment when the door was kicked in. She'd have only a split second to hit the shooter in the face with the retardant. She had to be fast.

Then the footsteps continued past the door.

Nina stayed rigid on the floor, still ready to hit the trigger. But the steps kept going down the hallway.

She relaxed a fraction, became aware of the thudding

of her heart against her chest wall and how cold and clammy her hands were. She'd never been this scared, wondering if whoever was on the other side was about to unleash a barrage of automatic gunfire through the walls.

"Clear," a male voice said from down the hall.

"Confirm, clear," said another.

Nina's heart leapt. Security? Were they checking the halls one at a time, clearing the building floor by floor?

The men came back, passing by the door. The far door opened and shut, then silence.

A collective sigh of relief filled the room, mixed with a couple of low groans.

"Shh," Nina said sharply, then lowered her voice to a whisper. "Stay still, stay quiet." Just because security had cleared this hall now didn't mean it would stay that way. Everyone had to stay put until the all clear was given via text, or if the police came to escort them out.

She was vaguely aware of Rylee typing into her phone a couple feet away. Nina hoped she was contacting Tate.

That hall door opened and closed once more. Nina tensed, her body going back into sentry mode.

The clear sound of a knock came. "Professor Cottrell, this is the Missoula PD," said a man's voice. "The building is secure, and you're free to come out now."

Nina stayed on the floor, refusing to relax her guard. Was it really the police? Or was it a trick to try and get Cottrell to open his door to the shooter?

Another door opened. Cottrell's? Voices swelled in a rush of sound, then the movement of dozens of feet on the hall floor.

More knocking. More voices. Working their way toward her door.

When the office beside her emptied and she still hadn't heard any shots, Nina waved the others back and got to her feet. She crept to the side of the door and waited there, ready to fire if it opened.

She almost jumped when someone knocked sharply on it. "Professor Benitez, this is the Missoula PD. The building is secure."

There still hadn't been any shots, so she slowly, quietly turned the lock on the door. Waited another few seconds in case anyone tried to barge in, then tentatively turned the latch. As soon as daylight showed between the door and the jamb, she whipped the extinguisher up, prepared to fire.

The door swung open to reveal a police officer in full tactical gear, his face covered by a black balaclava, presumably a precaution to protect the officers' identities. His gaze settled on her for an instant, then swept past her to scan the room. "You're all free to leave," he said to them. "An officer will escort you out of the building. Put your hands on top of your head, come into the hallway, and wait for further instructions."

Nina should have been relieved, but a strange sense of foreboding swept her instead. The idea of coming out into the hall and putting her hands on her head seemed worse, not reassuring.

"Hurry," the officer snapped. "We need to clear this building immediately."

Since he hadn't done anything threatening and others were streaming past in the hallway, she lowered the extinguisher and stepped out of the way, then faced her students, who were all crouched around her desk now. "Go ahead," she said, her voice a bit rough.

She waited until they had all filed past her into the hall, then grabbed Rylee in a tight hug. "You okay?"

"Yeah," Rylee breathed, squeezing hard. "See you outside."

"Yes." She let Rylee go, started to turn back for her laptop.

"*Leave it*," the cop commanded, "and come out

now."

Annoyed at his tone but understanding his urgency, Nina faced him and hurried out into the hallway, putting her hands on her head. The hallway was mass confusion. A torrent of people flowed past her, all rushing for the exit to the left.

"Nina!" Rylee was calling to her from near the door. A tactical cop was herding her and the rest of the group she was with through the exit.

"Doctor Benitez?"

Startled, Nina looked up into the masked face of another cop. Only his bright blue eyes were visible through the black balaclava, and he carried a rifle. "Yes."

"Come with me. I'm to escort you to a staff waiting area." He gripped her right upper arm and began walking her toward the exit at a rapid pace, pushing his way through the crowd.

Nina went along with him, hands still on her head and unable to answer her phone as it kept buzzing insistently in her pocket. "Was there a shooter?"

"I can't comment. Our team is still clearing the building. Hurry."

They reached the doorway. It was too narrow for the two of them to go through side-by-side.

The cop went first, towing Nina behind him. His scent trailed back to her. A subtle but distinctive mix of evergreen and spice.

An image exploded into her brain. A dark-haired man's face above her as he pinned her naked body down on the seat of a truck. Bright blue eyes revealed in the faint moonlight coming through the windows.

And that scent. All over her. All around her.

Her muscles froze. She stopped dead, only feet from the doorway

He looked back at her, his eyebrows drawn together in a fierce frown.

The bottom of her stomach fell out, fear and revulsion crashing over her.

Oh my God, it's him.

FUCK, SHE'D RECOGNIZED him. Vince knew it the second her gaze connected with his.

"*You.*" She tried to wrench her arm free, opened her mouth to scream when he wouldn't let go.

Vince had only a split-second to react. He hauled her closer with the hand on her arm, while reaching into his vest with the other. The cloth was hidden by his glove as he tugged her away from the door into the shadows of the building and quickly put his hand over her mouth and nose.

There were so many people around, the panic so thick he could almost smell it. No one was paying them any notice, and even if they had, the way he was holding her made it look like he was trying to keep her upright.

Those livid brown eyes spewed accusation at him, her fingers trying to pry his hand free from her face. Vince held that hate-filled stare as he kept his palm clamped across her nose and mouth, his dick flaring to life in his tactical pants.

Three seconds later her eyelids fluttered. Her clawing fingers slowed, then fell away from his hand. Her head lolled, then her body went slack. He caught her, threw her over his shoulder and stepped back into the stream of people flowing out of the building.

"Medical emergency," he barked, shouldering his way through the crowd. "Move aside."

The frightened mass of humanity slowly parted, the people he passed barely glanced at him and his prisoner. Elation pumped through him. This was even more perfect. There would be cameras, but his face was hidden and by the time anyone got around to analyzing the footage, he would be long gone.

And so would Nina Benitez.

Vince rushed through the crowd, carried her through the police cordon toward where the emergency vehicles were parked, lights flashing. But he veered right and crossed the area of lawn beside the parking lot instead, heading for the deep shadows and concealment offered by the thick shrubbery bordering the next building.

Nina remained limp, completely deadweight as he hurried through the shaded area, excitement ripping through him. He turned right at the narrow alley that ran alongside the building and headed straight for the campus maintenance vehicles parked at the end.

Pulling a keyfob from his pocket, he unlocked the second car on the right and glanced back.

The alley was deserted. No one was following them. No one had any idea what he had done, or what he was about to do.

He had to kill her, but not here. Not when he might be seen, and he had the perfect spot picked out. A place he hadn't used before.

He opened the trunk and loaded Nina into it, then quickly bound her wrists behind her before shutting the lid. A glance back reassured him that no one had seen him.

He'd done it. His plan had worked.

This time he was going to dispose of the body properly. He couldn't risk leaving any evidence behind.

He refused to lose everything now.

CHAPTER NINETEEN

T ate was in the middle of adding notes to a robbery case on his computer when his phone chimed with an incoming text. Seated at his desk, he picked it up and went cold all over when he read Rylee's message.

Clapp Building under lockdown. Hiding with Nina in her office. Have you heard anything?

Shit. "Avery!" He shot from his chair and strode through his open office door as he replied to Rylee. *No. Hang tight. Looking into it now.*

Avery stuck her head out of the office next door, frowning at him. "What?"

"Rylee says Nina's building is on lockdown. They're hiding in her office. Find out what's going on." He wanted answers, and would get them faster if they both looked into it individually.

Worry filled her expression. "On it."

She disappeared back into her office and Tate called Greg on the Missoula force. "What do you know about the lockdown at UofM?" he said as soon as Greg answered.

"Reports of an active shooter, maybe more than one. Tactical teams are en route."

"Is the threat credible?"

"Yes, though nothing's been verified. The threat's isolated to the Clapp Building right now, but the entire campus has been locked down for security reasons."

Dammit. "Nina and Rylee are both in Clapp right now."

"Oh, man, I'm sorry."

Yeah. Fuck. "I'm heading down there now. Can you alert whoever's in charge so I don't have to deal with security and red-tape bullshit when I get there?"

"Do you one better—I'll go and get you cleared now, then wait for you."

"Thanks, man." He just wanted to get down there and find Nina and Rylee.

"You bet. I'll keep you posted with any updates."

Tate ended the call and texted both Nina and Rylee as he hurried to the staff room. They both would have done lockdown drills at some point over the years, but it was totally different when facing a real threat.

Lock the door. Stay in the office. Get on the floor, stay away from the door, walls, and any windows. Be quiet.

The three officers taking a break inside the staff room all stared at him as he burst in and turned the TV to a Missoula news station. A breaking news story about the situation was already being broadcast.

Cell phone footage from someone in the mass of frightened people running through a hallway. Another one showing people pouring out of the Clapp Building, their faces panicked.

The situation looked like total chaos. People were funneling out the door in a disorderly stream, some breaking away from the officers trying to sort them into an or-

derly line, and veering across the grass while other officers rushed over to try and herd them back into line. He
didn't spot either Rylee or Nina in any of the videos.

Avery rushed in behind him. "Nobody can confirm
whether there's a shooter or not, but that's what was
called in."

Tate nodded. "I'm heading down there." He turned
away and headed for the door.

If there was a shooter on campus he wanted to be
there in person, and make sure Nina and Rylee got to
safety as soon as possible. Neither of them had responded
since his last text, and his mind was filled with all the bad
things that could either have or be happening right now.

"I'll come with you." Avery was right beside him as
they exited the building into the bright September sunshine.

"Gimme those," she said, snatching his keys from
him as they jogged to his truck. "I'll drive, you keep trying
to contact Nina and Rylee."

While Avery drove, Tate constantly checked his
phone for updates and alerts while watching more video
footage being broadcast from the campus. The tactical
teams were on site now. No one knew if anyone had been
injured.

The ride was tense, with the news on the radio and
Tate manning every update he could get on his phone.
Greg was on scene.

Tate's phone rang. His heart leapt, hoping it was
Nina or his niece, but it was Mason. "Hey, can't talk—"

"There's an active shooter at UofM."

"I know. Avery and I are already on our way down
there."

"You want backup?"

"I appreciate the offer. Keep you on standby?"

"You got it. You need anything, just call."

"Will do. Gotta go." They were twenty minutes out

of Rifle Creek when Rylee's number suddenly showed up on his call display. Tate snatched the phone up to his ear. "Rylee?" he said urgently.

"Yeah, it's me. I'm okay," she said, her voice a little shaky. "The police evacuated us from the building, and now I'm outside. They're still searching the building."

His heart slowed a fraction. "What about Nina?"

"We got separated during the evacuation, but she's okay too."

Then why hadn't she responded? "She's still not answering her phone or returning texts."

"I saw her put it into her pocket in the office. Maybe she's just busy talking to the police."

Maybe. "Keep an eye out for her, will you? Let me know if you see her."

"Of course."

"Was anyone hurt?"

"I don't think so. At least, I haven't heard that anyone was shot. There are some minor injuries because of people trampling each other trying to get out of the building, and someone tried to jump from a second story window to escape. What's going on? Did they say the shooter's still inside?"

"No, I haven't heard anything. I'm on my way there with Avery right now. We should be there in twenty minutes. I'll text you once I get there. Until then just do what the police tell you and stay vigilant. Is there any cover near you?" Because of him and Tala, she definitely knew the difference between cover and concealment, and how to use both.

"Yes, there's a concrete retaining wall maybe fifty feet away."

A short sprint if she needed to use it. "You know what to do?"

"Yes. You should have seen Nina, she was so calm. When the lockdown happened, she went out and herded a

195

bunch of people into her office, then covered the window and laid on the floor in front of us with a fire extinguisher, ready to blast anyone in the face if they came through the door."

Tate closed his eyes, picturing Nina doing just that. Putting herself between her students and a potential shooter with nothing but a fire extinguisher to defend them with.

He would have given anything to be able to wrap her up in a hug right now, keep her safe and tell her how proud he was of her. That he wanted her all to himself, and a future with her.

"Uncle Tate? You still there?"

He opened his eyes and stared at the road as Avery sped past a slow-moving car on the highway. "I'm here."

"Love you."

"Love you too, kiddo. I'll be there soon."

"She all right?" Avery asked when Tate lowered his phone.

"Yeah. She hasn't seen Nina outside, though."

"We'll find her."

Tate nodded, lost in his thoughts. This thing between him and Nina was still new, but it was real and intense. He'd been holding so much of himself back from her, and for what? She'd been open with him, made herself completely vulnerable while he hid what was going on inside him.

That wasn't right. He wanted the chance to *make* things right.

A few minutes from campus, he sent her one more text.

I'm almost at campus. Please let me know you're okay. Worried about you. Why wasn't she responding yet?

The entrance to campus was completely blocked off by emergency vehicles. Campus security had already set up a secure perimeter, not letting anyone in or out.

Avery had to park a long way away from Nina's building because of it. When they finally got to the perimeter Greg was waiting there for them with Rylee.

Tate pulled his niece into a fierce hug, thankful she was okay. She and Nina had both been through too much these past few weeks. "You all right?"

"Yeah, just…that was scary." She peered up at him. "Any word from Nina yet?"

"No." And that bothered him. Something had to be wrong.

"Team's just finishing clearing the building now," Greg said. "Still no reliable sighting of the shooter."

Tate released Rylee with a kiss on her forehead. "Stay here near the officers while Avery and I go find Nina. I'll meet you back here."

Rylee nodded and gave him a little push. "Go."

Tate, Avery and Greg ducked under the perimeter tape and headed straight to the mobile command post parked a block from Nina's building.

She still hadn't responded to him, and he was getting antsy. "Rylee said she and Nina were separated when they evacuated the building. A cop was escorting her," he said to Greg.

"We'll take a look at the security feeds and see if we can find her that way."

Tate and Avery showed their badges to the cop guarding the mobile command's door, then they went inside it with Greg. "Can we see the video from the second-floor hallway in Clapp?" Greg asked the woman seated at one of the computers after showing her his ID.

"Sure." She pulled up the link. "What time frame?"

"As soon as the tactical team starts evacuating the offices," Tate answered, leaning in.

The woman backed the feed up and hit play. Tate watched as the officers began emptying each office one by one down the hallway. He spotted Rylee as she came out of the third one.

"There she is," Avery said, pointing to Nina as she came out the door a few seconds later.

She had her hands on her head, was heading for the exit with everyone else, then a cop came up and took her by the arm. Tate's attention sharpened. There was no reason for the cop to be touching her. "What's he doing?"

"Escorting her," Greg said.

Why was he holding her arm, though? She was complying with procedure, wasn't hysterical or combative. "Follow them."

The female officer kept the video playing until Nina and the cop walked out of camera range. "Can you track them after this?" Tate asked, anxiety building in his gut.

Something was wrong, he felt it. She should have responded to him by now.

"Yep, just gimme a sec…" She typed a few commands and clicked on another camera.

The new feed showed the mass of people being herded out the ground-floor exits. He caught sight of Rylee first, then the tall cop farther back, his hand still around Nina's arm.

He pulled her through the exterior door. Tate lost sight of her for a few moments as the crowd flowed around her and the cop, but it looked like she'd stopped dead just outside the door and was staring up at him. Then the cop veered right and pulled her into the shadows.

Tate squinted to make out the shadowy shapes in the background, thought he saw the guy's hand move up toward Nina's face. "What the hell?"

He lost sight of them again for a few seconds. And when they reappeared, the cop was striding through the crowd with Nina draped over his shoulder like a rag doll.

"Oh my God," Avery said, and called over one of the superior officers.

An alarm blared in Tate's head. "Back that up," he said tensely. He and Avery leaned in closer as the woman replayed the last few seconds of the video.

"There," Tate snapped, hitting the cop's image on screen with his finger. "Right there. You see it?" The bastard's hand definitely came up to her face. Had he fucking hit Nina?

"Yeah," Avery muttered, watching intently.

The crowd obscured the view once again, and Nina appeared over the cop's shoulder moments later. "Again," Tate said, rage pulsing inside him.

He watched the snippet again, Avery tense beside him. "Stop," he commanded, staring at a tiny bit of something light-colored that appeared to be in the cop's hand. "Can you zoom in?"

When the tech did, the blood drained from Tate's face. "He fucking drugged her."

Avery met his gaze, her face full of shock, then she and Greg immediately left. Presumably to get help from whoever was in charge.

Tate turned back to the monitor, not wanting to believe what he'd just seen, but unable to refute it. "Can you follow them?" he asked, his heart pumping hard. He wanted to reach through the screen, rip Nina away from the cop and beat his face in.

"I'll try." The tech tried various feeds, but only managed to catch a glimpse of them as the cop carried Nina down an alley beside one of the buildings.

Tate watched in horror as the cop unlocked a car and opened the trunk. He inhaled sharply as the asshole put Nina into it, pulled her phone from her pocket, and tossed it behind the row of parked vehicles before shutting the trunk.

"Mother*fucker*," he snarled, curling his hands around the edge of the desk to keep from punching something. Raw fury exploded inside him.

Nina hadn't been ignoring him. She hadn't responded because she'd been abducted and locked in the trunk of a goddamn car.

"Did he take her?" Avery said, voice taut with anger and disbelief as she appeared beside him again.

Tate nodded, jaw tight. "Yeah. Trace that plate number," he ordered the tech, never taking his eyes off the screen as the cop got into the driver's seat and appeared to pull of his ski mask.

"Tracing," the woman said, typing fast.

As they all watched, the car reversed, turned, then drove down the alley and out of sight. Tate's pulse picked up. *No, no, no...*

He was aware of a small crowd gathered around them now, and the buzz of voices, but all he cared about was finding that vehicle. It wouldn't get through the police barricade or the perimeter. Would it?

"It's a campus-owned vehicle," the tech said. "And it has a LoJack."

Yes! "Trace it." He whirled to speak to everyone around him. "Stop that car. Don't let it out of campus."

"On it," a male officer said, and got on his radio.

Shit, what if they were already too late? The video in the alley had been taken at least fifteen minutes ago.

"Where is the suspect vehicle?" a deep, stern voice over his shoulder demanded.

Tate looked over his shoulder to see Greg standing next to an older cop who was clearly the officer in charge.

The female tech gave her superior an apologetic look. "I don't know, sir, I can't access the LoJack system from—"

Tate ignored them both, instead dialing someone at Missoula PD who could do it, even as Greg was on his own phone with someone.

Tate stepped past Avery and outside into the bright sunshine, panic and fury eating at him. Nina needed him but in order to help her, he needed to find her.

"I need you to track this plate involving a kidnapping at the University of Montana," he said after identifying himself. "I just watched the suspect put a woman into the trunk and drive off." Not just a woman. Nina. And he couldn't handle the thought of anything happening to her.

"Got it," the man said. "Hang on."

Tate's fingers were numb around his phone as he waited, a terrible feeling of helplessness invading him. Then Avery stepped out into the daylight, her face grim. "The driver made it through the perimeter seven minutes ago."

Tate cursed and broke into a run, heading for the spot where he'd left Rylee.

"They've got an alert out," Avery said, running beside him. "He won't get far."

He'd already gotten too far. And it was killing Tate not to be in pursuit right now. Nina had been unconscious, but when she came to, she would find herself trapped in the darkness.

Rylee was waiting in a patch of shade at the perimeter where he'd left her. "What's wrong?" she asked, jumping to her feet in alarm.

"Someone took Nina."

Rylee gasped and turned into Avery as his partner slid a comforting arm around her. "What do you want to do?" Avery said.

The local cops were tracking the LoJack signal now. "He's almost ten minutes ahead of us, and I'm not gonna sit here on my ass and trust the locals to find him in time."

"Let's go," Avery said, and started jogging toward where they'd left Tate's truck.

"Stay put with this officer until we come back for you," he said to Rylee, who nodded and stepped back to stand next to the cop he indicated. Tate took off after Avery, the sound of his shoes on the pavement blending with the thud of his heart in his ears.

They had to intercept that vehicle before it reached its final destination. Nina's life depended on it.

CHAPTER TWENTY

Nina jerked back to consciousness when she slammed into something. She sucked in a breath at the impact, automatically trying to reach out and steady herself. Her arms wouldn't work. Her brain was slow and sluggish, her eyelids heavy.

She had the sense that she was moving. Where...was she?

She fought to open her eyes. Her whole body felt heavy and lethargic. Why couldn't she move her arms? It was dark, and she was bouncing slightly.

Nina grunted as she bounced upward, her head and side hitting whatever was above her. When she landed, the fog cleared slightly from her brain.

A car. She was trapped in a trunk!

The active shooter evacuation. That cop—he'd dragged her off to the side and put something over her mouth.

Panic tore through her. She twisted to roll onto her back, trying to get her bearings.

There was a faint light coming from the left. She

squinted at it. A bit of plastic that looked almost like it was glowing slightly. The trunk release?

Sweat broke out all over her body. It was hot inside, with no air circulation, the sense of claustrophobia adding to the sensation that it was getting increasingly difficult to breathe. Where was this monster taking her? She had to get out before they got there.

Twisting onto her right side, she inched backward, pressing herself flat against the rear of the trunk. Her hands were bound at the wrists but her fingers were free.

The car slowed. She braced herself with her feet and tensed her muscles to try to keep from rolling as it turned the corner and began picking up speed.

Hurry, hurry...

She wiggled back into position, trying to find the release lever with her searching fingers. It was frustrating, not knowing whether she was close or not, unable to move her arms much, and every motion of the car made it that much harder.

Her heart raced frantically against her ribs as she felt along the plastic wall behind her. The car began to slow.

No! She had to get out. Had to run before he stopped. She wouldn't be raped again and then killed.

Her frantic fingers found something. She strained her arms upward at a painful angle, her shoulders aching, and touched the area again. A sort of T-shaped lever. She closed her fingers around it, the stifling air rushing in and out of her lungs with each shallow breath, and waited.

The vehicle slowed even more. Came almost to a stop.

Now.

She set her jaw and pulled the lever downward, almost losing her grip because of the awkward angle. But it was enough.

The trunk popped open, leaving her squinting against the sudden flood of light. There was no time to think. She sat up and swung her legs over the edge of the trunk, then jumped.

She hit the road on her front, barely managing to keep from smashing her face into it. The impact drove the air from her lungs, pain exploding throughout her body. And the car was turning.

Get up. Get up and run!

Pure adrenaline had her struggling to her feet as she took in her surroundings. They were on a quiet, country road in the middle of nowhere. Trees bordered either side.

Panic drove Nina into a run. Weaving a bit, her gait hindered with her arms secured behind her, and still under the influence of whatever he'd drugged her with.

Her legs were numb as she veered across the road and headed for the trees, hoping to hide. She'd reached the edge of the road when she heard the skid of tires behind her.

She risked a glance over her shoulder, her heart clenching in terror when she saw the car plunging to a halt in the middle of the road. He'd seen her! Would be coming after her. And as a cop, he'd be armed.

A bolt of terror streaked up her spine, turning her insides to ice. Frantic, she scanned for a place to hide as a door opened and running footsteps came from behind her.

Through the trees she spotted the edge of a small building. She raced toward it, running in a zig-zag route to make it harder for him to hit her with a bullet, desperate to put more distance between them and find a hiding spot.

He was coming after her, sounded like he was getting closer every second, his heavy treads thudding against the forest floor. Nina ran as hard as she could, desperate to reach the building. It was coming more into view now, and she saw it was actually a cluster of little cabins, like a campground or something.

The urge to scream for help clawed at her but she swallowed it back, not wanting to give her position away in case he didn't have a clear view of her. Instead she put on an extra burst of speed and darted across a thin strip of lawn toward the first cabin.

There were little alleys between them. She cut left around the first one, then left again, looking for a place to hide. But there was no one here. No one to help her.

She didn't dare slow, didn't dare try to hide in one of the cabins. She had to keep going, even though the fear clawed at her and her lungs burned from the exertion.

He didn't call out to her. Didn't yell any threats, and that almost scared her more. She couldn't hear him now but he had to be close behind her, so close she didn't dare risk looking back. She plunged headlong away from the last cabin toward the forest and veered right.

Her foot snagged on something. A cry locked in her throat as she went airborne. Unable to lift her hands to protect herself or cushion her fall, she hit the ground facedown and skidded across the mat of dirt and dry pine needles.

She winced, struggled upright and forced herself to her knees, the hot ball of fear trapped in her throat threatening to choke her. Branches snapped and cracked behind her.

A surge of terror drove her forward, running blindly through the forest as scrapes and cuts began to burn and throb all over her face. Blood dripped into her eyes. She shook her head but it didn't help clear her vision. She kept running—until her left foot hit nothing but air.

A tight scream ripped from her as she fell, landing on her side this time. The world turned in somersaults as she rolled down a shallow ravine and hit the bottom with a thud.

For a moment she couldn't move. Her lungs burned like they were full of acid, and pain obliterated her ability to think.

No. Get up!

Groaning, she rolled and pushed to her knees, managing to wipe the blood from her eyes by rubbing her face against her shoulder. She got up and staggered forward, totally disoriented.

Then she heard it. Water. Rushing water nearby. And the sound of that monster coming closer, somewhere above and behind her.

She broke into a limping run, aiming for the sound of the water. A small river or creek. If she could get to it, she might be able to hide her tracks, maybe buy enough time to find help.

The water came into view. A bank, sloping down to what looked like a small tributary of rushing water. She ran for it as fast as she could, frightened sobs choking her, tears blinding her.

At the edge of the trees, she ducked behind a thick trunk and paused, listening for the sound of her hunter. Once she left the forest and lost what little concealment it offered, she would be totally exposed for the few seconds it would take her to reach the water.

She glanced left, her heart leaping when she spotted the wooden dock about thirty yards away. The water must be deeper than she imagined. It was moving fast.

God, she didn't know what to do. Keep running through the forest, hugging the riverbank? Or risk heading for the water?

A sound in the distance behind her made her glance around the edge of the tree trunk. Horror sent her heart rocketing into her throat when she saw the cop racing through the trees—with a pistol in his hand.

THAT BITCH WASN'T getting away from him.

Vince plunged down the side of the ravine and skidded to the bottom, following the skid mark she'd left in the forest floor. He landed on his knees, jumped up and raced after her, his gaze pinned on the spot up ahead where he'd seen her dart between the trees, seconds before.

He couldn't believe she'd managed to pop the trunk release and jump out as he'd made that tight, hairpin turn in the road. He hadn't noticed the trunk, he'd been too busy navigating. As it was, he'd barely caught the flash of movement out of the corner of his eye as she ran for the trees.

Worse, he'd been forced to stay put for another fifteen to twenty seconds as a school bus passed by. That had given her enough of a head start to lose him initially.

But now he had her. They were all alone out here, there was no one to help her or hear her screams. If anyone heard the gunshots, they wouldn't do anything out here.

He had to kill her. He was going to end this here and now, all he had to do was get within pistol range, kill her, then disappear for a few days. He'd kept his face covered at the campus. They'd never ID him. His wife thought he was off hunting in the mountains. And he was.

For his first human prey.

Vince's long legs ate up the distance between them as he ran through the woods, dodging trees and fallen logs.

Up ahead, he caught a flash of Nina's red dress as she disappeared behind the screen of trees. The sound of the river was louder now, the smell of it growing stronger. He raced after her, excitement mixing with a rush of fear as his conscience tried to surface.

He shoved it aside, ruthlessly blocking it. There was no other way to save himself, he had to do this. Nina would be his undoing otherwise.

Another flash of red. Eighty yards ahead she broke from the trees and began running down the riverbank. Vince cursed and tore for the edge of the trees, arriving just in time to see her running for a wooden dock farther downriver.

He stared in amazement. Was she going to jump? With her hands tied behind her in that fast-moving water she'd probably drown, but he had to be sure she died.

Breaking from cover, he ran down the riverbank just as she reached the dock. He was within range now.

He stopped, his chest heaving. His hands trembled ever so slightly as he took aim and fired at the center of her back.

CHAPTER TWENTY-ONE

Tate's truck bounced and jostled as he raced it along the dirt road, but he didn't slow. He couldn't. Every second mattered.

A few minutes ago, the LoJack signal from the stolen vehicle had stopped in front of them somewhere down this country road bordered by forest on either side. Missoula PD had been dispatched but Tate wasn't waiting around for them.

All he cared about was rescuing Nina. Ever since that vehicle had stopped, his stomach had been a giant knot. Because stopping meant the kidnapper had reached his final destination—and Tate was terrified that would mean the end for Nina.

"We close?" he said to Avery, his tires kicking up a cloud of dust as they sped over the bumpy road. They still didn't know who the kidnapper was, but it had to be the guy who had raped Nina. Nothing else made sense.

"Yes. Should be just up here," Avery said, glancing up from her phone to look at the stretch of road ahead of them. "There, I see it—just at the bend in the road."

The maroon-and-gray vehicle was stopped in the middle of the road. Both the trunk and the driver's side door were open.

"See anything?" He immediately pulled to the left shoulder, putting the clues together in his mind as he slowed the truck. The driver had left in one hell of a rush. Why? What did it mean?

"No. Lemme out."

Before Tate had fully stopped, Avery jumped out and raced for the other vehicle, service pistol in hand. Tate yanked the keys from the ignition, ran around to grab his rifle from the back, then followed her, weapon up and ready. He wanted to be able to get off a long-range shot if necessary. *Where are you, Nina?*

Avery was circling the suspect's vehicle. "No sign of either of them," she called out, immediately turning to sweep the surrounding area with her weapon.

Tate did the same, anxiety twisting inside him. He'd been in combat and later served on SWAT. He'd been afraid before during an op. But never like this. Never where someone so important to him was in the hands of a monster who wanted to kill her.

It took all of his mental discipline to block that out and stay in op mode as he took in their surroundings. The ground was hard and dry. He and Avery spread out, looking for footprints leading away from the vehicle.

Tate spotted some leading into the trees beyond his truck. "Found something." Two sets, and they looked fresh. One smaller and daintier, the other wide and large like the treads of a work boot.

Avery hurried over, looked at the evidence, and nodded. "We can't wait for a K-9."

"I know. Follow me." He led the way into the trees, rifle to his shoulder, searching for any kind of sign that Nina or her attacker had passed this way.

"I see something up ahead," Avery murmured a minute later, positioned behind him and slightly to his right to watch their rear.

Tate craned his neck to see around a crooked tree ahead and spotted the outline of a building. *Nina.*

His stomach knotted as he ran toward it, soon realizing it was a group of small cabins. He didn't bother trying to be quiet as he ran. It was too damn quiet out here. Had the bastard dragged her into one of the cabins to kill her?

Turned out the cabins were deserted, however. That was both good and bad. If she wasn't there, it might mean she was still alive. But where had they gone? What had made the guy leave the car so fast, leaving it parked in the middle of the road where anyone could see it, without closing the door and trunk?

Frustration burned in his chest as he glanced around. Shit, they could be anywhere. "You go east, I'll head west," he told Avery. Splitting up wasn't ideal, but they didn't have a choice and he trusted that she could take the kidnapper out if she came across him alone.

"Got it."

She took off in the other direction as Tate hurried away from the cabins toward the trees to his left. This area was on a low bluff overlooking a tributary of the river. He headed toward the edge of it, hoping to get a better view of what lay below.

A distant gunshot echoed through the air.

His entire body tensed, his heart constricting in terror. *No. Please, no.*

"Tate?" Avery yelled back at him.

"Down there!" He raced for the edge of the bluff, facing the direction the shot had come from. When he got to the edge and looked down, what he saw made his blood freeze.

"Nina!" he screamed, her name torn from the center of his chest. She was running down a wooden dock in the red dress she'd put on that morning. And the tactical cop from campus stood maybe a hundred-fifty-feet from her, a pistol trained on her back.

"Nina!" he roared, terror and helplessness exploding through him. The cop was within range of Tate's rifle but it was a difficult shot and the angle was all wrong.

He raced along the edge of the bluff, trying to find a better angle.

The bastard hadn't heard Tate yell. Instead the cop tracked her and fired again.

Nina toppled forward.

Tate's heart lurched. *No!*

He watched in helpless horror as she fell off the end of the dock and plunged into the river.

****

The shock of the cold water hit Nina like a punch in the face. An instant after it closed over her head, she began to sink.

She hadn't caught a full breath before she'd jumped, the sound of the gunshot ripping a cry of terror from her. For a split second she'd thought he'd hit her, but the bullet had missed.

He'd been coming at her. Her only choice had been to jump and try to swim out of firing range.

The water was too murky to see anything. Her lungs burned already, the pressure excruciating. Having her hands bound behind her made it impossible to move her arms to steer or propel herself toward the surface. She was a decent swimmer but she kept dropping no matter how she twisted and kicked her feet, the current propelling her forward all the while.

Her flailing feet touched something. She bent her knees and shoved off of it, kicking hard, her face turned upward. What little air she'd had in her lungs was gone. The urge to breathe was overwhelming, a fire burning in her chest and a primal scream in her head.

Just as she was about to lose the battle, her head broke through the surface. She heaved in a desperate breath a heartbeat before the water closed back over her head.

Dammit, no!

She kicked hard, angling her body toward the surface. This time when she broke through, she twisted onto her back, struggling to keep her face above the water.

The current was strong, pushing her along at a surprisingly quick rate. Needing to see her surroundings, she bucked once to get her head fully out of the water.

She blinked the muddy water from her eyes and squinted. She was maybe thirty yards from the nearest edge of the riverbank. The dock was shrinking fast in the distance. And on the right…

A jolt of fear streaked through her when she spotted the cop racing after her along the riverbank.

The current tugged her back under. She fought her way back up, sucked in a bit of water with her next ragged breath and started coughing uncontrollably, her heart about to explode.

Her brain screamed at her to get out. She couldn't stay in the water. She'd drown.

Gathering her resolve, she turned onto her side and determinedly began kicking as hard as she could, angling her body toward shore. The water wanted to pull her back toward the middle of the river. She fought it, the cold and panic quickly sapping her strength.

Her legs and feet were numb as she propelled herself at an angle toward shore. A glance to the left showed she had enough distance from the cop now, even if she got out on the same shoreline he was on. She might be able to get up the bank and back into the woods to hide. It was her only option.

The current pulled her down. She sucked in a breath and dipped back under again, but this time the bottom was much closer. She shoved off it and surfaced, swimming for the bank now only a few dozen yards away.

When she tested the depth a few seconds later, her feet touched. She found her footing on the river bottom and waded her way to shore. Gasping for breath as she finally made it, she climbed out of the water.

The cold and exertion had her trembling all over. She shot a glance to her left, saw the cop still coming at her.

Gritting her teeth, she put her head down and forced her shaky legs into as much of a run as they had left in them. Her shoes were gone, the muddy bank squishy and slick beneath her bare feet. Water sluiced from her body, making her dress cling to her like a second-skin and adding weight her exhausted muscles didn't need.

The bank sloped gently upward, the trees beyond it beckoning to her. She was totally exposed here, the sense of vulnerability terrifying. Her damn dress was like a neon sign in the darkness. There was no way to get it off her with her hands bound. She had to get deep enough into the woods and disappear so that he couldn't see her, then find someplace to hide. Fast.

As she ran, she glanced down. Her footprints were well-defined in the muddy bank, and the water left a clear trail when she reached the dried grass beyond it.

She kept going, icy terror sluicing over her, expecting a shot to ring out at any moment. She was being hunted. Her only chance at surviving this was to outrun him and lose him in the forest long enough to hide somewhere he wouldn't find her.

The tree line was right in front of her now. She darted into the woods, careening through the trees, pain shooting through her feet as the rocks and sticks cut her bare soles.

She didn't stop. Glanced around, frantically looking for a place to hide. Nothing stood out and she couldn't slow down to look around.

Her heart was an erratic tattoo in her ears. *Don't stop,*

don't stop. He's coming.

Her skin crawled, the back of her neck prickling in a constant reminder of what was at stake. But she was tiring fast, the initial surge of adrenaline that had gotten her this far fading fast. She was shaking, gasping for breath.

A gunshot blasted through the quiet.

Her whole body jerked, her heart rocketing into her throat, blocking the cry forming there. Shit, he'd seen her, and he was too close! She had to lose him, buy some time.

She veered right and pushed herself harder, not willing to risk a glance over her shoulder as she wove her way through the trees. This damn red dress was going to get her killed.

A sob caught in her throat. She forced it down and plunged ahead, searching for some kind of cover. Her gaze caught on something off to the right. A large, half-rotten trunk. She swerved toward it, her feet on fire and her pulse thudding in her throat.

The trunk loomed closer. But when she neared it, she realized it wasn't thick enough. She'd never be able to hide behind it. She had to find something else.

Just as she raced past it, she spotted something else close by. A small outcropping of rock.

Nina headed straight for it, ducked behind it and dropped to the ground, curling into as small a ball as possible while trying to quiet her ragged breathing. Now that she'd stopped, a wave of helplessness and despair crashed over her.

This was it. She had nowhere else to go. Either the cop ran by without finding her, or this spot would be her grave.

Nina shuddered and squeezed her eyes shut, refusing to give into the burn of tears. She needed to get her hands free.

Angling her body, she looked for a sharp edge of rock, placed the center of the plastic zip tie binding her wrists against it, and began sawing. Small, quick motions, up and down, up and down...

The quiet was suffocating, her ears attuned to every tiny sound. Through the fear, her mind filled with thoughts of her family...and of Tate.

She loved him. Even if it was too soon. Even if they'd barely spent any time together. She knew her own heart, and right now it was bleeding at the thought of never seeing him again.

Then she heard something. Something was moving out ahead and to the right.

She held her breath, praying. Had he seen her?

The sound came closer. She began sawing at the zip tie faster. *Go past me. Go past me!*

"You can't hide, Nina! I'm going to find you."

The zip tie was partially cut now. Clenching her teeth together, she twisted her hands and pulled apart with all her might as she kept sawing.

Her hands broke apart. She shuddered, reached down behind her to pick up a fist-sized rock. If it looked like he'd found her, if he came close enough, she would try to bash him in the face and run—

"Stop, police!"

Nina gasped and froze, hope surging at the distant shout carrying through the trees. The urge to pop up from behind the rock and look around was strong, but she stayed where she was, hardly daring to breathe as the agonizing seconds stretched out.

Another shot exploded in the silence. She flinched. Who had fired at whom?

"Hands up! Drop your weapon!"

Her entire body went rigid as the sound of that second voice finally registered. One she would recognize anywhere.

Tate. He'd found her.

But now there was an armed madman standing between them.

CHAPTER TWENTY-TWO

Tate stopped and put his rifle to his shoulder, partially hidden behind a tree as he caught his breath. After the harrowing race down here to catch up, he finally had the bastard in his sights.

He'd lost sight of Nina over a minute ago. She was somewhere off to the right, hidden from view, and he wanted her to stay there until this was over. He was worried as hell she might have hypothermia after being in the water. He'd aged ten years watching her repeatedly going under in the water like that.

"Hands up! Drop your weapon!" he shouted. This ended *now*.

The shooter whirled to face him, shock and fury on his face at being caught.

Tate longed to put a bullet in the center of it but refrained, finger curled around the trigger. They would take this fucker in alive so investigators could wring every last bit of information about his victims and crimes out of him. Then lock him up to await the lethal injection he deserved.

Tate could hear Avery rushing up behind him, just

having caught up. "Backup's almost here," she panted.

Tate nodded once, raw fury rushing through him as he stared the shooter down. "Last chance," he called out.

There was no way the shooter could miss Tate's rifle. He had to know Tate had called in backup. But rather than drop his pistol and comply, the bastard whirled and fired at him.

Tate didn't flinch, the shot going wide, and followed as the shooter bolted through the trees. Tate dropped to one knee. When the shooter appeared in a small opening, Tate fired one round, hitting him in the back of the right shoulder.

A mingled cry of pain and rage filled the air. The shooter went down for a second but then popped up and kept going, crashing through the brush in a desperate attempt to escape.

Tate's jaw tightened. *Not. Fucking. Happening.*

"Ready?" Tate muttered to Avery.

"Yep."

She was right behind him as they raced down the slight incline and followed the shooter deeper into the woods. Tate couldn't see him, but he could see the movement of the branches and brush that marked the asshole's progress, giving away his location.

Tate was prepared to punch as many holes in the bastard's hide as necessary to bring him down. But a lethal one only as a last resort.

The shooter was slowing now. Tate closed the distance between them, noting the pistol was now in the man's left hand, his right arm dangling at his side, blood dripping down it. "Stop and drop your weapon!" he yelled. He wanted this over so he could go to Nina.

The shooter whirled and fired. Tate ducked, then stopped. Taking aim, he fired again, hitting the back of the man's left thigh.

Blood sprayed as an enraged roar echoed through the

trees.

"It's over," Tate said as he stalked forward, rifle to his shoulder. "Give it up." They were maybe fifty yards apart now.

Tate stopped just out of pistol range. The asshole was down, had nowhere to go. "Drop it, *now*," he barked.

Rolling to his side, the shooter stared back at him with utter loathing, his teeth bared in a feral grimace of pain. "Fuck you," he snarled. His left hand flashed upward, the muzzle of the pistol pointed toward his own head.

Tate fired, hitting him in the stomach instead of the chest. He wanted this bastard to live long enough to tell them everything they needed to know.

The shooter dropped back with a guttural grunt, his pistol falling to the ground. Tate raced for him, ready to fire again. This time the bastard stayed down, his hand going to the wound in his gut rather than for his weapon.

Tate ran up and kicked the pistol away. "Why'd you target Nina?" he demanded, standing over him.

Pain-glazed blue eyes stared up at him. Livid scratches marked his face. Tate hoped Nina had done the damage, but they looked old enough that it might have been someone else. Maybe Samantha.

The asshole opened his mouth. A garbled sound came out, along with a trickle of blood.

"I got him," Avery said, holstering her weapon and quickly dropping to her knees beside the guy. "Why'd you take Nina? Huh?" she snapped, pulling a pair of flex cuffs out of her pocket.

No answer. Just another guttural groan and more blood.

Avery looked up at Tate, her face set, anger burning in her eyes. "Go. Find her."

He nodded and turned back the way he'd come, leaving her to cuff the bastard and try to keep him alive if she could. If the asshole was going to die, Tate just hoped it took a long time to happen.

"Nina! Nina, can you hear me?" he shouted, turning in a slow circle. He had only a vague idea which direction she was in. "He's down and we've got him. It's over. Where are you?"

"Here."

He whirled, searching the undergrowth in the direction the faint reply had come from. His feet moved without conscious thought, carrying him toward her voice. "Nina, where?"

"Here!"

Her voice was stronger now, giving him hope that she was okay.

Tate broke into a run, following it. He still couldn't see her. But she had to be fairly close. "I'm coming."

He leapt over a large fallen branch and kept running, desperate to get to her. "I can't see you. Where are you?"

A flash of red appeared up ahead on the right. He raced toward it, his heart clenching when Nina stepped out from behind a rock outcropping. She had blood on her face. "*Nina.*"

Her face crumpled and her arms came up, a broken zip tie around each wrist as she reached for him.

Tate erased the distance between them in a few more strides and grabbed her, hauling her tight against him with a groan. "I've got you. I've got you," he breathed, his voice rough.

"Tate," she whispered, her arms looped around his neck.

Jesus, she was freezing. He let go of her just long enough to set his rifle down, then grabbed the back of her sodden dress and quickly peeled it off her.

She protested and tried to cover herself but he ignored it. "We have to get you dry and warmed up," he told her, dropping the wet dress before ripping off his shirt. He scanned her quickly for injuries. She was scraped and bruised in several places, but he didn't see any sign of serious injury.

He tugged his shirt down over her head and pulled it down to cover her. The material came halfway down her thighs.

Tate pulled her close again and wrapped his arms around her to warm her, closing his eyes as he took his first full breath since he'd seen that video of her being taken on campus.

Christ, he'd almost lost her. He would never let that happen again. He was all in, ready to give her his heart, and would do anything to keep her safe.

"Is h-he d-dead?" she whispered, teeth chattering. She was shaking so hard, partly from cold, but it had to be fear as well.

"I don't know."

"It w-was him. H-he's the one wh-who r-raped me."

Tate clenched his jaw and hugged her tighter, wanting to go back there and pound the fucker's face in. Was he an actual cop? Or just posing as one?

Tate was willing to bet the bastard had reported an active shooter in a bid to get to Nina. "It's okay now, sweetheart. He'll never hurt anyone again. I've got you."

She made a choked sound and buried her face in his chest. Tate's heart clenched. "It's all right now," he repeated, wishing he could make this all go away for her. "I'm going to get you out of here now, okay?"

A tiny sob came out of her, ripping his heart to shreds, but she nodded. "C-cold."

"I know, baby. I'll take care of you. Come on." He slung his rifle across his back, then bent and carefully gathered her up, one arm beneath her knees and the other wrapped securely around her ribs.

She immediately curled into him, hiding her face in his neck. Tate cradled her to him and started carrying her out of the woods, a complex knot of emotion building in his throat.

He loved her. And now that she was safe in his arms, he was never letting her go again.

****

What a bitch of a day, and it was barely half over.

Avery sighed and ran a hand through her hair as she walked away from the Fed she'd been speaking to. They'd begun questioning her the instant she stepped out of the trees with Nina and Tate where the emergency vehicles were parked on the road. She was drained, wanted all this to be over.

At least Nina was safe and being looked at right now. Everything had turned out okay in the end, but God, Avery had never been that scared before.

Hunting that animal down through the forest while he chased Nina was going to be permanently burned into her psyche. Now she was tired and just wanted to see her friend.

"Avery!"

She spun around, peered past the police tape as someone pushed their way in front of one of the cops guarding the perimeter set up on the dirt road she and Tate had raced up earlier. Shading her eyes with one hand, she was surprised to see Mason standing there.

The cops weren't letting him through, and much as he irritated her, she wasn't going to leave him standing there when he'd come all this way and was clearly worried. She hurried over, holding up her badge. "He's with me," she said to the cops, and they let him through.

Mason ducked under the tape and closed the distance between them, the brim of his black cowboy hat hiding his face in shadow. "What happened?" he demanded, stopping a foot from her and setting his hands on his hips.

The sheer power of him hit her, the tightly coiled energy rolling off him palpable. A wall of strength and tightly leashed violence ready to unload on a target. "Nina's okay. Kidnapper's en route to the hospital, sporting a few bullet holes courtesy of Tate." She peered up at him as he visibly relaxed, struck again by the intensity of his bright blue gaze. "What are you doing here?"

"Tracked Tate's phone." Then he wrapped his arms around her and pulled her into a tight hug.

Avery was too stunned to resist, even as her body tensed. Then went hot, all over, in a way that had nothing to do with perimenopause.

Pressed against that warm, hard wall of muscle, those ridiculously sexy arms around her, all her nerve endings suddenly burst to life. She automatically laid her hands against his back, his body heat helping to chase away the chill inside her.

"You okay?" he murmured, his cheek pressed to her temple.

He smelled as delicious as he looked. And his obvious concern took her aback.

She'd seen Mason in playful mode. Teasing and flirting mode. Borderline arrogant mode. But she'd never seen this protective side of him, the lethal operator that was so much a part of him coming through.

Arousal and something deeper, softer swept through her. Something dangerous.

She cleared her throat and stepped back, doing her damndest to hide her reaction as she put a bit of space between them. "Tate's being interviewed, which means Nina's alone. I need to be with her."

Mason nodded, his jaw flexing, that piercing blue gaze locked on her. "I'm glad you're okay. All of you."

She put on a smile. It was hard to remember why she'd made up her mind to dislike him when he was like this. She couldn't keep her guard up against this side of him for long, so she needed to be careful. "Me too. I don't know how long we'll be, but at least a while more. Do you want to wait, or…?"

"Nah, if everything's good here, I'll head back. Just wanted to be sure you guys were all right."

"I appreciate that. Can you go check on Rylee? We left her on campus, and it'll be a while before Tate or I can get to her."

"Of course." He reached up to graze his knuckles gently against her jaw, those blue, blue eyes on hers. "See you later, angel eyes."

Avery stood there frozen for a second, heat sparking across the skin he'd just touched, her eyes drinking in the sight of him as he walked away.

Blowing out a breath, she spun around and went to find Nina. In future, she needed to stay the hell away from Mason Gallant before she was tempted to do something she would no doubt regret later.

CHAPTER TWENTY-THREE

Nina was still shivering when Avery finally showed up at the ambulance parked at the edge of the road beside the forest. Tate had stayed with her while the paramedics looked her over, then while she'd called her parents to let them know what had happened and that she was okay.

They were understandably freaked out and were flying out first thing in the morning to come here. Then Tate had to leave her to talk with the police, and ever since she'd felt colder without him holding her.

"Hey, sweetheart." Avery reached out to hug her.

Nina let go of the blanket with one hand to embrace her friend. "Hey." She squeezed hard, clung a moment, then let go.

Avery's golden eyes assessed her critically as she sat beside Nina on the edge of the ambulance deck. "You hurt anywhere?"

"Not really. J-just bruised and scraped all over. Especially my f-feet." She straightened her legs to show Avery the bandages covering them. Her friend had been busy talking to various law enforcement people while the paramedics treated Nina. Running through the forest barefoot like that had taken a toll on her tender soles. "They hurt the worst."

Avery nodded, then met her gaze. "I couldn't get anything out of him before he passed out."

That was unfortunate. Not that Nina had expected him to confess to anything. "Is he going to die?"

"I'm not sure. But I think so. Tate hit him in the stomach, to take him down without killing him outright."

"I hope it h-hurts like hell."

Avery grinned, then frowned when Nina shuddered. "You're still freezing."

Nina nodded. Someone had given her sweats and a jacket, but even all of that and the blanket from the paramedics wasn't doing the trick. "I can't s-seem to w-warm up." Her jaw shook, making her teeth clack together for a moment.

"Well, let's see if I can help with that until Tate gets back."

Nina huddled close to her friend, sighing at the feel of Avery's arms around her. It felt good to be held right now, but as much as she loved her friend, it was Tate's arms she wanted around her.

"Was he… Was he the one who raped you?" Avery asked after a moment.

"Y-yes."

"When did you recognize him?"

"When he d-dragged me out of my b-building."

"He was wearing a mask."

"His s-smell." She wanted to gag just thinking of it. If she ever smelled that cologne again, she would throw up instantly.

"His smell," Avery murmured, her voice full of approval. "That's incredible, but it makes perfect sense, since smell can trigger powerful memories. For me it's the scent of bacon frying. Reminds me of my dad cooking Sunday breakfast. I used to lie in bed on Sunday mornings, breathing that in and waiting for him to call us down, but mostly hoping he'd call us too late for us to make church later."

Nina chuckled softly. "For me it's my m-mother's f-flan. The smell of the caramel sauce."

"Flan." Avery looked down at her, quirked an eyebrow. "That's something you haven't made for the twisted sisters yet. Like to see them make anything out of *that*."

Nina grinned, then laughed softly. It felt so good, warming her insides and chasing away the deep chill. "Good c-call."

"What are you two laughing about?" a deep, delicious male voice asked.

Nina snapped her gaze to Tate, drinking in the sight of him as he strode toward them. Her heart skipped a beat, rolling over in her chest. Her hero. Tall, strong and today he'd saved her life. "N-next step in our dessert war," she explained.

His lips quirked, then he lowered himself to sit on Nina's other side. "Mind if I take over the warming duties for a bit?" he said to Avery.

"Yeah, I do mind," Avery said, leaning in to envelop Nina in a hug. "We'll make a Nina sammich."

Nina giggled softly, joy filling her with more warmth. She leaned into Tate's big frame and sighed at the feel of her man and best friend surrounding her.

No one spoke after that. Tate and Avery continued to hold her between them. Gradually the shivers began to slow. Her muscles no longer jerked. Exhaustion hit her, lulling her into closing her eyes.

She must have dropped off to sleep, because the next thing she knew, Tate's voice reached her.

"Wake up, sunshine."

Her eyes snapped open. They were still sitting on the back of the ambulance deck, but they were alone now. Her heart lurched as everything from earlier came flooding back.

She swallowed, forcing the fear back. She was safe now. Tate had seen to that. "How long have I been sleeping?" Her voice was raspy. She had a kink in the side of her neck. And the soles of her feet felt like they were on fire.

He drew his fingers through her damp hair, his face only inches from hers. "A while."

"Where's the Avery part of the me sammich?"

A grin curved his lips. "She had to go take care of a few things. And now we do too."

Nina looked past him to where Avery was talking with several police officers and FBI agents. "FBI? When did they get here?"

"Let's just say, better late than never." Tate kissed her temple and shifted his hold, sitting her up more. "We have to do a few more interviews before we can leave. Are you up to it?" His gorgeous hazel eyes were full of concern. "If not, they can come talk to us tonight."

"No, I'd rather do it now and get it over with." She wanted this done, so they could get out of here and go home.

She reached for his hand. Hers was all scraped and bloody, but he didn't seem to mind at all, curling his large, warm fingers around hers. Dread and vulnerability twisted inside her. "Will you stay with me?"

Raising her hand to his lips, he pressed a kiss to her knuckles. "Through everything."

Something hitched in her chest at the way he said it, the serious look in his eyes. He'd just given her a vow, and she had the feeling he meant he'd stay with her through a lot more than the police business.

The urge to tell him how she felt pressed against the

inside of her ribcage, expanding outward until it felt like her chest would explode. But she was prevented from saying anything by an FBI agent heading straight for them.

Tate squeezed her hand gently in reassurance. "We'll get this done and then go home."

Home. Whether to her place or his, she didn't care, as long as she got to be alone with him.

The entire process after that took a lot longer than she'd expected. By the time everything was done the sun was setting. She shivered, pulling the folds of the blanket tighter around her as she digested everything she'd just learned.

The monster who had put her and other women through hell was Vince Reimer, a cop on the Missoula police department. Married, with two young daughters.

It made Nina sick. He'd used his skills and know-how to pick and choose his victims, and had orchestrated the attack today by calling in the fake active shooter threat. As one of Missoula's tactical officers, he'd known he would be one of the first people on scene and have direct access into the locked down building.

All to get her. To silence her and prevent her from identifying him. Currently he was being operated on. His chances of survival were fifty-fifty.

Tate looped an arm around her shoulders and tugged her into his side. "She's exhausted. Are we done here?" he said to the two Feds they'd been talking to for the past half-hour, a bite to his tone.

The older one looked at Nina, then nodded. "Sure. You can head out now. We'll contact you tomorrow to follow up."

Thank the lord.

"Let's go," Tate said to her, then scooped her up and carried her to his truck where Avery was already waiting inside.

"Good to go?" Avery asked from the back as Tate set

Nina in the front passenger seat.

"Yep. We're outta here." Tate shut Nina's door and went around to the driver's side.

Avery reached forward to wrap her hand around Nina's shoulder and squeeze lightly. "Warmer now?"

"Yes. Just tired." So damn tired. It felt like a week since she'd last slept. "He was a local cop."

"I know, they told me. Here." Avery handed up her wadded-up jacket. "Use this as a pillow."

"Thanks." She settled herself against the doorframe as Tate turned the truck around and headed back toward town.

He glanced over at her, smiled, and reached out to stroke his fingers down the side of her cheek. "Sleep, baby. I got this."

She smiled back, then closed her eyes and let sleep take her, knowing on a bone-deep level that she was safe. Tate was beside her. And the monster who had hunted her was gone, and would never hurt anyone ever again.

She woke when strong arms slid around her. She gasped and stiffened, Vince's face flashing before her eyes for a moment.

"Just me," Tate whispered, lifting her out of the truck. "We're home."

Nina blinked and looked around. It was almost dark and they were in Avery's driveway. She curled her arms around Tate's neck and leaned into him as he carried her toward the side pathway.

"If you guys need anything, just let me know," Avery said, heading for the front door.

"Will do," Tate answered, then nuzzled the side of Nina's face. "I'm gonna feed you, then get you cleaned up and into bed."

"Sounds heavenly."

Inside her suite, he set her on the couch and tucked

her throw blanket around her before making them sandwiches. They ate quickly, then he picked her back up and carried her to the master bathroom.

"Bath, or shower?" he asked.

"Bath." She didn't want to stand up right now, her feet hurt too much.

In the bathroom he filled the tub and helped her strip. "We'll keep your feet out. I'll do them separately," he told her, taking out a facecloth from the vanity drawer.

Nina didn't answer, just enjoyed the pleasure of watching him move, the muscles in his back and arms flexing. "Thank you for rescuing me," she said after a few moments.

He stopped, turned to face her. "Don't thank me for that. You saved yourself by getting out of that trunk and then running for it. By jumping into the river even though your hands were tied behind your back. If you hadn't done all that, I wouldn't have been able to get him in time." He cupped her cheek in his hand, his eyes searching hers. "I'd do anything to keep you safe. You know that, right?"

Her heart squeezed so hard it hurt. "Yes," she whispered. "So that means you'll stay with me?" She didn't want to be alone. Definitely not tonight. Maybe not for the foreseeable future.

Empathy flashed in his eyes, then his expression turned serious. "I'm not going anywhere, sunshine."

I love you. Love you so much. Somehow, she held the words back.

It wasn't until later, after her bath when he'd tucked her into bed and climbed in next to her and propped his head in his hand to study her in the soft lamplight, that she knew something had shifted between them. Her heart began to beat faster at the look on his face. There was a softness in his gaze that she'd never seen before. Because he'd never allowed her to see it until now.

"I never expected anyone like you to come into my

life," he murmured, easing his thumb across her cheek.

"A sexy, brilliant physics and astronomy nerd?"

He grinned. "Yeah." Then his expression sobered. "I've been holding back because of my own issues, but I'm done with that. I want you and no one else."

Nina searched his eyes. "You want to be exclusive?"

"Hell yes. I want you all to myself."

Ohh, she liked where this was going.

His gaze was steady on hers. Unflinching. "Because I'm in love with you."

Nina sucked in a stunned breath even as joy exploded inside her. "Tate," she whispered, instantly tearing up.

"Aww, damn, don't cry," he said, wiping her tears away.

She shook her head, grabbed his hand and pressed it to her cheek. "Happy tears," she whispered. "And oh, God, I love you too. So much." She wound her arms around his neck and hugged him, letting out a soggy laugh. "I can't believe it. Those are literally the last words I expected to hear from you today."

He chuckled low in his throat and gathered her close, banding those hard, powerful arms around her. Emotion flooded her. He was so strong. Strong enough to protect her, stand beside her.

And better yet, strong enough to overcome his fear and surrender his heart to her.

"I wasn't going to say it yet. Thought it was too soon." He sounded almost embarrassed. "But it's how I feel."

She shook her head, swallowing the lump in her throat. "It's never too soon to say what's in your heart."

"Well, good, because I love you."

It sounded even better that way. Nina eased back to wipe at her face and drew her fingertips over the stubble on his jaw, unable to stop smiling. This had been both the worst and best day of her life. How strange and incredible.

"See? Told you you're a closet romantic."

A rueful grin curved his lips as he leaned in for a kiss. "Guess you bring that out in me, sunshine."

EPILOGUE

Pausing in Tate's homey, log-walled kitchen to close her eyes a moment, Nina took in a deep breath and smiled. Ahh, the sweet sound of silence.

She loved her family to death, but she was glad they'd finally left because she wanted her space back, and she wanted alone time with Tate. Rylee was also gone now, having moved back to campus. She had a new roommate, and seemed to be doing well so far with weekly visits to a trauma counselor.

Tate was currently at a business meeting with Mason and their friend Braxton, who was checking in via video call from somewhere in the Middle East. They'd all agreed that the property Tate had chosen would be ideal for their plans, so they were making plans together for what came next.

Nina was excited for them. Tate was still leery of quitting his job, and Avery sure didn't want him to leave. He'd stay on as detective for now, but if all went well, he'd be part owner of Rifle Creek Tactical in a few more months.

She hummed to herself as she bustled around the kitchen getting everything ready. By the time Tate came home she wanted everything finished and waiting for him. He'd been taking care of her these past two weeks with her family, and after all of that he deserved something romantic done for him too.

As she carried the bottle of champagne in its ice bucket to the sliding door that led out to the back deck, the doorbell rang. She set it on the kitchen table and hurried down to answer it.

Nina's eyes widened. "Bev. Pat. What are you two doing all the way out here?" Tate's house was a solid nine-minute drive from their neighborhood, so there was no way they'd just come here for the heck of it.

"We stopped by your place but Avery said you were here. So we came over to give you this." Pat smiled as she handed Nina a basket. "Your flan was so delicious, we couldn't possibly outdo it. So we thought we'd start over." She winked at Nina.

Nina took the basket and pulled back the gingham cloth. She laughed. "Kale?" Eww. How was she supposed to make something sweet and delicious out of that?

Pat nodded, eyes twinkling. "From our garden. You're really good. We decided we need to challenge you more."

"Well. Challenge accepted." She shook her head. "It was really nice of you to come here just to see me."

Pat waved it away. "Don't be silly. We miss seeing you. I hope you'll stop by for tea and goodies next time you have a minute."

"I'd love that. And maybe you could give me some pointers about gardening. I'd like to put a small one into Avery's backyard as a surprise, to thank her for everything she's done for me. Something low maintenance she won't have to fuss much with, because she's busy."

Pat's face lit up. "We'd love that! Wouldn't we,

Bev?" she said, turning to her sister.

Bev pushed past her sister and handed Nina something else. "I made these for you and Tate," she said softly, almost shyly.

Nina opened the little box, inhaled and smiled. "Peanut butter chocolate chip?"

"Chocolate chunks," Bev said. "I know how much you love them."

Aww. "That was so sweet of you, thank you."

Bev nodded, her cheeks turning pink. Then she shocked Nina by pulling her into a hug. "We're just so glad you're okay, and that the asshole who attacked you is dead." She gave Nina a maternal pat on the back.

Nina didn't know what shocked her more, the hug, or hearing Bev say asshole. "Thank you. I'm glad too."

Vince Reimer had died a couple of days after surgery. Investigators had only gotten minimal information from him about other cases, but it was safe to say he'd raped more than ten young women from the university over the past two years. They'd never know the true number because so many women didn't report rape out of fear of being judged or blamed.

"All right, all right, enough mushy stuff," Pat announced, pulling her sister away. "Time to go home and let Nina think about how to improve upon our challenge ingredient."

Nina stood on the doorstep and waved as they drove away in their little red Volkswagen beetle, smiling. Was this the greatest community ever, or what?

She turned to go back inside, then stopped when she heard Tate's truck coming up the street. He pipped the horn at Bev and Pat, who honked back, and pulled into the driveway. He climbed out and shut the door, giving Nina a sexy smile that had her heart knocking. "Did they stop by?"

"Yes, with another offering." Nina held up the basket. "The rivalry continues."

He chuckled and came up the steps to wrap his arms around her waist. "Hey, sunshine," he murmured.

"Hey." If her voice sounded breathless it was because he made her heart pound. "How was your day?"

"Good. And I just saw something very interesting on the way home." His eyes twinkled.

"Really? What?"

"As I was driving past Mrs. Engleman's house, who should happen to come out the front door tucking his shirt into his pants?"

Nina gasped. "No *way*. Curt and Mrs. Engleman?" Nina had only met her once, but she seemed really prim and proper, and a little standoffish.

"Yep." He chuckled. "Dude grins at me and waves, then sauntered to his truck, looking mighty pleased with himself."

Nina laughed. "I love it. Curt and Mrs. Engleman…"

Tate kissed her softly, then raised his head to gaze into her eyes. "Mason's out with Ric somewhere. So does that mean we're finally alone?"

She grinned. He'd been so great with her family, and incredibly tolerant when everyone had been here together at once—the most frustrating part being that they hadn't been able to spend the night together because of her old-fashioned parents.

They'd been forced to sneak sexy rendezvous here and there, which was exciting in a sense, but she was *so* ready to spend the whole night in bed together without any interruptions. "Yep. They should be boarding their flight home any minute."

"Good." He scooped her up, lifting her from the ground. Nina squealed in delight and looped one arm around his neck as he carried her over the threshold.

When they reached the kitchen, he stopped. "What's

all this?"

She slid out of his arms. "I didn't quite get it finished before Bev and Pat arrived. But come outside anyway." She set the basket on the table and grabbed his hand to tow him out onto the deck.

"Seriously, what *is* all this?" he said with a laugh as she led him down the steps to the backyard.

She'd laid out a large blanket beside the fire pit, which already had a fire going in it, and pillows and blankets. It was the end of September now, and the nights got cold. This high up in the mountains, fall was already here, and the past few mornings they'd woken to frost covering the ground and leaves.

"This is to show you how much I love and appreciate you," she said. "Come on, sit down." She tugged on his hand.

Grinning, he did. "Now what?"

"Now you stay put and relax while I finish getting everything ready." She bent forward to drop a kiss on his lips, then hurried back inside.

Five minutes later she carried out the bucket of champagne and a fully loaded plate. "Here you are." She gave him his plate. "Medium-cooked fillet mignon with hollandaise sauce, roasted asparagus and a fully-loaded, twice-baked potato."

He took it from her, his face full of surprise. "My favorites."

"I know." She made it a point to know all his favorite things. "And after we eat, we're gonna stretch out on the blanket and watch the stars come out."

"Sounds good to me."

"Good. Be right back." She scampered back in to grab them champagne flutes and her own plate, then hurried back down to join him. "There," she said with a smile as she curled her legs under her and poured them each a glass of champagne. "To us."

He touched his flute to hers and took a sip, a slight frown on his face. "You didn't have to do all this."

She shrugged. "I wanted to."

They ate their meal together, talking about various things. "So the meeting went well, I take it?" she asked.

"Went great. The guys are totally on board and the financing looks good. We're gonna put an offer in on the property."

"That's awesome. And, speaking of awesome, just wait until you see what I've got for dessert." She bounced her eyebrows suggestively and lowered one sleeve of her dress just enough to show him her new purple lace bra she'd bought on a recent shopping trip with her sister. She'd been saving it for tonight, their first night alone in weeks.

Tate's gaze heated. "I'd rather have that for dessert instead."

"Even if I made chocolate-pecan pie?"

He groaned, giving her an accusing look. "That's my favorite."

"I know." She grinned suggestively. "I know *all* your favorites. But here's the beauty of this—you can have *both*. Even at the same time if you want."

He laughed and set his plate down, then set hers aside and dragged her into his lap to hug her tight. He was already semi-hard beneath her bottom. Arousal stirred in her blood, sending a wave of warmth through her. "This is amazing, sunshine."

"What is?"

"Just...everything. No one's ever done anything like this for me before."

Nina's heart hitched. "Never?"

"No. I think I like it."

That made her smile. "Good." She kissed him, holding his handsome face in her hands as she poured her heart into it.

Just as the heat in her blood burst into flame, he stopped and pulled back, one hand curved around her nape. "I have something for you."

"What?"

"Stay here." Before she could say anything else, he was up and heading for his workshop at the back of the yard.

Nina sat up and waited, watching as he came out with something in his hands a moment later. He crossed the lawn, knelt down beside her and handed her something wrapped in a cloth. "Here."

Wondering what he was up to, she took it with a grin and pulled the cloth away. She gasped. "Oh, Tate." A small wooden box with a picture of Saturn carved into the lid. She looked up at him. "Did you make this?"

"Yeah. Open it."

She did, making a sound of wonder when she saw the sun carved on the underside of the lid, and the message carved into the bottom right above a key he'd placed there. *You are my sunshine.*

Nina bit her lip, tears flooding her eyes. "Tate," she whispered, overcome with emotion. That he would make something like this for her, something so sentimental and poignant, touched her deeply. "It's beautiful."

She sniffed, wiped at her eyes and picked up the key. "What's this for?"

"For you, so you can move in with me."

Nina stared at him, totally caught off guard. "Are you...sure?"

"I'm sure."

She frowned at him. "This isn't just because I made you fillet mignon and chocolate-pecan pie, is it? Because that's definitely only a special occasion thing. Don't be expecting that every night."

He chuckled. "No. It's because I love you so damn much, and I can't stand being away from you. I want you beside me every night, and when I wake up every morning."

Oh, hell she was going to ugly cry. For him to say something like that this soon was huge. "Can I put glow-in-the-dark stars all over our bedroom ceiling? I want to build a map on it."

His lips quirked as he pretended to consider it. "I'll allow it."

"Then I'd love to move in with you."

He kissed her, a low growl rumbling up from his chest as he tipped her over and spread her out on her back on the blanket. "I love you, sunshine."

"Love you t—" She sighed as his tongue delved into her mouth, one hand gliding down to cup her breast through the thin fabric of her dress.

"Howdy, neighbor," said a chipper voice.

Nina jerked, her eyes flying wide at the sound of Curt's voice coming from the other side of the fence. Tate was on top of her and the skirt of her dress was almost up at her waist. Could he see them?

"Hey, Curt. Go away, Curt," Tate called over his shoulder.

Nina let out a squeak when the top part of Curt's face appeared over the top of the fence.

His eyes widened. "*Oh*! Oh, sorry. Have a good night, then. We'll catch up later." He cleared his throat and walked away.

Nina's laugh dissolved into a soft moan as Tate resumed kissing her, that hot, hard body blanketing hers, his hips wedged between her splayed thighs, putting delicious pressure right where she wanted it.

"Gotta love that guy. His timing's almost as bad as Mason's," Tate muttered against her lips, then set about showing her the stars.

Nina gave herself up to it, reveling in every touch, stroke and caress. *This* was what true love felt like. *This* was everything that had been missing before.

Tate was the only man for her. He owned her heart, and had her trust and respect as well. This was her happily ever after, and she was going to make the most of it every single day.

—The End—

Dear reader,

Thank you for reading *Lethal Edge*. I hope you enjoyed the start of the Rifle Creek Series. If you'd like to stay in touch with me and be the first to learn about new releases you can:

Join my newsletter at:
http://kayleacross.com/v2/newsletter/

Find me on Facebook:
https://www.facebook.com/KayleaCrossAuthor/

Follow me on Twitter:
https://twitter.com/kayleacross

Follow me on Instagram:
https://www.instagram.com/kaylea_cross_author/

Also, please consider leaving a review at your favorite online book retailer. It helps other readers discover new books.

Happy reading,
Kaylea

LETHAL TEMPTATION

Rifle Creek Series
By Kaylea Cross
Copyright © 2020 Kaylea Cross

CHAPTER ONE

Avery stopped typing notes on her computer to snatch her phone from her desk when it rang. She stilled when she saw the number of her main police contact in Billings, and took a deep breath before answering.

She'd been waiting for this call. Dreading it for days. "Detective Dahl."

"Avery, it's Jim. I have some news for you."

"Hi, Jim. Go ahead." She braced herself for the possibility of bad news.

"It's about Mike Radzat."

"Yes." Her stomach tensed, her fingers tightening around the phone.

"The National Appeals Board met this morning, and they've made the decision to—"

To overturn the Parole Commission's decision and grant Radzat parole. So that dangerous, manipulative piece of shit could target more innocent victims.

"—deny his appeal."

Thank you, God. She leaned back in her chair, slowly relaxing. "That's great news." She wanted him to stay in prison for as long as possible. "When will his next parole board hearing be?"

"Likely in another two years."

Hopefully he'd be denied parole then too. "Thanks for letting me know."

"Of course. Have a good day."

"You too." She set her phone down on her desk with a relieved sigh. Until now she hadn't realized just how anxious she'd been about the situation.

She looked up at a brisk knock on her partially open office door. Her work partner, Tate, stood in the doorway, wearing dress slacks, a charcoal-gray button-down, and a few days of bronze stubble on his jaw. His expression was somber. "We're being dispatched to a domestic violence call."

Avery pushed up from her desk and took her service pistol from the drawer, sliding it into the holster on her hip. "Where's everyone else?" They were detectives, not patrol officers, but the Sheriff's Department here was small enough that they were often spread thin, so everyone had to pitch in where needed.

"Busy."

She hurried after him down the hall toward the main doors. These kinds of calls were thankfully rare here in Rifle Creek. It had been a long while since she'd had to respond to something like this, and she hadn't missed it. She'd always hated them.

One in five officer "line of duty" deaths occurred while responding to domestic violence calls. They were by far the most dangerous kind of call for an officer to respond to, and she was thankful to have Tate with her.

They'd been partners for just over seven months now, and they'd become close right from the start. She trusted and felt safe with him. And not only was he a former Marine Raider with combat experience in addition to his years as a law enforcement officer, he was also in love with Avery's best friend.

There was no one else she'd rather have watching her

back in a situation like this. "Where's the domestic at?"

"Summit Park. Neighbor called it in."

New, fairly affluent neighborhood on the ridge above the creek. Just went to show that domestic violence didn't discriminate—it affected all demographics, and all walks of life.

They exited the building into the bright October morning sunshine and hurried for his gray Ford pickup. "What was that call about when I showed up at your office?" Tate asked. "You looked relieved."

"Just got word that the inmate I testified against in Billings a few years ago has officially been denied parole."

"Radzat?" He unlocked the doors for them.

"Yeah." Serial assaulter, thief and drug dealer. "For once, our justice system got it right." Even though she'd done everything in her power to keep him behind bars, she'd been worried they might let him out early.

During the parole hearing she'd testified that he shouldn't be granted parole—ever. Mike Radzat needed to stay behind bars right up until the last day of his sentence. He'd been committing violent crimes since the age of twenty-three, and he'd only been put away for the things he'd been *caught* for.

Having worked as a patrol officer in Billings for several years prior to becoming a detective, she had arrested him at least ten times, and each crime had been increasingly violent. No surprise to her that he'd wound up being arrested for aggravated murder soon after, having carved a rival to pieces with a machete.

"How long's he got left in prison?" Tate asked as he steered out of the parking lot.

"Eighteen years." She shook her head. "He had every chance in the world to straighten out. He came from a good family and had all kinds of support and opportunities. Instead he threw it all away."

"At least he's not getting out anytime soon."

"That's the silver lining."

They were quiet for a few minutes, until Tate turned off the two-lane highway. "So, Mason's moving in tomorrow night, huh?"

Her good mood took a dip. Oh, God, she didn't even want to think about Mason. The man unsettled and confused her. And he was about to become her basement suite tenant, because rental suites in Rifle Creek were sparse, and she could use the money. "Yeah. Now give me the rundown on this situation we're responding to."

Tate outlined what the caller had told the 911 operator about the domestic violence incident. Sounded like the middle-aged couple had been in one hell of a fight if the neighbor had been concerned enough to call the cops. Husband was a lawyer, wife an interior decorator. The caller didn't know if the wife had been injured, but had feared enough for her safety to make the call.

As they approached the neighborhood, Avery mentally readied herself for the unknown situation they were about to walk into.

"Ready?" Tate asked as he pulled up to the sprawling, two-story brick house.

"Yep." She got out and walked with him up to the front door, hand on the butt of her service weapon. The neighborhood was quiet, most of the driveways empty with the residents at work, though she noticed the next-door neighbor peeking at her and Tate through a gap in the curtains as they headed up the front walkway.

Tate rang the doorbell. Electronic, with a camera. When no one answered, he rang it again, and rapped on the door.

"Hang on," came the irritated reply a few moments later.

"Mr. Zinke," Tate said when the homeowner finally opened the door.

Avery studied him in silence. Forty-three-year-old male, clean cut, with brown eyes and dark blond hair. Same height as her, right around six-feet, with a wiry build. The dress slacks and shirt hinted that he was on his way to work.

Zinke didn't budge, the door opened only wide enough to frame his face. Avery didn't see any visible scratches or marks on it. "Yes?" he said, still sounding irritated.

Avery and Tate held up their badges. "Rifle Creek Sheriff's Department. We got a call about a domestic disturbance at this address," Avery said in a no-nonsense tone. "We'd like to speak to you and your wife."

His face tightened as he stared at her. "She's not here."

Uh-huh. Then how come both cars were still in the driveway? "Can we come in?"

He eyed them with suspicion. "What for?"

"We want to ask you some questions."

A muscle ticked in his jaw, then he relented and stepped back. "Fine, but make it quick. I need to get into the office for a meeting."

Tate went in first. Avery followed, using her heightened awareness to get a read on the situation. The wife was nowhere in sight. And the place was spotless, furnished and decorated to perfection, like a show home. "The report said you and your wife were in a heated argument."

"Who reported it?" Zinke demanded.

"I don't know. Was there an argument?" she asked.

"Yeah. So?"

Avery already disliked this arrogant sonofabitch. And it didn't bode well that his wife wasn't visible. "Where's your wife right now?"

"Out. And it was nothing." His cheeks flushed, but not from embarrassment. Oh, no, this asshole was pissed right off at having his behavior witnessed and reported.

"Where's your wife?" Tate pressed.

"Out," he snapped, no longer even trying to maintain a civil façade. "Look, whoever reported it was overreacting. I raised my voice, so what? I was mad. It's over now."

"Do you have any weapons in the house or on you?" He wasn't wearing a holster, and there were no visible bulges in his clothing. Avery patted him down to be sure.

His jaw flexed. "In the gun safe in my office."

"Which is where?" Tate said.

He jerked his chin toward the hallway. "In there."

"Show us." They followed him to the office and verified that the firearms were all accounted for.

"I'm going to check the rest of the house," Avery told Tate.

"She's not here," Zinke snapped.

Avery ignored him and did her job, looking in each room on the lower floor for weapons or any sign that the wife was here. When she found nothing, before heading upstairs she came back to join Tate in the living room.

"Did you assault your wife, Mr. Zinke?" Tate asked.

Zinke's face turned even redder. "*No*. Now are we done?"

A muted thud sounded above their heads. All three of them paused. Avery watched Zinke closely. "Is someone else home?" she asked. Whoever it was, they'd been hiding.

"No. Was probably the cat," he muttered.

Right. "I'm going to look upstairs," Avery said to Tate, pushing to her feet.

Zinke shot to his, blocking her way. "I didn't give you permission."

Avery arched an eyebrow at him, not the least bit intimidated. "Under the circumstances, I don't need your permission."

Zinke made a move to block her as she stepped past

him, but Tate was there, placing himself between them with a solid hand on Zinke's chest. "You stay here with me. Sit down."

Zinke glared, his eyes burning with anger. "You got a warrant?"

"Don't need one if we suspect someone might be hurt."

"I'll be reporting this," Zinke growled, jaw tight.

"Be my guest," Avery muttered to herself as she hit the stairs. She kept her hand on the butt of her pistol, attuned to every sound, watching for any sign of movement above her.

The upstairs landing led down two hallways. One to the guest suites, which were empty, and one to what she guessed must be the master.

Her pulse sped up as she walked toward the master bedroom. "Mrs. Zinke? I'm Detective Avery Dahl, Rifle Creek Sherriff's Department. Are you all right?"

No answer. But then Avery caught the faint sound of something moving inside.

She entered the room. "Mrs. Zinke?"

Silence.

Screw this. Avery drew her weapon and began a more thorough sweep. The master suite was huge, and immaculate. Sweet perfume scented the air. "Mrs. Zinke?"

The bathroom was empty. So was the walk-in closet. What the hell? She'd heard something hit the floor up here not two minutes ago, then movement.

She stopped, spotting a faint smudge of dirt in the carpet. A potted orchid rested on an occasional table above it. The stain in this immaculately kept home was like a red flag. Pointing Avery directly to the built-in cabinets beside it.

She turned toward them and crouched down to pull one of the cabinet doors open, weapon ready.

A tiny gasp answered.

Avery's heart clenched at the sight revealed in the beam of sunlight streaming through the window behind her. A blond woman was curled up in a ball inside, her face half-hidden in shadow. But the visible part of it was all Avery needed to see.

She holstered her weapon and got down on her knees to peer inside. "Tracy?"

The woman didn't answer, her face wet with tears, her left eye swelling shut. She was trembling.

Avery extended a hand toward her. "It's all right now. I'm Detective Avery Dahl. Come out and let me help you."

The woman's one-eyed gaze darted frantically around the room.

"My partner has him downstairs. You're safe now."

"N-no," Tracy whimpered. "Don't—d-don't arrest him."

Avery gestured with her hand. "Just come out and we'll talk. I need to see that you're all right." Because clearly, she wasn't.

Tracy put a trembling hand in Avery's. Avery helped her out, and smothered a sharp intake of breath when she saw the woman fully in the light.

Zinke had busted her lip open. Her pink blouse was covered in blood. A welt was forming on her cheek below the swelling eye.

Tracy sniffed and wiped gingerly at her face, her gaze on the floor.

"You're hurt," Avery said, keeping her tone gentle even as she wanted to race back downstairs to watch Tate cuff Zinke and tell him what a piece of shit he was for beating his wife.

The woman shook her head. "N-no. I slipped in the sh-shower."

"Tracy." The woman looked up at her, the shame and fear there making Avery's gut tighten. "You and I both know you didn't slip in the shower."

Tracy began to cry softly.

Avery gently took her over to sit on the edge of the wide, king-size bed and got on her radio. She called dispatch for an ambulance, ignoring Tracy's protests. If Zinke had beaten her this badly, she might have fractures or even internal injuries that needed to be checked.

Just as she finished, Zinke's enraged voice shattered the quiet from downstairs. "You can't fucking prove anything!"

Tracy jerked, her entire body going rigid. Avery grasped her hand and gave her a reassuring smile. "Listen to me. I want you to stay right here, okay? I'm going to check on my partner, and then I'll be right back. Don't move."

She turned and raced for the door. Zinke was screaming and swearing at Tate as she ran down the stairs. His enraged stare snapped to her the moment she came into view. Avery held it, a rush of triumph hitting her. "I found her and called for an ambulance," she said to Tate. "Cuff him."

Tate drew the cuffs from his belt and reached for Zinke's wrist. Zinke snarled and took a swing at him.

Tate blocked the punch and sidestepped. Zinke stumbled past him, his momentum throwing him forward as he caught himself on the coffee table, scattering a pile of mail everywhere. "You wanna add resisting arrest on top of everything else?" Tate snapped, grabbing Zinke's arm to twist it behind him.

Zinke whirled, the glint of the blade in his hand catching in the light.

Tate! Avery didn't have time to shout the warning. She launched herself at Zinke, hitting him square in the back.

They landed with a thud on the coffee table, Zinke taking the brunt of the impact. Avery instantly locked her hands around the wrist wielding the blade—a freaking letter opener they'd missed under the mail.

She twisted sharply while Tate wrenched the bastard's other hand up and behind him, one muscular arm pinned against Zinke's nape.

Zinke screamed, thrashing. The letter opener hit the floor.

"I got him," Tate said as he held Zinke there, totally calm.

Avery released what she sincerely hoped was Zinke's broken wrist and kicked the blade across the floor. Then she shoved off him, heart racing as Tate kept the asshole subdued and cuffed him.

Tate yanked Zinke to his feet and started Mirandizing him. Avery whirled toward the stairs, stilling at the sight of Tracy Zinke standing halfway down them. Her one open eye was wide, her tear-streaked face pale, one hand at the base of her throat. "No," she pleaded.

At the sound of her voice Zinke's head snapped around to face her. "You fucking *bitch*!" he screamed. "You did this!"

"Shut up," Tate growled, giving him a rough shake before shoving him toward the front door.

"I told you to stay out of sight until they were gone!" Zinke yelled at his wife.

Avery rushed past them to take Tracy by the arm. "Come upstairs with me."

"No," Tracy cried, turning back toward her husband. "Where is he taking him?"

"He's being arrested for domestic assault, resisting arrest, and attacking a police officer."

"No, you can't," she begged. "You can't, he'll—" She broke off, dissolving into tears.

Avery hurried her up the stairs and into the master bedroom. Backup was on the way, should be here any minute. "I'm having some paramedics come look at you. For now, just come sit and tell me what happened."

Tracy continued to cry, a devastated, heartbroken sound that made Avery's insides tighten. "He—he d-didn't mean it," she sobbed. "It was an accident."

No, it fucking wasn't. And Avery would bet everything she owned that this wasn't the first time, either. Not even close.

"I won't press charges," Tracy blurted through her tears, a hint of defiance breaking through her fear.

Avery quelled a rush of frustration. So many women refused to press charges against their abuser, for a variety of reasons. But there was enough evidence to charge and convict him, so hopefully that wouldn't matter. "Tracy. I understand that you're afraid right now, but you don't need to think about any of that yet. Right now, I just need you to take some deep breaths, calm down, and talk to me."

She sat quietly, letting Tracy calm down, waiting for the tears to stop. "There. Now please tell me what happened."

"It… It was just a s-stupid argument," Tracy began.

Avery listened, taking detailed notes. But ten seconds in, it was obvious Tracy wasn't telling the whole truth. "So you see, it was partly my fault," Tracy finished in a whisper.

"No, it wasn't," Avery said in a low voice, holding back the rest of what she wanted to say. Her phone buzzed in her pocket. She pulled it out to see Tate's message that Zinke was on his way to the sheriff's department in the back of a squad car, and the ambulance was ten minutes out.

Avery replied for him to stay outside. She didn't want anyone else to come in here and make Tracy clam up even more.

"Can I get you anything?" Avery asked her in the quiet.

"No." Tracy sighed and bent her head, rubbing her fingers over her forehead. "He didn't use to be like this," she whispered. "When we first got together, he was wonderful. But…"

"But?"

"After we got married, things changed. *He* changed." She looked up at Avery, her battered face full of misery. "Does that sound crazy?"

An echo of pain twisted through Avery, an old hurt flaring back to life. Different from Tracy's. But still valid. "No. It doesn't sound crazy at all."

She knew all too well how suddenly a man could change after putting a ring on a woman's finger.

End Excerpt

About the Author

NY Times and USA Today Bestselling author Kaylea Cross writes edge-of-your-seat military romantic suspense. Her work has won many awards, including the Daphne du Maurier Award of Excellence, and has been nominated multiple times for the National Readers' Choice Awards. A Registered Massage Therapist by trade, Kaylea is also an avid gardener, artist, Civil War buff, Special Ops aficionado, belly dance enthusiast and former nationally-carded softball pitcher. She lives in Vancouver, BC with her husband and family.

You can visit Kaylea at www.kayleacross.com. If you would like to be notified of future releases, please join her newsletter: http://kayleacross.com/v2/newsletter/

COMPLETE BOOKLIST

ROMANTIC SUSPENSE
Rifle Creek Series
Lethal Edge
Lethal Temptation
Lethal Protector

Vengeance Series
Stealing Vengeance
Covert Vengeance
Explosive Vengeance
Toxic Vengeance
Beautiful Vengeance

Crimson Point Series
Fractured Honor
Buried Lies
Shattered Vows
Rocky Ground
Broken Bonds

DEA FAST Series
Falling Fast
Fast Kill
Stand Fast
Strike Fast
Fast Fury
Fast Justice
Fast Vengeance

Colebrook Siblings Trilogy
Brody's Vow
Wyatt's Stand
Easton's Claim

Silent Night, Deadly Night

PARANORMAL ROMANCE
Empowered Series
Darkest Caress

HISTORICAL ROMANCE
The Vacant Chair

EROTIC ROMANCE (writing as *Callie Croix*)
Deacon's Touch
Dillon's Claim
No Holds Barred
Touch Me
Let Me In
Covert Seduction

Manufactured by Amazon.ca
Bolton, ON